PRAISE FOR THE WILLOW

"A tender, loving, and ultimately hopeful story of how
we move forward from unspeakable trauma."
—Sarah Darer Littman, author of *Deepfake*

A heartbreaking and ultimately affirming story of grief,
love, and what happens after the very worst
happens…. While pain and heartache are
an all-too-real part of THE WILLOW,
readers will connect with Kirsten as she
finds her way through the worst kind of loss.
—Annie Cardi,
author of *The Chance You Won't Return*

THE WILLOW

WENDY M. MCDONALD

THE WILLOW

Published by Table for 7 Press

ISBN: 978-1-7369254-4-7 (paperback); 978-1-7369254-5-4 (ebook)

Summary: High school senior Kirsten Madsen loses her young sister Astrid in a school shooting. Overcome with grief and guilt, Kirsten retreats into an imaginary world in which Astrid is still alive and gets to grow up.

[1. psychological drama 2. death 3. sibling loss 4. trauma 5. LGBTQ+ 6. grief 7. school shooting]

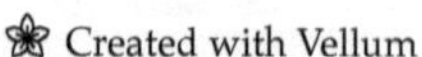 Created with Vellum

for Dan — I love you because

for Penelope and Zephyr — I am forever in awe of you both

and

for my brother Daniel (1974 - 2017) — I miss you

CONTENTS

BEFORE

"Kyurp?"

"What's up, Frog Breath?"

She tugs off the green kid-sized gardening gloves I bought her because she always wants to help me garden. "When's snack time?" She whines a little, but it's probably out of boredom.

I pull off my own gloves and heave myself up the hill a few yards to where I've left my phone on the hearth of the fire pit. It's later than I thought. "We missed snack time. Go tell Mom we're ready for lunch."

Astrid hop-skips up the hill and onto the deck, then disappears through the side door. She comes back out with Mom and a lunch of cold fried chicken, Market Basket macaroni salad, edamame pods, and lemonade. She'd eat it for every meal if Mom let her. We spread everything out in a sunny, sorta-flat spot above the hole and secure the blanket with a few rocks from the pile near the edge of the creek. I drop onto the blanket and swig a lemonade halfway down. Astrid sits across from me, grabs a drumstick, and gnaws on it.

"Kyurp's letting me help dig the hole," she says, mouth full.

Mom eyes the mound of dirt, then the hole, which isn't nearly big enough yet. Well—it's not nearly as deep as it needs to be. It's actually almost four feet wide.

"I know," I say, choosing a thigh from the plate. "There's an enormous rock under there. I'm trying to find the borders. Then I can dig down and use the crowbar to lever it out—I hope." I've planted enough shrubs to know, if the rock is much bigger than a backpack, I'll have to pick a new spot for Astrid's willow.

Mom leans over and brushes my bangs to the side. I smooth them back down with my free hand.

Astrid takes another drumstick. "Can we have this for my birthday dinner tomorrow?"

"Of course," Mom says. "Would it be your birthday without Wicked Chicken and edamame?"

"Nope!"

Mom tweaks Astrid's nose, then looks at me.

I shrug, sucking on an edamame pod. As repetitious dinners go, fried chicken is easy to take.

When we're done eating, Mom clears the picnic away. Astrid and I pull our gloves back on. Grabbing the trowel, Astrid kneels at the uphill edge of the hole. "Dig on this side?"

"Yep. I think that's our best bet."

By the time I find the bottom of the rock, it's nearly four. I trudge up the hill and bring back both crowbars. With them, I ease the boulder up inch by inch. Every time I gain enough space, I throw my weight into bracing it and give Astrid the go-ahead. Quick as a tadpole darts through the shallows, Astrid wedges small rocks beneath it. We don't even smash any fingers.

Finally, it's standing on end, an eighteen-inch-long version of the uprights at Stonehenge. Panting for breath, sweat soaking through the brim of my cap, I survey my dig site. The sharp, late afternoon sun lights the amber granite chunk to a blazing orange.

"Go get Mom and Dad," I tell Astrid, and she skitters up the hill. "We're tipping it out downhill," I say, once they join me.

Together, we lever the rock up until its own weight works for us. It hits the ground with a thud I feel through my shoes. The three of us roll the boulder to the edge of the creek while Astrid supervises from uphill.

By the time the willow is planted and watered, it's too late to do more than shape the mulch into a decent berm. Mom and Dad watch for a minute, then head inside to order the Sunday pizza from Zesty's. Astrid skips around, singing the theme song from her favorite show, *Lily's Pad*—"… down by the pond-shore, playing in the cattails… that's Lily's Pad!"—and chasing the earliest fireflies until I'm done with the mulch.

As the creek succumbs to dusk, frog song rises, bouncing back and forth—*gao, gao… gao, gao*—and Astrid crouches at the edge of the creek.

"Ready, Frog Breath? Let's clean up before dinner."

"You're my favorite big sister," she says, turning away from the creek as I stand and brush the mulch off my hands.

"I'm your *only* big sister."

Holding the empty mulch bag and my spade in one hand, I let her climb up for a piggyback even though she's really too big.

She wraps her arms around my neck and links her hands. "I know. You're still my favorite."

"Why?"

She giggles. "Um… because you give me piggybacks."

"Piggybacks," I grunt, pitching forward and starting up the hill.

"Yeah. And because you let me have some of your coffee."

"So, you love me for my piggybacks and coffee?"

"Uh-huh."

My legs feel like overcooked asparagus.

As we reach the top of the hill, she gives me a squeezy hug from behind. "And because you planted my tree for me." She slides down and runs up the deck stairs and toward the house. "But sometimes just because," she shouts over her shoulder.

2

MONDAY MORNING

ASTRID BURSTS through the back door, singing the *Lily's Pad* theme at the top of her lungs. Her knees are stained by grass, dirt, and mulch, and decorated with several fresh cuts and scrapes. She pulls off the froggy-green gloves and drops them on the floor.

"Kyurp! You gotta come see what I did for my tree!" Her voice rises with excitement that practically explodes, her goofy grin spreading across her face.

From her usual spot in the booth, Mom smiles and eats another spoonful of yogurt. Beside her, the presents for Astrid's sixth birthday are piled behind the plastic tray of everything-free mini cupcakes for school and Astrid's new green play dress. Astrid isn't allowed to open presents until our family party this evening—but even I wish she could open one now, because I'd hand her mine. I hunted every-where for a *Lily's Pad* lunchbox and backpack, finally resorting to ordering something custom on Etsy. It cost two weeks' pay from my job at Dirty Knees.

I have a little time before school, so I set my charm bracelet on the counter with a *plink* and let Astrid lead me outside. Just two yards above our side of the creek that burbles casually toward the Merrimack River, the willow waits, a gentle spring breeze tickling its stringy branches. Around it is a haphazard circle of stones.

"Hey, Frog Breath, how long did it take you to drag these from the rock pile?"

"Not that long."

"Did you do the fairy dance?"

She shakes her head, her dark brown braids branches whipping in a storm. "Fairy dance?"

"A tree takes years to grow, and the more fairy song a tree gets, the bigger and stronger it grows. Like my apple tree. But we have to call them with a special dance. Ready?" I guide her in skipping sloppy circles around the tree again and again, until she collapses onto the damp grass, her face flushed, hair pulling free of the braids and clinging to her cheeks.

"You have to invite the fairies every day," I say.

"Will you do it with me?"

"Sure. Sometimes, at least." I point to the patch of irises bobbing in the cool June breeze. I notice Astrid has relocated the metal statue of a birdwatching frog I bought for the front flower garden—now it's nestled into the bed of irises. Even in the shade, their velvety, purple petals are so vibrant it's as if the sun is already shining on them. "See how the flowers are dancing?"

She looks over and nods.

"The fairies are coming. We need to leave now so we don't scare them away."

Astrid grabs my hand and drags me up the slope, chattering on about how she's going to make me a surprise in art today and I can see it when I pick her up. Ever since I got my license, I've picked her up after school. Before that—starting in seventh grade—I came home right away a few afternoons each week to babysit.

Back in the kitchen, Mom looks up from reading *The Globe* on her tablet. "Get the food from Wicked Chicken this afternoon?"

"Pick up Frog Breath, pick up chicken. No problem. What time are Uncle Nick and Brent coming over?"

"Six, I think. Dad and I should be home by six-thirty, traffic willing."

I nudge the step-stool toward the sink. Astrid climbs up and washes her hands, humming the *Lily's Pad* theme song once through as she soaps and scrubs and rinses. "Josie and I might go out this weekend for our six-month anniversary. Not the Emily Snow concert—that's Friday with her and Oakley. Also, I need to talk to you and Dad about this new greenhouse they want my help with at work."

"What greenhouse?"

Astrid holds out her dripping hands, and I hand her the towel. When she hands it back to me and hops off the stool, the towel is sopping wet. We need to teach her to shake some of the dripping water into the sink.

"One Maura wants to start, growing year-round greens for local restaurants. If she does it, it'll mean more hours."

"That sounds like a great opportunity," she says, smiling.

I fasten the charm bracelet Mom and Dad gave me before Astrid was born. The day they brought her home, they gave me a simple silver disc with a braided border and the words *big sister* engraved on one side. Every year, on her birthday, they give me a new charm. It's their way of recognizing how much I do to help out with her. Ever since her fourth birthday, Astrid's insisted on picking out the charms herself. This year —she keeps telling me—she wrapped it herself, too. All week, she's moved it from one hiding place to another.

"I hid your new charm real good, Kyurp," she says, climbing onto the bench across from Mom at the table and eyeing the cupcakes.

"Will you help me look for it?"

"No way." She smiles that face-exploding smile of hers. "It's going to take you forever to find. Maybe even a whole week."

Oakley knocks at the side door, then opens it and steps in. "Hey! Ready?" My best friend Oakley and I met in kindergarten and by the end of the year, when we won first prize in the speed relay on field day, we were as inseparable as honeybees and wildflowers. She flashes me a wide smile as I shoulder my purse and backpack and head for the door.

"Don't forget the chicken," shouts Mom as I bolt.

"Cluck, cluck!" I call back. But I'm already thinking about Josie.

Callahan's Ice Creamery is a tiny, old, converted Cape across the road from the bottom of Winslow Mid-High's driveway. Our town is about an hour northwest of Boston, squished in-between Lowell and a bunch of other towns that are actually large enough to have Independence Day parades every July. Winslow is so small, our middle school and high school are on the same campus. Callahan's is the big hangout for everyone from ninth grade on. It's on maybe an acre of land right on the Merrimack, with houses on either side. The back-yard has a gazebo, a dozen picnic tables, and wooden stairs leading down to more seating on the rivers-edge deck. The front yard is a gravel parking lot. In the back windows, speakers blare a Top-40 TuneStream station loud enough for customers to hear, but not so loud the neighbors will complain.

It's almost three—I should leave soon to go pick up Astrid, but whenever I get there on time, she just begs me to let her go back in and hang in the cafeteria with the other pickup-kids—including her best friend Lexie Oh. Lexie's dad is always one of the last parents to arrive. Sometimes if I'm on time, I park and walk in to say *Hi* to Uncle Nick—he's the elementary school principal and Dad's best friend since high school. Then Mr. Oh finally shows up sweating and muttering about getting stuck in traffic on the bridge, even though there are like four other bridges he could've taken. So most after-noons, I push the envelope a little—Astrid and Lexie have this game where they pretend to be Lily Frog and Shelley Turtle from *Lily's Pad.* This way, we both get to hang with our friends. Everybody's happy.

Emily Snow's latest single, "I'm Gonna Crash," comes on as Oakley and I snag one end of a table on the lawn. Brent and two of his friends are at the other end. As usual, Brent is wearing a shirt that has some obscure science joke on it, and his dark, too-long hair half-hides his eyes. He and his friends are playing around on their phones, probably trying out Brent's latest co-op game. He glances over as we sit and gives me a quick smile.

I pump my plastic spoon up and down in my frappe and watch the parking lot. Oakley waves her own spoon across my field of vision. "Hey. Earth to Kirsten."

"Sorry. What?"

"My mom said I can borrow the good car for the concert. I'll pick you up at four, then we'll get Josie."

Josie shows up right then, not dressed for lacrosse and paying so much attention to her phone that she bumps into an awning support. She snorts, smiles, and brushes her pixie bangs off her forehead. Her straight, black hair falls right back down. Damn, that's cute. She looks around for me and lets the smile linger on her face. I wish she'd let my hand linger in hers for half as long. My fingers twitch around my spoon as I smile back, pushing the wish away. I can't even wave at her—she'll freak out and say I'm being obvious—but I'll do anything to stick with Josie until she's ready to come out. Even in a small town, it's possible to surround yourself with people who love you and who will fight for you. Pocketing her phone and running a hand through her hair again, she heads over.

Oakley waggles her eyebrows at me and turns to inject herself into Brent's conversation. I slide over a bit to open a seat and offer Josie the kiddie size double-chocolate brownie—her usual order. She digs out a huge brownie chunk. "Happy six months," I say, softly. "How long can you stay?"

"Not long. The bus leaves at 3:30, and I still have to change."

I reach over for her free hand, but she pulls it away, then stops. She glances around.

I sigh. Everyone at this table knows we're dating—but it's the risk of someone else noticing, I guess, that keeps her in check.

Slowly, she eases her hand back across toward mine, and takes hold—right there, out in the open. The warmth of her touch sends a tingle through my fingers. I stare at my pale hand in her light brown one, resting on the chipped green picnic table like it's nothing—even though it's everything.

My heart skitters and flits, a butterfly.

"Are you sure?" I ask, my voice low.

"Mostly," she says. "It's like you said before—I'm almost eighteen. What am I going to do, let my mom dictate my love life forever?"

"Did you tell her? What'd she say?" I face Josie—it'd be so cool if she came out at home and things were better than she expected. We wouldn't have to always meet at my house, or take Oakley or Brent as a disguise when we see a movie. We could go on a real date without having to drive into Boston.

A squall of sirens rises and fades in the distance. Josie shakes her head. "I'm not that brave. Not yet. I just…" she nods toward Oakley and everyone else at our table—people who have known us both forever. People I've been out to for years. It's obvious—to them, at least—what Josie and I are. "It's not like anyone here is going to tell my parents."

"I've said that exact thing to you like a million times."

She gives me her don't-bullshit-me look and I laugh.

"Okay, like… five or six times? And, not to be ungrateful or anything—" I flash her a flirty smile "—but why is that suddenly a good argument for a little PDA?"

She gives her head a fast shake and glances down at our hands. She laces her fingers with mine. "Coming from you all those times, it felt more like pressure than logic, but I joined this online forum my Uncle Stu recommended and got pretty much the same thing. I mean, I'm *so* not ready for my parents to find out, but I will be someday. It's a step, you know?"

I dance a little in my seat. "It's an excellent step. I'll enjoy exploring it with you."

"Omigod," she says, laughing and looking right at me like she almost never does unless we're totally alone. She looks like she wants to kiss me. For a moment, I think she's about to lean over and do just that—

Then an emergency alert goes off.

We jerk apart and scramble for our phones along with everyone else, trying to silence the screaming signal that's never relevant to our lives.

ACTIVE SHOOTER ALERT
Winslow Elementary, Winslow, MA
Police responding. Tune to local news.

"Astrid!" Leaving my frappe on the table and Josie sitting there holding her phone, I race for my car. I'm shoving the key in the ignition when the passenger door opens and Oakley folds herself into the seat. Her face is tight and her hands shake as she buckles the seatbelt.

"I need to pick up Luther." She pulls her braids back with a scrunchie and thumbs through an app on her phone, probably looking for more information or texting her parents.

My text notice buzzes. I grab my phone and open the messenger app, glancing between the screen and the road.

Oakley snatches it out of my hand. "What, do you want to get us killed?" She glances at my screen. "Your mom wants to know if you've got Astrid."

I tighten my grip on the steering wheel. "Shit. Shitshitshit."

"What do you want me to tell her?"

"I don't know. 'On my way?'"

Oakley types the message, hits SEND, then puts my phone in the storage tray beneath the radio.

There's a rusted-out Buick in front of us going five miles under the speed limit, and the typical New England road is a winding, solid-double-line exercise in patience. As we follow the road along the river toward the double-arched red bridge that everybody uses as a landmark, my heart pounds in my chest and my knuckles turn white from clenching the steering wheel. Oakley's legs jitter like she's holding herself back from jumping out and running all the way to the elementary school.

The Buick has a trailer hitch with a tennis ball crammed onto it and a faded red Good Sam Club sticker on the bumper. Oakley reaches over and lays on the horn. "Come on, Good Sam. Speed up or get the fuck out of the way."

I push Oakley's hand away and pound the horn myself, shouting uselessly at the Buick's driver. "Move! Turn!"

An ambulance siren swells behind us and I edge to the right. It crawls past, straddling the center line, and I want to fall in line behind it and get past the Buick. But I stay where I am like a responsible driver.

"Check the news. Check Twitter."

Oakley thumbs her phone screen. "It's all over the internet. Shots fired. Active shooter. But that's it, over and over. Nobody knows."

My mouth goes dry. This can't be happening—not in our tiny little town. Not to us.

The Buick slows to a near stop, then turns into a parking lot. Finally! My text alert buzzes again as I floor the gas, even though there's a line of traffic ahead, near the top of the hill. I should've picked Astrid up on time today. Screw her *Lily's Pad* game with Lexie.

Oakley braces herself against the dashboard as I come to a halt, joining the line of cars. Up ahead, Nuthatch Road peels off to the right and the traffic follows it. Beyond that, I can see the heart-stopping strobe of emergency lights. Now Oakley actually does jump out and run.

"Hey!" I shout. I pull over onto someone's lawn and shut the car off, leaving the keys on the dash. Grabbing my phone, I run after Oakley, catching up at the base of Winslow Elementary's winding driveway.

Oakley is kicking and struggling and lunging against a pair of officers who look like they'll never sleep again. Catching my breath, I take in the barriers and tape, the emblems on the dozens of squad cars blocking and lining the driveway: Winslow, but also Lowell, Tyngsboro, Dunstable, Dracut, Chelmsford, Westford, and… Nashua?

They sent patrol cars across the state line from New Hampshire?

Everything is in focus at once—but I can't focus on any one thing that makes sense.

My attention jumps from the crowd of patrol cars to a bicycle ditched on the curb, to the row of oaks and maples that line the edge of the woods several yards away. Leaves rustle in the light breeze. An Irish setter lopes into the grassy strip between the curb and the tree line, dragging its leash. I stare at its long, coppery fur. Where's its owner? What if it chases a squirrel into the road and gets hit by a car—or by an ambulance? What happens if an ambulance hits a dog and crashes? What if the person inside dies because of someone's escaped dog? I look around, but nobody seems to notice the dog.

My phone, buzzing in my hands, snaps me out of my head. I realize I'm walking toward the dog and stop, glancing down at my phone. The text bubble from Mom says Text me when Astrid is safe.

My hands shake as I unlock my phone to reply. Why did I stay so long with Josie?

I send I don't have her yet. They won't let us through

But the message just spins.

"Miss, we've evacuated the children. You need to go to Winslow Indoor Gym. That's the reunification point." An officer with a Chelmsford badge and a grimly calm voice takes me by the arm and turns me around. We step through a sour-smelling spatter of vomit in the road. I realize my own gut is all twisted up and I feel like I'm about to lose my frappe.

"My sister…" Pulling away from her, I dart for the school, making it all the way to the first bend in the driveway.

From here, I can see the fire trucks and ambulances outside the school. There's a woman standing in the grass, phone to one ear, shaking her head. A group of parents and older teenagers are talking to several officers and firefighters. They gesture toward the building. A pair of ambulances crawl toward the car-clogged bus lane, their lights flashing, but sirens off.

The officer I escaped from catches up to me. "Miss, you'll need to come with me…"

Her radio crackles. From it, I hear, "Where the hell is the medivac?"

Punching in Mom's number but getting the all-circuits-busy message, I let the officer lead me back to the sawhorse barriers strung with yellow tape.

"My sister's waiting…"

We pass an EMT sitting alone on the curb. He's sobbing into his hands.

I want to throw up. I want to go home. I want…

I want everything to be okay.

I shake my head to clear it.

"Kirsten," shouts Oakley, still flanked by officers. "That's my friend. I'll get a ride with my friend."

"Winslow Indoor Gym," they remind us as we race back to my car. It doesn't matter that we've left it empty. It seems like half the cars on the road are empty.

Two miles. It's only two miles to the gym.

In the seat beside me, her legs jittering again as if running would make everything turn out okay, Oakley tries her phone over and over, but she still can't get through to anyone. Shaking so hard I can barely hold the steering wheel, I stare at the car in front of me, seeing nothing beyond its brake lights as we inch our way past Evergreen Ridge Plaza, all the way down Groton Street and onto Collins Road. We have to park alongside the landfill on Collins and jog the last half-mile to the sports center. Other people—classmates, parents—clutter the road alongside us. Brent's car creeps by, then squeezes into a spot against the brambles and wild blueberry shrubs along the left side of the narrow road. He climbs out and falls into pace with us, his face pale.

"Dad's phone keeps going straight to voicemail."

Taking in the tense throng around us, I shake my head, my stomach still in knots. "He's the principal. He's probably swamped dealing with whatever's going on."

"Yeah," Brent nods. "That's probably it."

We jog the rest of the way in silence.

AFTER

3

MONDAY AFTERNOON

THE DOORS of the front entrance are a natural choke point, and it looks like the police are still setting up. A single pair of officers flanks the doors, holding clipboards which (I assume) tell them who's allowed to pick up which kid. My name will be there. So will Oakley's. Brent pushes forward. "Officer. I can't reach my dad—Nick Broderick. He's the principal."

The officer nods. He surveys the crowd, then turns to the second officer. "I'll be just a minute." Taking Brent by the arm, he leads him inside and to the left, where the golf bays and karate dojos are.

Behind us in the crowd, someone shouts, "He got in! Let us in, too! Our kids are in there!" Several people shout their agreement. There's pushing, and people shouting at others to calm down, then more pushing and shouting.

Oakley and I lock elbows and link hands. Hers are as clammy as mine. We're jostled up alongside the lone remaining officer and into the doorway. He tucks his clipboard beneath his arm. "I need help out here," he shouts over his shoulder, but we're already past him, on our way down the stairs on the right. I don't even know if it's where we're supposed to go. Maybe we should have gone left, like Brent.

The perimeter may be leaky, but inside—downstairs, it's a chaos of organization. The comforting order of shoes, sweat, and adrenaline is buried beneath an unfamiliar tang. The facility director and his staff have roped the two full-sized fields off into six sections—one for each grade. They've set up tables, and officers with clipboards are stationed behind them.

An employee, in his red polo with the black collar, lugs a case of water toward one field. Oakley nods her head toward the storage area beneath the stairs, where more water and snack foods are stacked. We each grab a case of water and head past the officers and tables toward the fields. I guess, if you look like you know what you're doing, you can get away with almost anything.

Around the perimeter of the fields is the track where Oakley and I run a few nights each week during the winter. Beyond it, two more officers block the exit to the lower parking lot with clipboards. A father hustles his daughter toward the officers. It's my calculus teacher, Mr. d'Elia. Did he get past the officers upstairs the same way we did? He's crying. I turn away.

We set the water down on the bleachers in the center aisle and separate, Oakley heading to the right, where signage indicates the upper grade classes are gathered. I head left, to the lower grades.

I trip on the rumpled artificial turf as I slip beneath the netting and scan the field of sniffling, crying kids. There are more makeshift signs—copier paper taped to lacrosse sticks jammed into the tops of orange cones—with classroom numbers and teachers' names, arranged in front of clusters of kids. Some clusters have two cones but only one teacher. Men and women in business-casual attire sit cross-legged on the floor, talking to small groups of children. I guess they're counselors. There should be more teachers, more kids... more noise.

Instead, conversations hiss around me like a raging, storm-swollen brook on the verge of overflowing. Sobs echo across the space, crashing into each other.

My breath comes fast and shallow. There's a lump in my throat that I'm certain will choke me if I can't swallow it down. I find Miss Kirby's sign. Counting the kids' faces, I try to pick out Astrid's braids and dark eyes. Six. Half the pick-up kids are missing. What does that mean?

I glance at the other classes; they're all missing pick-up kids.

I turn back to the kindergarten classes. Who's missing? I don't see Hunter Adams, but Astrid says he misses school a lot. His family's a mess.

From our neighborhood, I recognize Trevor McLaughlin, who Astrid says steals extra graham crackers and juice boxes from the snack tray. And Stephanie Byars, who Astrid swears ate crayons and threw them up in a perfect, carnation-pink circle right in front of the coat hooks. I see Jeremiah Martin, the towheaded brat next door who always runs across the property line and bites Astrid whenever she gets too close to that side of our yard. He's chewing on his own hand.

There's Lexie—one pigtail sticky and stiffening, a reddish-brown stain across the same side of her light pink dress—clutching a bottle of water and an unopened bag of Cheezy Whalez. I don't see Astrid.

I don't see Astrid.

My breath catches in my throat, my heart racing the 100-meter, and I start into the cluster of cross-legged children—but someone stops me. Shorter and even more boy-figured than me, her plain brown hair is streaked with gray but still in the pixie haircut she's had since I was in her class. She's wearing a too-big Winslow Indoor Gym sweatshirt instead of one of her usual tailored cotton blouses.

Miss Kirby. She fixes her bulgy blue eyes on me and I look away, my heart still racing as I search for Astrid.

"Kirsten." Her voice is softer than I remember, and clipped with something. What is that? "How did you get down here?"

"Astrid. I'm supposed to pick up Astrid." My voice sounds tiny, like I'm a lost-in-the-mall child. From the clump of kindergartners, there's a whimper. I glance over. Jeremiah chews furiously at his hand. Lexie's thumb is in her mouth. She hasn't sucked her thumb in over a year. I crouch down to comfort Lexie and help her ease her thumb back out, but Miss Kirby takes my hand and tugs me gently up.

She leads me towards the edge of the fields. "Kirsten…"

I stare at her and take a gasping breath in. I shake my head. "No…not Astrid…" Astrid is signed up for two weeks of Irish Step camp this summer, plus her first-ever week of Girl Scout day camp up in Dracut. Next weekend, I'm helping her work on her swaps. We're making pipe-cleaner frogs from a tutorial I found online.

I look back at Astrid's class. Lexie stares at me. Whose blood is that on her dress? In her hair?

I count the kids again. Six. Who's not here? Why don't I remember all their faces? Hunter Adams. Who else? I don't know… I don't know… please not Astrid…

Miss Kirby nods at the other kindergarten teacher, then leads me off the field, toward the stairs. Where is she taking me? I need to find Astrid.

She beckons to an officer, and when he joins us Miss Kirby says quietly, "This is Kirsten Madsen. Her sister Astrid…"

I shake my head *No* and take a step back.

The officer turns to me, taking me by the elbow. "Miss Madsen, I'm Officer Boulard. Let's go upstairs."

"Where, upstairs? The room they took Brent into? What's in that room? Is my sister in that room?"

On TV, they always take you to a special room for Bad News. Is Brent up there, right now, getting Bad News? I don't want to go up there.

"Come on upstairs with me. We have a room set up with some privacy."

Bolting for the trash barrel by the snack counter, I vomit my chocolate frappe into it. Even though I'm sweating and sputtering, spitting into the trash, my muscles go icy. I'm shaking so much my knees buckle, and I cling to the rim of the barrel for support, panting fast and shallow like a stressed cat.

Officer Boulard rests a hand on my shoulder. "Let's go upstairs. You can talk to Mr. Almeda."

"The school counselor?" I shake my head and stagger away. "No…" I know what this is, and I won't let anyone rip my family apart. I won't let it happen.

The space around me rocks and swims and suddenly I can't breathe. No air comes in, no air goes out. I start coughing so hard I have to put a hand on Miss Kirby's shoulder for support. Miss Kirby wraps an arm around me and together, she and Officer Boulard ease me over to the nearest bench as my vision goes foggy and white. Stupidly, I think, *this must be what drowning is like…*

No.

Wait.

This isn't happening.

My face is wet. Am I crying? Why am I crying?

I take a few deep breaths, wipe my eyes with the sleeves of my t-shirt, and stand.

The gym tilts and spins around me for another moment, then my vision clears and everything comes into sharp focus, like I'm seeing the world in soap opera mode on a new TV.

I turn to Miss Kirby. "Where's Astrid? I always pick her up. She's probably wondering where I am..." I start back toward the field where the kindergarteners are. Then, from the tiny lobby at the top of the stairs, comes Oakley's voice, high and shrieking. "I'm not going in that room—just tell me where my brother is—Luther Washington!"

I stop, because just like Oakley, I know—and I'm holding my breath.

Then I feel Astrid's arms wrapped around my waist. "Kyurp!"

My breath rushes out in a whoosh, and the world closes in around me until all I can see is Astrid's hair, her braids sloppy from the day's activities. Her hair still smells of green apple from last night's shampooing. All I can hear is the wobble in her voice.

I bend over, scooping her up, holding her to me like she weighs nothing—like she's a figment of my imagination—but the warmth of her sweaty body against mine and the pressure of her legs wrapped tightly around my waist wipe away every other care I've ever had, and I can't stop crying. "Astrid... oh, God..."

"They made me close my eyes. I lost my backpack." Her tears and snot run onto my shirt, but all that matters is getting her home.

"I know, Astrid. It's okay." I stroke her hair. Damn, it's a mess. I'll have to comb it out.

"But it had my field day paper. And the thing I made you in art."

"It's okay. It'll be okay. You can make me another thing."

I carry her up the stairs and turn away from the karate dojo they took Oakley and Brent into, grateful the door is shut and I can't see them. I don't want to risk eye contact. I'm not ready to know what they're facing. Not for certain.

I switch Astrid to piggyback and hold her hands tight as she leans into me. Pushing past the officers at the door, squeezing through the crowd, we head toward my car.

I'm holding onto Astrid.

I can't let Astrid go.

4

MONDAY EVENING

I sɪᴛ with Astrid until she falls asleep in my bed, sucking on Mr. Ribbit's left front foot like when she was in preschool. My head is pounding from too much crying and I have no idea how I'm going to get any rest tonight but I guess it doesn't matter.

Astrid's okay.

Joining Mom and Dad in the kitchen, I duck beneath the booth the way I used to when I was Astrid's age, and into my spot between Dad and the inside wall. Dad and Mom are holding hands across the scarred wooden tabletop. They just sit there and stare at the empty air.

Astrid's presents are still piled at the back of the booth, like an offering to all the kids who will never get presents again. I'll help her open them tomorrow. It'll distract her.

The scenes in other houses must be very different.

Oakley texted me earlier. Her family is still waiting to hear about Luther's surgery at Lowell Memorial. He's okay—or he will be—and was lucky enough to not need the airlift into Boston.

But Brent?

We were here, in the kitchen—the lights bright against the darkness outside, just like they are now—when I first met Brent. I'd been peeking out the back window every few minutes as we got ready for Game Night.

"Kirsten, stop," said Mom, for the fifth time. Or maybe the tenth. She waddled through the kitchen toward the dining room, tugging me away from the window with her free hand as she passed. "They'll be here when they get here."

"But we get to meet him tonight," I said, letting her have her way. She was seven months pregnant, after all. I pulled the box of popcorn from the pantry and removed three packets. Unwrapping the first packet, I placed it in the microwave and hit the POPCORN button.

Dad set a stack of board and card games down on the dining room table and went back to the front closet for more.

"Erik, don't you think you're being a little overenthusiastic?" asked Mom.

Dad laughed. "The kid better get used to it, if he's going to be staying with Nick."

Mom shook her head and emptied the bag of M&Ms she was carrying into the bowls dotted across the table.

I snuck another peek out the window. "They're coming!" Behind me, the buttery scent of popcorn filled the air as kernels began bursting.

"What's his name again?" asked Mom.

Before Dad could answer, Uncle Nick rapped on the storm door, then walked right on in. The boy who followed him was about my age—but shorter, skinnier, and with pale skin and messy, longish dark brown hair that hung into his eyes. He wore a ratty pair of sneakers, jeans, and, under an unzipped hoodie, a brand-new T-shirt that had a conical robot on it. The caption read *R2-D2? I loved him in* Star Trek.

I didn't recognize the robot, but I smiled anyway. The shirt was funny enough only knowing two-thirds of the joke.

Nick put his arm around the boy as they stepped up into the kitchen. "Madsen crew, this is Brent. Brent, meet Kirsten— she's in the sixth grade, too; she'll be at the bus stop with you next week—and Erik and Maren."

Brent nodded. "Hi," he mumbled.

The microwave beeped. I put in the next packet of popcorn, then emptied the first into one of the bowls waiting on the counter.

"Brent, come pick the first game," said Dad from the dining room, where he stood with the second stack of games in his hands. "I highly recommend *Tornado Alley,* but if you don't like card games, we can always go with *Evolution.* In that one, you get to build your own species."

"Um…" Brent looked at Nick.

Nick urged him through the kitchen. Mom squished herself into the booth as they passed, a huge grin on her face. "So nice to meet you, Brent." She waved, like some sort of idiot.

Dad, Nick, and Brent surveyed the games while I finished making the popcorn and Mom set out glasses of ice and a few two-liters of soda.

By the time I'd brought the popcorn into the dining room, Brent had loosened up a bit and taken a seat beside Nick. Dad was already dealing the first hand of *Tornado Alley.*

I sat across from Brent and Nick while Mom took the seat opposite Dad. She mock-glared at Dad and Nick. "I only ask that you both remember, there are three other people at this table. No ganging up on everyone and cheating like you do when you play on the app."

Dad laughed. "Cheating only works on the app, Maren. Why do you think we like it so much?"

"There's an app for this game?" asked Brent.

Nick nodded. "I'll show you tomorrow." He surveyed the cards in his hand. "Ooh! Great hand. Thanks, Erik!" He leaned toward Brent. "Save your StormChaser card and your JetStream card. And if you draw the F-5, guard it with your life. Anything else, you can discard for an extra draw on your turn."

Brent nodded and took a deep breath. "Okay. Can I check the rules if I need to?"

Dad slid them across the table toward him. "Sure thing."

"Don't worry," I said. "Dad and Nick play hard, but they hardly ever win unless they're playing the app. Mom almost always wins in real life."

"One of these days..." Dad beaned Mom with an M&M. Mom squealed and beaned him back.

Brent cracked a smile, and beat the pants off everyone, his first game.

That was over six years ago. Tonight, there's no laughter, no joking or horsing around. Dad wraps his free arm around me but otherwise doesn't move. I don't hug him back. What hangs in the air between us now is the fact that we escaped hell, but our friends didn't.

We get to go on as if nothing ever happened. Why does that make me feel numb?

Brent got here around nine o'clock. Mom already had the futon in Dad's office set up; Brent just went in and shut the door. He didn't even eat anything.

I'd fed Astrid around seven, then let her play games on my phone while Mom, Dad, and I picked at leftovers from the fridge, finally giving in to the gnawing in our stomachs.

Tucking Astrid into my blankets, I promised we'd get Wicked Chicken tomorrow and do her birthday dinner then.

"And macaroni salad and edamame?" she asked.

"Would it be your birthday dinner without them?"

She shook her head *No*. I nestled Mr. Ribbit in beside her and she started in on his sucking foot.

The clock over the kitchen sink ticks the seconds out, the only sound in the room.

Tick, tick, tick...

Marking the seconds we still have together.

The phone rings. I jump. Mom sucks her breath in sharply.

We let the machine get it again, expecting more of what we've been subjected to all evening—*so sorry to hear... Tragedy for our entire community... Anything we can do to help... Praying for you all*—but it's an automated district call.

"This is a notice from the superintendent of Winslow public schools, Dr. Linda Ruiz. In response to today's violence on the Winslow Elementary School campus, all Winslow Public Schools will be closed for the rest of the week. This includes all extracurricular and athletic activities. Parents of Winslow Elementary students will be notified of district plans regarding the remainder of the school year once a decision has been made." There is a pause, then the message continues. "Our prayers are with all the families affected by this horrific event. Thank you."

Dad stands, walks over to the phone, and turns the speaker volume off. Then he switches off the ringer, too.

"I'll take care of Astrid this week. Keep her occupied," I say, sliding out of the booth.

"What?" Mom asks, but I don't respond, and I don't hear Dad's answer, either. I'm already turning the corner to the living room, where I sit in the middle of the floor, in Astrid's TV-watching spot. A warm circle of light from the reading lamp by the couch cuts through the darkness, but it's too much. I turn it off and return to Astrid's spot. Wrapping my arms around my knees and staring at the small cluster of framed photos in front of the picture window, I let myself sink into the soft, late-spring darkness until it colors my mood.

What good will prayers do? They won't bring back Uncle Nick or anyone else who died. They won't help Luther—only surgeons can do that. I pull out my phone to text Oakley but what is there to say? Where do I start? Somehow, texting feels both essential and crass. I need to reach her—find some way to hold her through this—but the colorful bubbles seem like balloons at a funeral. I close the app and shove the phone into my back pocket.

Outside, beyond the picture window, headlights slide by and move on.

Dad plods down the dark hall to his den. The door clicks open.

Mom comes in and sits beside me. "Kirsten…" Her voice is tired and breathy, her eyes swollen from crying. She takes my hand but I pull it away.

"Don't."

"We'll get through this together."

I let out a sharp laugh. She stands and sighs.

"We'll talk later," she says, then heads down the hallway until the gloom swallows her.

Finally alone, I let my gaze range the room, resting on the collage of Mom's and Dad's wedding photos by the front door. I can fit the images in place as easily as a puzzle of the United States. Even though I can barely make out the details from here, my eyes are pulled to the photo of Dad and Uncle Nick, his best man. I don't really need to see it to know they're in a corny, suggested-by-the-photographer pose: both in their tuxes, with Dad pretend pitching and Nick crouched, catcher's mitt in hand.

Beside the wedding collage is another, of me: three, in my pink ballet tutu; five, on the big-kid swings at the park with Oakley; six, beside the newly planted apple tree that sprouted my love of gardening; ten, as a sunflower for Halloween…

There's no photo collage of Astrid.

It's not that we don't have pictures of Astrid, it's just that they're all on our phones.

Maybe Astrid and I can do that, this week—upload a bunch of photos and get prints made, so she can have a collage by the front door, too. That'll help keep her busy while Mom and Dad help Brent plan Nick's funeral.

Feeling less tortured now that I've got a game plan, I stand and pad toward my room at the end of the hall. Dad's den is silent, but the door is open and I peer in. He's sprawled stomach-down on the futon, one arm slung over Brent. The master bedroom is empty, and I find Mom on Astrid's bed, curled into a ball and clutching one of the frog-face throw pillows. I cover her with one of Grandma Madsen's crocheted afghans and shut the door behind me.

In my own bedroom doorway, I stand for a minute watching Astrid sleep, listening to her adenoidal snores and loving every single one for the first time. Pulling on an old concert tee, I sneak into bed beside her. Usually, I leave my charm bracelet in a little shell on my dresser but tonight, I can't stand the thought of taking it off. Astrid stirs, then curls against me, still sucking on Mr. Ribbit. I watch her sleep until I drift off, myself.

They gave me the bracelet the day they told me Mom was pregnant.

I had my suspicions, though—after all, I was already in the sixth grade. We'd had a sex-ed class in fifth grade—at least, enough of a sex-ed class that I knew what it meant when Mom started puking out of nowhere and kept on puking, even though me and Dad never got sick. Plus, I kind-of remembered when Oakley's was mom's pregnant with Luther, and she suddenly couldn't stand the smell or taste of pork. Oakley still refers to it as The Summer Without Ribs.

After Mom's "stomach bug" had dragged on for over two weeks, they told me.

They were sitting there, together on the couch, when I arrived home from a sleepover at Oakley's one Saturday morning early in October.

"Kirsten, honey? Come here and sit with us for a minute." Dad patted the spot between them. Mom was sipping hot yellow Gatorade—the only thing she'd kept down since Wednesday. So disgusting.

"Yeah?" I lowered myself to the reserved space. "Is everything okay?" I already knew it wasn't *okay*-okay, but I still needed to make sure all Mom's puking wasn't something horrible.

"You know how Mom's stomach has been bothering her lately?" Dad began.

I didn't want to sit through five minutes of build-up, so I jumped in. "Is Mom having a baby?"

Mom made a snort-laugh. "I told you she suspected…"

Dad shook his head and did that shrugging thing he always does when Mom's right. "You did."

"The thing is," Mom said, "I'm having a hard time with the morning sickness. It's a lot worse than I had it with you. We're going to need you to help a little with meals, since Dad usually gets home too late to start supper."

I'd never made much more than a microwaveable pasta bowl or hot chocolate, but I nodded. "You'll have to show me what to do."

"Let's not torture Mom more than we have to," said Dad. "I'm going to try and get home earlier a few nights a week, but I can't guarantee it. So, I'll teach you the basics, and we'll find some easy recipes that you can do on your own. But we'll need to avoid chicken for a while, since—"

At that, Mom made a *hurk* noise and scrambled off the couch, bolting toward the bathroom.

"…apparently, even the mention turns Mom's stomach," Dad finished, laughing a little.

We brainstormed basic meal ideas—spaghetti and meatballs, tacos, three-bean chili with canned beans—and after a few minutes, Mom came back in. Clearing her throat, she sank back into her spot on the couch. "Did you give her the thing?" she asked, and Dad picked up a small wrapped box I hadn't noticed on the table beside him.

"Mom and I thought, since you'll probably be helping out a lot—we wanted to recognize the fact that this baby is a surprise for all of us, and that your life is going to change, too." He pressed down on the stick-on bow, then handed me the box.

I stared at the tiny package. Oakley and her little brother Luther fought a lot, but Oakley also went after anyone who picked on him—which happened a lot, since he's such a rule-follower. Last year, when it was his turn to be Kindergarten Bathroom Monitor, he made himself a little cop-style badge out of a jar lid from the recycling bin and wore it around his neck on a piece of string until his teacher said it wasn't safe and made him take it off. Oakley made him a cardboard one he could wear on his belt, and he kept on strutting around, reminding everyone, including his parents, to wash their hands. Maybe a little brother or sister wouldn't be so bad. Maybe it would even be fun, after a while.

"Are you having a boy or a girl?" I asked Mom, running my fingers along the edge of the box. They'd picked out lavender paper with darker purple dots—my favorite color.

"Oh, honey, we're only a month in," Mom said, laughing. "We won't know that until January—maybe February."

"Oh." I plucked the bow off and stuck it on top of Dad's head, the way Mom and I always do. Maybe they'd let me come to the appointment where they find out. Would they get one of those black-and-white pictures that looks like an alien blob, and show it around to everyone as if people can make out where the legs and arms and head are? I tore off the paper and lifted the lid off the white cardboard box. Inside was a link-style silver charm bracelet.

My Astrid bracelet.

5

TUESDAY MORNING

*K*YURP*, you hafta get up.*

It's too early, Frog Breath.

It's not. And you need to look for your charm.

Later.

Now.

Why now?

Remember the first one I picked out all by myself?

Yeah, it was the snowflake.

For Emily Snow.

And Mom helped you hide it.

Right. Remember where?

Wasn't it in a bag of Cheezy Whalez?

Uh-huh. Now c'mon.
Get up and look for your new charm.

Will you give me a hint?

Nuh-uh. You hafta find without me.

I don't want to find it without you.

You have to.

The sun is blazing through the window and it takes me a moment to remember why I don't have to freak out about being late for school. It's after ten, so Astrid's probably been up for hours. Scrambling up, I peer through the window. She's not out at her willow, either. I grab some shorts from the floor and tug them on, then venture down the hall, past Dad's empty den. Brent is gone. Did he go home? The Brodericks' house is on the other side of the block; our back yards actually meet in the middle of the creek that bisects the small patch of woods.

In the living room, I sink into my usual seat on the couch. Everything is exactly the same as it was last night, but somehow, it feels different. As if I've never been in this room before. But the couch is the same overstuffed green-and-white striped couch we've always had. Dad's easy chair is still the same shabby leather recliner he bought secondhand before dating Mom. The small bookshelf, stocked with all the photo albums Dad inherited from his parents, stands beneath the picture window, a selection of DVDs we've recently watched stacked neatly to the left of the framed photos: Astrid's kindergarten picture, Mom and Dad's wedding photo, and my senior portrait. Is it the light that's different? Or me?

Astrid wanders in, wearing her frog boots and pajamas.

I turn on the TV and call up an episode of *Lily's Pad* for her, then return to the couch.

I pull out my phone and scroll through some texts that came in before I woke up. They all say the same kind of thing—so sorry... text if you need me... can't believe this happened... There's even one from my boss, Maura.

> **Maura:** Kirsten, I'm so sorry to hear about Astrid. Please don't worry about coming in until you're ready. Jeff and I will cover your shifts. Just text if you need anything.

She must not realize Astrid's okay—just scared. But I'm not about to be rude, so I keep my reply basic.

> **Kirsten:** Thanks, Maura. It's unreal. Mom and Dad will be glad to have me around to help while they're preoccupied with funeral plans

Pocketing my phone, I watch Astrid watching TV. She's sprawled on her stomach on the floor, her legs bent up at the knees like always. It's the episode where Mama Frog makes Lily and Shelley take Tad with them when they explore the nearby woods. Lily and Shelley scare Tad by hiding in a tree-stump, only to leap out, screaming, *A bat! A bat!* Tad cries, *Don't let it eat me Lily! Don't let it eat me!*

Astrid kicks her feet back and forth, as if unmoved by Tad's trauma, and giggles.

On-screen, Lily and Shelley roll around in the soft, leafy mulch, laughing and pointing at Tad.

"That's not fair," I say.

"It is, too." Astrid turns to face me. "Tad's a baby. He's always breaking Lily's toys and getting in the way. He doesn't even know bats don't hunt in the day."

"He's still little. He'll learn as he grows up."

"Some kids don't grow up." Astrid stares at me for a long moment, then blinks and turns back to the show.

Mom's voice drifts in from the kitchen. I follow the reassuring sound and find her at the kitchen table, on her phone. Astrid's gifts are still piled against the wall. Mom's brown eyes are puffy from crying all night, and the way she's hugging herself with her free hand makes her look like a child scared to find herself suddenly alone in the dark. There's a small prescription bottle on the table beside her coffee-in-progress. The label says ATIVAN. Isn't that for panic attacks? Oakley's mom took it for a while, when her mom and aunt both had breast cancer. When did my mom start having panic attacks?

"…Wednesday, to figure everything out," she says.

In front of her on the table is one of those grocery-store notepads with near-useless magnets. I lean over and read what she's written on it:

Wed—2:30 pm
Randall & Torres Funeral Home, 43 Merrimack

Nick—Thurs AM — 9?—First Unitarian, Chelmsford

Astrid—

That must be to work out the details of Uncle Nick's funeral. Will Brent go to the funeral home with them? Or are Mom and Dad shouldering that burden for him? When she gets off the phone, I'll answer the Astrid question: Sure, I can watch her. No problem.

She glances up at me, a tight smile flickering across her face, and nods toward the coffee pot. I pour myself a cup and dose it with my usual ton of sugar and splash of half-and-half. On the counter are trays of mini muffins and picked-at coffeecake. Mom never buys stuff like this. People must have brought it by for Brent. I choose an apple cinnamon muffin and eat it in two bites as I look out the window above the sink. Dad sits on the deck, staring toward the bottom of the backyard. He's still in yesterday's clothes, his sandy hair standing up on one side and smushed flat on the other.

"No, don't rush up," says Mom. "Wednesday afternoon is fine. Just let me know what time to meet the train."

She must be talking to Grandma. Grandma always comes up from New York by train and stays in the den. But Brent's staying in the den, now. I stare out the window at Dad, trying to gauge what he's looking at. Maybe the willow, or the foot-bridge that connects our yard to Nick's yard—Brent's yard, now.

Dad asleep on the futon, one arm slung over Brent—Mom, curled around Astrid's frog pillow—

Mom hangs up the phone as there's a tentative knock at the side door. I turn away from the sight of my broken dad and toward the door.

When I pull the curtain aside, Josie is there, wearing cutoffs and a Bruins tee, her lacrosse bandanna covering her hair. She must've rolled out of bed and come over, only stopping for the box of Dunks she's holding. Beyond her, lining the curb like trash cans, are television vans. I bet it's twenty times worse at Oakley's or Brent's.

I open the door and she slips in. "Kirsten, I'm so sorry…"

I shut the door and Josie follows me up the three steps to the kitchen. She sets the Dunk's box on the counter. "Hi, Mrs. Madsen. I'm… so sorry…"

"Thank you, Josie," says Mom. Her voice sounds thin, like she's already said *thank you* too many times for something she never wanted. "Thank you for being here for Kirsten."

I look at Josie, giving her a parents-are-so-embarrassing eye-roll. "Come on back."

"Of course," Josie says, her gaze ranging between me and Mom before it settles on me and she offers an uncertain smile.

Usually, when I realize everyone in the family is off doing their own thing in their own space, I'm grateful for the space and the privacy. Today, as Josie and I tread down the hallway, past the open den door, Astrid's TV show fading as we round the corner to my room, I feel a pang of guilt—*you're abandoning them.* I push the nonsensical thought away. Mom is there for Dad, and Astrid's too wrapped up in her show to focus on the change in routine. It's fine.

I shut the door on all of it and flip my bedspread across the sheets. Josie and I sit, side by side, on the rumpled bedspread. We're awkwardly silent, sneaking glances at each other.

Finally, I have to break the silence before it smothers me. I shift, turning toward her, and we blurt in sync: "Sorry I bailed on you yesterday…" "I wish I knew what to say…"

We do that nervous laugh thing, then both say, "you go…" then, "no, you…" then, "sorry…" and then we both stop, because how else do you break out of a loop like this?

I take a deep breath and pick up a throw-pillow that fell to the floor sometime overnight. It's a photo-collage pillow, one of a matched pair Oakley's mom made us last year, full of photos of me and Oakley reaching all the way back to kindergarten. I trace a finger along the lines where one image meets the next. *I'll make one for Astrid and Lexie,* I think. But my throat tightens as soon as the thought comes. Why?

"Kirsten?" Josie touches my shoulder. The slight pressure of her hand is warm and comforting, but there's a strange sadness deep inside me, like some secret core has cracked, and I just keep staring at the pillow. "I'm so sorry…" Josie says.

"Me, too," I respond. Something shifts in my head and the need to escape from this house surges inside, making me fidget. I turn toward Josie again.

"Hey," I say, standing. "Want to go for a run? We can swing by Oakley's and see if she's heard anything about Luther." In the moment it takes her to answer, I'm halfway across the room, plucking my sneakers from the shoe-pile in my closet and sitting on the carpet to tug them on.

"A run? Sure." She wags her feet, making her drugstore flip-flops flap. "I'll need to grab my running shoes from the trunk, though. And we should probably cut through the back yards. Some of the reporters are pretty determined."

I nod, secure my hair into a ponytail, and open the door.

On our way past Astrid's room, I peek in. She's on the floor, playing with her *Lily's Pad* action figures. "No, Tad," she says, in her Lily-voice. "That's dangerous."

"Hey, Frog Breath? Josie and I are going for a quick run. Stay out of Mom and Dad's hair. Got it?"

She keeps playing, making Lily hop onto a log made from an empty toilet paper roll.

"What? Astrid's okay?" Beside me, Josie pokes her head around the edge of the doorway, then pulls back, a frown flashing across her face before becoming a tight smile. She runs a hand through her hair. "Um... lemme get my gear," she takes a backward step down the hall.

"Meet you in the kitchen," I say, lingering in Astrid's doorway and watching her play. "Astrid? Did you hear? Don't bug Mom and Dad."

"Don't bug Mom and Dad," she echoes. As Lily guides Tad back across the log and into a patch of shrubs made of crumped-up construction paper, Astrid switches back to her Lily voice. "See, Tad? If we hide under here, the predators can't get us."

She'll probably still be here playing when I get back. "Great. I'll fix you lunch when I get home." I head for the kitchen.

Josie's leaning against the counter, her sneakers on the floor beside her. Oakley's in the booth, across from my mom.

"...last night, but I thought I was imaging it..." says Mom, then drops off when she sees me. "Oakley's here," she says, her tone suddenly light.

Oakley's Mom's slow cooker is on the counter, warming what smells like her shepherd's pie. Our moms swapped favorite recipes years ago, and Mom must be making it for the Washingtons, but it's weird that she's not using our slow cooker.

"Are you guys okay?" I ask Oakley.

Oakley faces me; her warm brown eyes are puffy and blood-shot. "Not really. You know Luther... always looking out for everyone else." She shakes her head.

I let out a self-conscious, snorty laugh. Oakley is right: only in the fifth grade, Luther already considers himself in training to be a firefighter or an EMT... or, he sometimes says, a police officer. He's all about helping people. All about following the rules. So why is he in the hospital instead of here, pushing his glasses up his nose and going on about how Oakley was supposed to drop him off at so-and-so's house before coming here—or, whatever?

"The fool picks that moment to be a hero. His teacher told me he pushed five kids into the bathroom…"

She melts into my arms. "I'm sorry…" I mumble.

"Oh, God…" She breaks into loud, body-wracking sobs, finding fresh tears from depths I'm grateful I don't need to access in myself. "I swear… I promise… if this could just be a dream… if he could just be okay… I'll never kick him out of my room again.… Please… oh, please…" I hold her awkwardly, rubbing her arms and her back, as she chokes on her own efforts to breathe. Josie reaches behind me and places a hand on Oakley's shoulder.

Oakley and I are both crying over Luther. Mom leans across the table, reaching one hand toward each of us. Oakley's words sputter out between gasps. "Oh, God… I can't believe… I shouldn't be… how are you…? …How can you even bear it?"

"Let it out, Oakley. It's okay. It's not a competition." Mom stretches and puts a hand on Oakley's arm. "Why don't you three go for that run? A little physical exertion might help."

In the back yard, Josie pauses beside the willow. "Is this Astrid's tree?"

I brush a hand along the whippy branches. "A weeping willow. Like from *Lily's Pad*."

Oakley takes my free hand and squeezes. "K, I'm so sorry…"

I shake my head. "I don't want to think about it." Can't think about what might've been. *Won't.* "Let's just get out of here."

We follow the creek through the back yards to where Oakley parked her dad's old car out of sight of the news vans. We drive around aimlessly for over a whole thirty-minute music sweep, talking about nothing—stupid stuff, like the finals prep we're missing, who's having graduation parties, and what jobs we have lined up for earning college money. Eventually, we find ourselves in the empty overflow lot behind the high school.

She shuts the engine off. I think we're all afraid to talk about yesterday again, but it's unsettling how none of us are our usual selves. How long will that last? I mean, things have to go back to normal—or, as normal as they'll ever be again.

We sit quietly for a while before it seems we all decide together, subconsciously, that it's time to run. We leave the car like climbing from a pool of quicksand, stumbling toward the football field and the wide pink track.

We start slow, at practically a walk, and after the first circuit, Josie and I follow Oakley's lead as she picks up the pace one lap at a time. After a while, she pulls ahead and we end up staggered, falling into our own rhythms.

My sneakers meet the track—*cushcushcushcush*—and I focus on a spot several yards ahead. Sweat stings my eyes, trickles down my back, wrinkles the clasp of my bra. *Cushcushcushcush.*

The early summer air smells of lilacs and cut grass, as comforting as marshmallows toasted over the last few red-hot charcoal briquettes. My muscles warm, relaxing into the predictability of my movements: my stride steady, my arms pumping, my breathing deep and regular.

Cushcushcushcush.

Eventually Oakley slows to a walk and retires to the field, where she stretches out near the 50-yard line, face up beneath the bright, clear sky. One lap later, Josie joins her.

I keep running. I'm not sure why. Maybe it's that I've escaped the trauma, and it's the only thing I can do to lessen the guilt itching at me like poison ivy in an unreachable spot. I keep replaying yesterday afternoon in my head: ice cream with Josie, the drive to the school, the feel of Astrid's weight against me as I piggybacked her all the way to the dinky Ford Mom and Dad bought me…. Every time a what-if threatens to invade my thoughts, I push it away, knowing that Astrid's okay. She's okay. I keep running—one more, two more, three more laps—before I take one last lap at a walk and join my friends.

Oakley's lying there, eyes shut to the world, tears running into her ears. Josie's positioned head-to-head at a slight angle to Oakley, shielding her eyes with one hand.

"What we do, now?" I asked, panting a bit as I stretch out on my back in the empty spot in the obtuse angle between them. Reaching out, I take Oakley's hand, then Josie's. Oakley's hand is warm and unresisting. She squeezes once. I squeeze back.

We lie there for I don't know how long. Heads together and legs extended in three directions, we're an asterisk, a starfish, a crosshair, a compass, a clock...

A peace sign.

We'll be a safe harbor for each other.

We'll get through this together. Even if Josie's not ready to come out to the world. Even if all I can do for Oakley is show up and run. I'll do that. We'll run until there's nowhere left to go.

News vans line the curb, leading the way to Brent's house like ants to sugar. Oakley keeps driving, turning right and parking halfway down the block. We cut through the back yards, sneaking along the creek to keep out of sight as I lead the way toward the Brodericks' deck door. Oakley and Josie lag behind a little. When I turn to hurry-up them, they've stopped walking and are huddled together. *I think we should tell her parents*, Josie says, then straightens and smiles when she sees me gesturing. She hustles forward, Oakley on her tail and giving me a pensive look.

Brent answers the deck door, still wearing yesterday's jeans and t-shirt. Even though he went right to bed after coming over last night, from the huge dark circles under his eyes, it looks like he didn't sleep at all.

I shut the French doors behind us as he slides into his usual chair at the round kitchen table. I sit beside him. Oakley and Josie tackle the pile of dishes in the sink: Oakley rinses and Josie loads the dishwasher.

Brent glances at me. "So, your parents and I talked this morning. Dad always said if anything happened…"

I nod. I was right, last night—Mom and Dad are officially Brent's guardians now. "Are they going to set you up in the den?"

"That's what we talked about." His voice is low and rough with exhaustion. "Since I'm just across the back yard, they said I can sleep here when I want. I'm supposed to come over every night for dinner, though."

Never again will I walk past the den to see Nick and Dad sprawled on the futon, shouting at the TV during a Sox or a Pats game. Somehow, it feels incomprehensible that either team will ever play again, but I know that's not right. I know the Sox will say something when they play tonight—dedicate the game to Winslow victims, or take up a collection, or something.

"Are you? Going to sleep here?" I don't think I'd be able to. Or—maybe I'd want to sleep in Nick's bed to keep him close to me for as long as I could.

He shrugs. "I don't know. It's home, you know? Even if it's really not, anymore."

"I'm sorry," I say. It sounds so meager, like the seed of a willow. But a willow's roots reach far in their search for water, so maybe it's not completely stupid to hope Brent will understand how much my *sorry* means.

Oakley rummages through the trays of food and desserts already cluttering the counter, scoops something into a bowl, microwaves it, and slides it in front of Brent. She sits on his other side and wraps one arm around him. Josie leans against the counter, holding one hand in the other and glancing at me, then away again.

"I'm not hungry," Brent mumbles, but takes the fork and picks at the food, anyway. It's some weird corn-noodle-beef casserole that looks more like steaming dog food than anything else. He takes a few bites.

The landline trills. Josie lunges across the counter and grabs it before it can ring again. She listens for a moment, then says, "No comment," and punches the end button. Before setting it back in the cradle, she examines the handset and silences the ringer.

Brent leans back in his chair, a grimace eclipsing his easy-going features.

Oakley answers a knock at the deck door, and Brent's best friends tumble into the kitchen. Oakley shuts the door behind them.

"Wasn't that the guy from Fox Five?" Sean mutters, his freckles disappearing into his flushing face as he gets more worked up. "'What does it feel like?' That's fucking sick, dude! What does he think it feels like?" He's holding a green cardboard container of blueberries. "Mom hit the Parlee farm stand first thing. Said you need to eat right." He rolls his eyes and sets the carton on the counter.

Tomás pulls me into a hug. "Sorry about your sister, Kirsten."

I shake my head and twist out of his embrace, standing.

Glancing up from the dog-food casserole, Brent offers a smile that only plays at his mouth. "Hey."

Tomás and Sean flank Brent, pull him out of the chair, clap him on the biceps, and slide into brief, boyish hugs.

"Dude," says Tomás. "You okay?"

Brent shrugs and sits back down.

Tomás and Sean grab bottles of water from the fridge and a Dunkin box from the selection on the counter before claiming the seats around Brent. They're sweaty, Tomás's curls plastered across his forehead and Sean's wild, red hair slicked back like it's the 50s.

Oakley takes the last seat, pulling it out so she can see both me and Brent, and I hop up onto the counter near Josie. "Did you guys run here?" I ask. Josie takes a blueberry muffin from the tray on the counter and carefully peels away the paper wrap. I slide the blueberry carton toward me, unwrap the wax paper from the top, and hold the carton to my nose. The earthy scent reminds me we haven't taken Astrid berry-picking yet this summer. Every time we go, it's the end of the world if we don't also pick up a bag of the mini doughnuts they make with whichever fruits are in season.

"Mom and Pop are at the hospital. My sister Xiomara teaches third grade—she was in the caf. Last I heard, she was near the end of the line for surgery," Tomás reports. "But that's good. It means she's stable. She's going to be okay."

Tomás takes a Boston Kreme as Sean goes for a jelly. "I'd hate to be a surgeon at Lowell Memorial or Nashua General right now," says Tomás. "They must be exhausted." He flicks his eyes from me to Oakley, then to Brent, but Brent is staring at his fork.

"Exhausted," I say, staring at Brent staring at his fork.

Oakley plucks a strawberry frosted from the box. "Exhausted," she mumbles.

Sean nods. "My mom's driving all over the place, getting food and stuff for people. She said to tell you she's making you a lasagna for the freezer." He jerks his head toward Brent, then takes a too-big bite of his doughnut. Jelly leaks from the corners of his mouth.

Oakley curls her lip. "You just gotta be gross, huh?"

Sean shrugs, still trying to get a handle on his overfull mouth. Tomás glances at Oakley, his mouth twitching, then reaches into the box and grabs another Boston Kreme, shoving the whole thing in his mouth at once. He makes no attempt to prevent the chocolate and cream from oozing out as he works to gain control of the doughnut.

Once he finally conquers it, Sean stands and examines the grocery-store pies on the counter. "Blueberry... apple... strawberry-rhubarb... or pumpkin?"

"Who the fuck makes a pumpkin pie in June?" says Tomás, around the last of his doughnut. He and Sean exchange looks, and Tomás gestures with both hands. Sean collects three forks from the drawer and returns to the table, plopping the pumpkin pie in the center and shoving the dog-food casserole aside.

Brent shakes his head a little as Sean hands around the forks.

Sean gives him one of those boy-punches. "You gotta eat, dude."

Brent sighs and picks up his fork. He takes a small forkful right from the pie plate and brings it slowly to his mouth. After that first bite, he leans forward and the three of them attack the pie with gusto, shoveling huge forkfuls into their mouths.

Oakley leans back in her chair, catches my eye, and raises an eyebrow.

The kitchen fills with the grunts and squelches of three boys eating like they've never had pie before.

Less than two minutes later, the tin plate is empty of everything but a raisin-sized piece of burnt crust.

"Holy shit," murmurs Josie. "Did that just happen?"

Tomás jerks his chin toward Brent. "Better?"

Brent nods, and we all fall silent for several minutes.

Josie picks the blueberries out of her muffin, eating them a few at a time. Then she smushes the cake into doughy balls and builds a burial mound on the counter between us.

Brent digs the fork through the now-cold casserole, levering up chunks as dense as New England clay, then letting them plop back into the bowl.

I can't tell what he's thinking. I consider how Dad is today: heavy-limbed and dead-faced, looking through me instead of at me. Brent seems the same. Oakley looks over at me and bursts into silent tears. What did she do last night, while I was curled up in bed with Astrid, watching her breathe? Did she cry? Throw things?

Picking a blueberry from the Parlee carton, I put it in my mouth, letting its tang blossom across my tongue before eating it.

Oakley's phone rings. She holds the phone to her ear and the rest of us watch her, trying to figure out how Luther's surgery went. Her dark, freckled face shifts from relief to sadness to determination. She hangs up and fiddles with the phone for a few moments before speaking.

"They couldn't save his eye. But he's awake and pissed at being forced to start with Jell-O instead of Flamin' Hot Cheetos," she says, with a small smile.

"Who knew there was a market for Flamin' Hot Jell-O?" I say, but nobody even smiles.

I select another blueberry and squish it between two fingers. The slick purple juice stains my skin, the tiny seeds gritty between my fingers. I lick my finger clean, pick a third blueberry and squish it, then a fourth. The juice trickles down my fingers, tickling my palm.

Oakley stands, grabs my sticky hand, and squeezes it between both of hers. "Kirsten..." she says, and starts bawling all over again.

6

TUESDAY AFTERNOON

IT'S after four by the time I get home, cutting through the back yard from Brent's house. On the way, I turn the hose on for the willow. Mom and Dad are squeezed onto the couch, asleep in each other's arms. I find Astrid in her bedroom, still playing with her *Lily's Pad* figures like I expected. She's changed into a pair of flannel jammies and pulled on her fluffy, frog-green bathrobe over them.

"Hey Frog Breath. What's up?" I study the scene she's created with her toys. It looks like Lily and Shelley are hiding beneath a half-fallen log. Astrid has a gang of predatory birds positioned all around the log—there's no escape.

She looks up at me. "I'm cold."

"Want some hot chocolate?"

She nods and follows me into the kitchen, where I heat up some water in the microwave and pour it over the powdered drink mix, adding an ice cube and enough mini marshmallows to cover the surface of her drink. I make myself one, too, and we sit silently at the booth, sipping the drinks bit-by-bit from teaspoons until they're cool enough to take straight from the cup. So what if it's June? I eye the pile of gifts still on the table.

"Mom and Dad didn't help you open these yet?"

She shakes her head.

I sigh. "They're a little preoccupied."

She nods.

"Do you understand what happened yesterday?" I ask. Maybe I shouldn't be doing this, but Mom and Dad are obviously overwhelmed. Even the meal for Oakley's family is still here, in the slow cooker. It's not like them to goof up on something like that. But then—we've never dealt with anything like this before. It's unfamiliar territory for all of us and out of everyone, I'm the least affected. I'm okay picking up the slack.

Astrid slurps up a half-melted marshmallow. "Hunter's dad wasn't supposed to pick him up anymore. Why'd they let him come into the school?"

I heard something about that on the radio as we drove back from the high school fields—but I'm not really sure what the deal is. I don't remember seeing him at the indoor gym that afternoon when I picked up Astrid, and I wish I could pretend the whole thing hadn't happened. "Yeah, well... I don't know about that part. I mean, do you understand what happened with kids getting hurt? Why I had to get you from the sports club?"

"Kids got killed," she whispers, looking down.

"Yeah. They did."

"Some grown-ups, too."

"Yeah. And a bunch of other kids and grown-ups got hurt. So... that's why you can't go to school today. Or, for a little while. Until they figure out exactly what happened and probably find another place to have school—at least until the end of the school year. Maybe next year, they'll let kids go back to Winslow Elementary."

They won't, of course. They'll reclaim the old building—Riverview Elementary—from whoever's leasing it and the kids will go to school there.

Astrid nods, and we fall back into silence until our hot chocolates are finished. I stare at the gifts still waiting for some love from her. Maybe it would do Mom and Dad some good to have Astrid's birthday.

"Hey, Frog Breath," I say, pulling the gifts towards the table's edge. "I'm going to wake Mom and Dad. Go change out of your jammies and back into play clothes, okay?"

She starts toward her bedroom, singing "Down by the pond-shore… in the weeping willow's shade… that's Lily's Pad…"

In the hope some noise will tug Mom and Dad awake, I clear away the hot-chocolate cups loudly, letting them clatter against each other, and banging the pantry door shut. When I enter the living room, though, they're still asleep.

"Mom? Dad?"

Mom startles awake and sits up, stretching. Dad mumbles something and starts snoring.

"What time is it?" asks Mom.

"Nearly five."

She stands and stretches some more. "Thanks for waking me." She pulls one of Grandma's afghans over Dad and heads toward the kitchen. "Brent should be here around six. Help me convince him to sleep here a few more nights?"

"I'm pretty sure he's already planning to," I say, following her.

She sees the pile of Astrid's gifts, pulled forward, and takes a deep breath before pushing them back against the booth wall.

I pull them forward again. "Astrid deserves a birthday," I say. "None of this is her fault."

Mom stares at me, her mouth open and this look in her eye like she can't decide if she should yell at me or cry.

Finally, she says, "You want to do this today? Now?" Her voice is wobbly and wet.

"We can't let what happened overshadow her birthday completely."

"I don't understand," she says, slowly. "What exactly do you think is going on?"

"You guys are overwhelmed trying to help Brent," I say, then realize that they're both ripped up over Nick's death, too. I'm such an idiot—no wonder they're practically zombies. "How about if I open them with her after dinner? I'll help her do it in her room, and I'll clean everything up."

"Kirsten…"

"What's going on?" Dad asks. He's standing in the kitchen doorway, squinting against the fluorescent light. His hair is even more smushed-up than it was this morning.

I pick up one present. "Astrid's birthday? I know you guys are trying to be there for Brent right now, but someone needs to be there for Astrid. I can do that."

Dad looks from me to Mom. There's a long pause as they do that parental-eye-conversation thing, then Dad turns back to me.

"You want to help Astrid open her presents." His voice is flat.

"Yes. She didn't get to last night. I promised her we'd do it tonight, complete with her Wicked Chicken dinner. I'm surprised she didn't tear into everything on her own this afternoon."

He steps slowly into the kitchen, toward me. When he reaches me, he takes the gift I'm holding and sets it back on the pile, moving in practically slow-motion. He pushes everything back against the wall. Again.

"Just give it a little more time." His voice is quiet, but there is a finality to it I'm not used to. "Just a few more days. Please. Then… we'll have Astrid's birthday."

Right then, Astrid comes skittering into the kitchen behind Dad. She slips between him and Mom, grabbing onto my hand. "Ready for presents!"

One look at Mom and Dad tells me I'm the one explaining this to Astrid. Great.

I sit in the booth and hold both her hands in mine. "Hey, Frog Breath? I know what I said, but…" I glance at Mom and Dad. They're standing there, in the middle of the room, holding hands and watching me, Dad's forehead furrowed by a weird look on his face. "You know, right now we need to help take care of people like Brent. People who are sad."

Mom starts crying.

Astrid nods. "But I can still have my birthday, right?"

I take a deep breath. "Well, yes… kind-of. Do you think you can wait a little longer? Just a day or two? So we can help our friends? Then we can have your birthday."

"With my birthday dinner?"

"Definitely with your birthday dinner."

"And Callahan's ice cream?"

"Definitely with Callahan's ice cream."

Astrid considers it seriously, her eyes on the pile of presents. "There was an episode of *Lily's Pad* where Mama Frog promised to take Lily swimming with Shelley. Then Tad got hurt, and they had to go to the doctor instead. But after Tad was all better, Mama took Lily and Shelley swimming." Astrid nods. "I guess I can be patient. Like Lily."

I smile and stand. "Thanks, Frog Breath. I knew you would understand. Let's go get cleaned up for dinner. Brent will be here soon."

As I shuffle her off down the hall to the bathroom, she keeps chattering. "Can we go to the Mixed-up Park with Lexie tomorrow? There's a game we play that only works there..."

"I'll have to check with her dad, but maybe..."

Behind us, Dad mutters something to Mom. I don't hear his words, only the low rumble of his voice.

"Maybe you're right. We'll talk about it at dinner," replies Mom. "I think it would do us all some good."

By the time Brent arrives for dinner, Astrid is back in the living room watching *Lily's Pad* and I've set the table for five. I put Brent next to Dad, in Astrid's usual spot, and tell Astrid her new spot is between me and Mom. As I pour Astrid a glass of milk and plop a smallish spoonful of shepherd's pie onto her plate, Mom slides a cookie sheet bearing a grocery-store pie into the oven. We never have dessert right after dinner like that. The pie in the oven, and Mrs. Washington's slow cooker insert on a hot pad in the middle of our table, are two more things wrong about today.

"What are you doing?" asks Brent, eyebrows raised.

"Helping Astrid."

Brent watches me add a spoonful of peas to Astrid's plate. Then he takes a deep breath and glances at Dad before taking his seat.

Dinner is weird—it's mostly the sound of forks scraping across the ceramic dishes. Mom has this stiff smile plastered on her face and Dad says barely anything beyond *pass the peas* or *is there any more broccoli?* Brent keeps his head down, like he's never been more interested in shepherd's pie.

I tried to fill the silence by asking Astrid questions, but she's more interested in getting back to her cartoon. Just as I'm wondering if she really understands what happened yesterday—even though we talked about it—a metallic *bang!* rings out in the kitchen.

Astrid jumps in her seat then freezes, her eyes open wide.

I pull her onto my lap.

"Astrid," I say softly. I smooth her hair, even though it's already tidy. "Hey, Astrid. Frog Breath. It's okay. You're safe. It's just the cookie sheet, in the oven."

She whimpers and shakes her head *No.*

Holding her tight, I glance at Brent. His head is still down. He's probably thinking about Nick, wondering if he'd have the same reaction as Astrid, if he'd survived.

Brent shouldn't have to witness this.

I scoot my chair back and stand, scooping Astrid up with me. She wraps her arms around my neck and buries her face in my shoulder, still whimpering.

I lug her down the hall, murmuring, "It's okay... I promise you're safe..." and turn toward her room, but she shakes her head again. "I want to sleep in your bed."

Nodding, I head toward my room instead. She snuggles down into my blankets and I hand her Mr. Ribbit.

"Astrid, you know you're safe now, right?"

She doesn't respond.

"Astrid, it's just a noise from the oven. You've heard it before. It's just a noise."

Finally she says, "It's scary now."

"I know." I sit on the bed beside her. "Can you fall asleep on your own? Or do you want me to stay and sing 'Weeping Willow'?"

"Stay. But I don't need you to sing. I'm not a little baby."

This is the first time she's ever wanted me to *not* sing it. Will she ever want me to, again? Or is this where it ends? "I don't mind. I'm surprised you didn't ask me to sing it last night."

"I don't need you to sing to me anymore. Just stay."

I sigh. "Okay. I'll stay for a while."

And I do. I sit on the floor, leaning against the bed.

The first time I ever got her to fall asleep, she was only a few weeks old. Mom wasn't even back to work yet. Dad was stuck in a massive traffic jam on 128, and didn't want to lose more time by stopping at Market Basket, but Mom was freaking out about hamburger buns or the wrong kind of cheese or something—I mean, worked up to the point of crying, over burger fixings.

"Mom," I said. "Just go yourself."

"Kirsten, you don't understand," she said. "It's not that simple."

"Why not? You've left me home for more than an hour before. Oakley babysits Luther all the time."

She sniffled and looked at me. "Are you sure?"

"Astrid's asleep. If she wakes up, I'll change her and feed her and wear her in that baby-carrier if you're not back yet."

"But I haven't showered in two days…"

I handed Mom her Red Sox cap. "Nobody will notice. Just… put on a shirt that doesn't have baby puke all over it."

She plucked at the hem of her ratty shirt, but didn't move.

"Mom, I'm thirteen. I won't drop her."

But almost exactly the instant Mom's car left the driveway, Astrid started fussing.

I picked her up and made cooing noises the way Mom and Dad did. Changed her diaper. Cuddled her and warmed up a bottle in a bowl of hot water and tested it on my wrist.

Feeding her helped for like five minutes, then she started crying again, so I burped her—I think. It was hard to tell with all the crying.

She completely hated the baby-carrier thing—screamed even louder, turning all blotchy and radish-red. If her screams weren't so close to my ears, the whole thing would've been funny.

So I started doing that bouncy-swingy-dance move, which helped a little. I felt stupid, though, dancing to screaming instead of music, so I pulled up the new Emily Snow album, pumping it through Dad's new remote speaker. The second song was a cover of an old folk tune, and Astrid quieted almost immediately into hiccups.

That song was the only one on the album I couldn't stand.

But I put the song on repeat and sang along.

> *...so lay me down, my love,*
> *down for the long sleep—*
> *'neath the weeping willow, sweeping willow tree—*
> *leave me rest, my love*
> *and do not weep for me...*

Mom got home during the second run-through of the chorus.

"Kirsten! Can't you choose something more appropriate?"

"She likes it," I said.

"You can't sing that to a baby." She plopped the bag of burger buns and pre-sliced cheese on the dining room table and reached for Astrid, but I kept swooping around with her.

"Why not?" I laughed because Mom was right—it's a pretty depressing song. "I can't help it if she likes it. She cried almost the whole time you were gone, no matter what I tried, until this came on."

Mom scowled and scooped Astrid out of my arms. Astrid started crying again.

"I told you," I said, smirking. "Give her back. I'll keep her quiet while you start dinner."

Ever since then, whenever Astrid can't fall asleep, or wakes up with a nightmare, she asks for that song. Since Mom refuses to sing it, and Dad can't carry a tune any better than a bottomless bucket carries water, I'm the only one who can calm Astrid down.

The song turned into one of those sister-bond things, and it's part of why she chose a willow when I asked her what she wanted to help me plant for her sixth birthday. Last year, she wanted to plant lily pads in the creek, but let me convince her to go for a rhododendron underneath her bedroom window. I think she just liked the way *rhododendron* sounded.

I hum a few bars of the folk song anyway and Astrid mumbles, "I said, *don't*"

Sitting quietly with a kid, waiting for them to fall asleep, is as boring as football. Time stretches, every minute lasting longer than the one before. Finally, her breathing becomes slow and deep, and I shut the door gently behind me as I leave.

Returning to the dining room, I can tell the conversation has picked up. Were they censoring themselves before, because of Astrid? I guess that makes sense. None of the rest of us were in the school when it happened. None of us really know what Astrid saw. And how do you ask a kid to live that again?

Mom coughs a little as I swing around the corner. Passing behind her to reach my seat, I pat her back the way she used to pat mine when something went down the wrong way.

My dinner is cold by now, but I dig back in, anyway.

"What are you talking about?" I asked.

Brent says, "Um…" and glances at Dad.

Dad, pushing his peas into his potatoes, says, "There are some counselors—social workers and psychologists and therapists—who have open hours tomorrow for people who need to talk about what happened."

I nod.

Dad takes a deep breath and continues. "I think—I think we should all go."

I take a forkful of cold broccoli—*ugh*—and chew while I think.

It makes sense. Astrid could use someone knowledgeable—someone trained in these things—to talk to. It would help Brent and Dad, too. And maybe talking to someone would help me figure out how to be there for everyone, including Oakley.

"Okay," I say. "But how do you want me to explain it to Astrid?"

Dad drops his fork and it clatters against his plate. He rubs his eyes.

Mom puts a hand on his shoulder, but looks at me. "I'll...talk to her." She rubs Dad's arm. "It'll be all right. It's a good idea, Erik. It'll help."

We finish the meal in silence.

I'm on my stomach in the living room, using a yardstick to clear the underside of the couch. I've already found six broken crayons (in various shades of green), a dried-out brown marker, and one of Astrid's outgrown bedroom slippers. Everything is coated in dust, dirt, and crushed-up Cheezy Whalez.

Mom's footsteps pass, and the front door bolt lock *clacks* into position for the night. It's late—too late to have all the lights on and be running the regular vacuum. The hand-held mini-vac sits on the couch cushion, where I can grab it easily.

"Sweetie?" says Mom.

"Yeah?"

"What are you doing?"

"Looking for Astrid's charm. She still won't help me find it."

The light shifts as she sits on the floor beside me. "Kirsten…"

I sit up and look at her. Her hands are trembling. "It's not here, anyway," I say.

Mom nods. "What exactly do you mean by 'Astrid won't help'?"

"She says I have to find it on my own."

"She says…" She stares at Astrid's filthy, too-small slipper, then picks it up.

Shrugging, I say, "It's fine. I'll find it. There are only so many places she could've hidden it by herself. Wait—you didn't help her, did you?"

Brushing crumbs and dust off the slipper, she shakes her head *No*.

"Then I'll find it." I say, reaching for the mini-vac and using it to suck up the mess I've made.

Mom stands like she's suddenly as old as Grandma. "Sweetie…" she says.

I glance up at her. Between us, the hand-vac whirrs, crumbs clattering through the funnel and into the tiny bag. She leans over and brushes my bangs out of my face. I smooth them back down.

She sighs, then smiles stiffly, like it hurts. "You know we'll get through this, right?"

I nod, running the vacuum over another patch of crumbs. "I know, Mom. The four of us, together."

7

WEDNESDAY MORNING

ASTRID LINGERS at the edge of my garden. She keeps running up from the play set at the bottom of the hill, pacing back and forth along the side where the tomatoes, peas, and corn are. I can't see her, but I can hear her sighing extra-loud and saying, "I WISH there was SOMEone to PLAY with. Kyurp? Are you in there?"

"Yeah, Frog Breath. I'm in here." But I'm busy. I've been busy since just after breakfast. The day is bright and hot, with a slight breeze I can just feel in the vegetable patch, where I'm picking squash bugs off the undersides of all my summer squash and zucchini plant leaves. And the cucumber, watermelon, and pumpkin leaves.

"When are you going to be done?"

"Not till almost dinnertime, Wart Face." I scoot along the row and lift the first leaf of the next plant. This one's clear. I lift another.

"DON'T call me Wart Face."

"Then don't bother me." This leaf has several of the large, brownish-black beetles scattered across the underside. When I was little, I was convinced I could hear them munching. Now, I just want them off my zucchini plants.

"But. I'm. Borrrred."

"Then come help me." I pluck the beetles off the leaf and drop them into my can of soapy water.

"I can help?" Her voice perks up.

I sigh. I swear, I was never so annoying. "Uh-huh. Open the gate. Be careful where you step." I scoot to the next plant.

There's a lot of muttering while Astrid opens the makeshift chicken-wire gate and closes it behind her. Then there's an awful lot of rustling. Then nothing.

"Frog Breath?"

"Kyurp?" She sounds scared. Is there a critter in here? I haven't seen signs of anything larger than a mouse.

"What's wrong?"

"I don't wanna come."

Plopping the bug I've just found into the water, I stand and make my way to Astrid. She's in the middle of the bush beans and bell peppers.

"I'm over this way," I say, gesturing toward the spot I've been working in.

She eyes the vines, but takes my hand and lets me lead her. We brush past an unruly cluster of leaves; they scrape against her leg and she squeals, grabbing my arm with both hands.

"Ew! Ew, ew, ew!"

I hide my laugh.

"It's just a watermelon vine, Frog Breath." I tug my arm, but she won't allow it to come free.

"It's scary! I don't wanna be near it."

"It's not scary. You like watermelon. Mom lets you use the melon baller on it."

"It's not the same. Watermelons are from the store. I see them there."

"The watermelons in the store come from a plant just like this one." I bend down and shift a leaf so she can see the blossom. "See? This flower is where the fruit comes from."

She gives me a doubtful look. "That's not a watermelon."

This time, I do laugh. "Bees will help turn it into a watermelon."

She scowls. "I don't like bees. They sting. And I don't like that plant. It's prickly. And scary."

"Well, this is where I'm working right now."

"I changed my mind. I'm not bored anymore."

I roll my eyes. "Fine, then. Go. But I'm not playing with you today."

She lets go of my arm and eyes the path to the gate. "Carry me out."

"No." I just want to get back to pest-picking. That's the sucky part about not using chemicals—you still have to get rid of the bugs, somehow. And I think I maybe can hear them munching, after all. "You can see the gate from here." I point, turning back to my bugs.

Astrid stomps a few paces, then shrieks, the leaves rustling around her. The light dims, and I glance up.

The vines have exploded in size—twistingwrithingsnaking through the air, tentacles sprung from a dozen snapping jaws, whipping Astrid through the air like she's nothing. An unceasing wail echoes all around me—Astrid? Or the mouths?

I stab at the writhing, thick-as-me tentacle-vines with my trowel as effectively as with cardboard. "Astrid!"

"Kirsten!"

"Astrid, fight back!"

Something grabs me by the shoulders, and I thrash back and forth—I can't let it take me. I need to break free and rescue Astrid. It looms over me, until the only thing left in my world is me, fighting against the vines—fighting my way toward Astrid.

"Kirsten, wake up. Please. Wake up."

The garden disappears, replaced by Dad's hands on my shoulders and Mom sitting beside me on the bed. Astrid isn't here.

"Kirsten? Sweetie?"

"Mom?"

Her breath whooshes out in relief. "You were having a nightmare," she says, smoothing my bangs down. "Screaming like…" she shakes her head.

I stare at her, at Dad. "It's gone." I'm too old to have nightmares, too old to climb into bed between them. Besides, they have enough to do, helping Brent plan Uncle Nick's funeral. I don't want them to have to stay up and try to make me feel better.

"Just like that?" Dad sits in my desk chair.

I nod.

"What was it about?" he asks.

"I don't remember. It's totally gone."

"Well…" Mom squeezes my hand. "Come get us if you need us. But try to get back to sleep."

I roll over, alone in bed, and think about the dream—about how I couldn't do anything to free Astrid from the plant-beast, or even save myself.

Is that what it was like in the caf? Did everyone feel helpless? Did Uncle Nick die not knowing if he'd stopped the shooter?

My twin bed feels huge and empty without Astrid snuggled beside me. I get up, pull my quilt and pillow off the bed, and venture into her room. She's there, splayed out and snoring, and my mind quiets instantly. I find a spot on the floor and cocoon myself. Her snores ease me into sleep and sometime later I'm roused by knocking on her open door.

"Kirsten?" It's Mom. "I got us an appointment at ten."

The therapist's office is in an old mill building in Chelmsford. There are a bunch of shops on the first floor, a restaurant, and a personal trainer's gym space. We climb the stairs to the second floor and pass a dentist's office, then an optometrist's and an accountant's. The floor is uneven and pitted, so we have to watch our step. On the walls, the original eight-inch posts are exposed every twelve feet. Like the floors, they're pitted. Clusters of old, thick staples flagged with bits of paper cling to the rough wood in places. I want to reach out and run my hand along the wood, but it probably isn't as smooth as it looks. I'd end up with a splinter. Instead, I lean toward one post, inhale deeply, and imagine I can still smell the damp, spicy scent of the forest where the beam once lived.

Mom, Dad, and Brent are ahead of me, and they don't see me and Astrid stop. I take Astrid's hand and we jog several steps to catch up. They're at the door to the therapist's office. The sign on the solid wooden door reads STONY BROOK MILLS FAMILY PSYCHOTHERAPY.

Mom called early this morning to make sure they were partic-ipating in the open-office-hours thing. As soon as she woke me up, I changed and bolted out the front door for a quick run down to the Merrimack trail and back. Just a little over a mile, but it helped me clear my head and figure out what to say to Astrid.

I told her we were going to a feelings doctor. How else do you explain therapy to a six-year-old?

Inside the large waiting room, the light is bright enough to read by, but low enough that other patients probably can't tell if you've been crying for nearly an hour when you leave. There are several small, round, white noise machines scat-tered around the perimeter. Their hiss is irritating at first, but settles into the comforting sound of rain pounding on a roof. Brent, Astrid, and I take seats while Mom and Dad check in with the receptionist, then fill out a bunch of paperwork. Dad helps Brent, then Brent is called back.

Mom and Dad sit silently. Mom's gaze darts around the room, then she looks at Dad and reaches over, holding his hand. Dad stares at some invisible point on the floor. Beside me, Astrid fidgets, swinging her legs beneath the seat. I pull out my phone and text Oakley while we wait.

> **GreenThumb:** Is Luther home yet?
>
> **28SecondsLater:** Dad just called. They're on their way now
>
> **GreenThumb:** Want me to come over when I'm done here?
>
> **28SecondsLater:** Done where?
>
> **GreenThumb:** We're at a therapist's office. Mom and Dad thought it would help Brent and Astrid
>
> **28SecondsLater:** ...
>
> **28SecondsLater:** Oh
>
> **GreenThumb:** Should I come over? I can bring Astrid

28SecondsLater: ...
28SecondsLater: You want to bring Astrid?
GreenThumb: Sure. I thought it might be a distraction for Luther. Plus, I'm looking for any excuse to escape. Grandma Villi is getting in later
28SecondsLater: ...
28SecondsLater: Sorry. Not a good day. I'm not sure Luther will be up for visitors. Plus Mom needs my help here
28SecondsLater: Want to run tomorrow, though? The reception for Nick is at our place after the funeral. Maybe after the crowd is gone, we can hit the Merrimack trail
GreenThumb: Sure. I'll bring my gear & let Josie know

It's like I said: even if all we do is run, at least I can be there to do that.

Astrid tugs at my sleeve, and I lean over.

"This isn't Dr. Steve's office," she stage-whispers.

"It's a different kind of doctor," I whisper back. "Remember? You talk to them about feelings and stuff."

I pull up Tic-Tac-Toe on my phone and let her beat me every round for a while.

Mom leans toward me. "Sweetie, let me and Dad go in first and explain the situation."

"Sure. We'll be fine out here."

Finally a short, Black woman comes out. "Madsen family?"

Mom and Dad stand and follow her.

Astrid and I play a few more rounds of Tic-Tac-Toe before switching to Dots. After a while, the therapist comes back out, smiles, and motions for us to join her. Her lipstick is a shimmery lavender that Oakley would love. She's got tight, curly hair cut super-short in a way Oakley would *not* love. "Hi, Kirsten. I'm Jamaica Knox," she says, as we follow her through the doorway.

"Nice to meet you," I mumble. Astrid hops along behind me as I follow Jamaica into a rat-maze hallway.

There are several offices back here, each with their own little white noise machines outside the door. The room we're shown into has a pair of shabby floral-patterned sofas and two prints on the wall of tropical beaches. There's a small bookshelf with two plastic plants on the top shelf and a bunch of self-help books and little positive sayings in tiny frames on the lower shelves. The plants are dusty. Mom and Dad are together on one couch, holding hands. I sit stiffly on the other, my knees together and my hands on my knees. Astrid suctions herself to my side.

Jamaica closes the door and relaxes into her office chair. She picks up the notepad and pen from the desk beside her.

"Your parents were telling me that your family is here today because of Monday's events at Winslow Elementary."

I nod, my head bouncing on my neck like I'm one of those novelty bobblehead figures. Beside me, Astrid squirms.

Jamaica surveys the four of us. What does she think of our family? Is she judging us for coming in so quickly? Are we wasting her time, when she should be talking to families like the Washingtons? How does this work, really?

"Kirsten, why don't you tell me a little about where you are, now?"

"I was there," I say. "I pick up Astrid after school every day, so I was there, outside the school where the police tape was. And they sent me to the community gym, so I went there like they told me and… it was all full of little kids crying and covered in blood. My best friend had to go in a room and find out her brother got hurt—but I thought at first he died. Brent's Dad—my Uncle Nick—did die. And at first I couldn't find Astrid. I couldn't find her. She wasn't with her class, and her teacher pulled me aside and then Astrid… she was in the bathroom or something, I guess, or with the wrong class. But she found me and I picked her up and fought through the crowd to get her out of there and bring her home safe."

I smooth Astrid's hair, even though it's fine. One of the little picture frames has an image of a butterfly in it, with the words *Just when the caterpillar thought the world was over, it became a butterfly.*

But the caterpillar was right. The world it knew *was* over.

"It sounds like that experience scared you," says Jamaica. She gazes at me.

"Yeah…"

I'm shredded up inside from the memory of Astrid's class-mates—Lexie's bloody pigtail; Jeremiah chewing his own hand. I'm making a fist. Why am I making a fist? *Push it all down; shove the tears away.* I have no reason to cry. Am I still scared? Maybe. But I don't know why.

Astrid tenses a little. I realize I've stopped smoothing her hair and start again. Shouldn't there be toys or something in here for kids to play with? Maybe I should hand her my phone so she can play Plotting Penguins or something.

Jamaica shifts in her chair. "Kirsten, I'd like you to try an exercise with me. Can you do that?"

"Okay," I say, then give a short, nervous laugh. "I guess." Is she going to make me close my eyes and do a trust-fall or something?

"Good. Okay. I'd like you to look around this room and point out five things you see that are green."

"You want me to point out green stuff?"

"Can you do that?"

"Um… yeah."

I glance at Mom, but she's just got that tight smile on her face that's more grimace than anything else. She's sitting on the hand that Dad's not holding.

I take a deep breath and look around. "Well, there's that fake English Ivy plant and the fake African Violet. Does that count as one or two?" And is it bad that I pointed out that they're fake?

She smiles. "Two. What else do you see that's green?"

I search the room. "Your mug is green."

She nods, gesturing for me to continue.

"And… um… that little sign on the shelf that says BREATHE… and…"

My gaze lands on my parents. Dad is wearing a crappy pair of shorts and a t-shirt with holes starting along the neckline. "Dad's Celtics cap," I say. "Does that count? That's five."

Dad starts taking the cap off, then reseats it. His mouth is a line. His eyes look like I've betrayed him somehow, but that doesn't make sense.

"That's good, Kirsten," Jamaica says.

It occurs to me she probably has like ten things in here that are green, so she can do this with people. I look over at her, but I can't read her face. "Why did you have me do that?"

"It makes a person take a minute to ground themselves in their surroundings. You can use a color, like we did, or you can use sounds, or textures… anything that helps you focus on your immediate surroundings. Can you tell me how it made you feel?"

"Um… I don't know. I noticed stuff in your office I didn't notice before. I guess it distracted me from being all…" All what? I fall silent and shrug.

"It's an excellent exercise that you can do on your own, whenever you're feeling anxious or overwhelmed."

"Oh. Yeah. I guess I do feel less tense."

She jots a note on her paper. "You said you picked Astrid up from school every day."

On the other sofa, Mom nods and jumps in. "Our work schedules… Erik's and mine… we've relied on Kirsten for a lot in the afternoons ever since Astrid was born. Even more once she got her driver's license." She sighs and shakes her head. "Maybe we expect too much…" She frowns.

"What do you think of your parents' expectations, Kirsten?" asks Jamaica.

I get annoyed sometimes at having to pick up Astrid every afternoon, but it's not her fault she was a surprise. And we have that wait-till-the-last-minute system worked out, just between us. "I don't know. I mean, it's okay. Astrid's not really a pain most of the time, and my parents are cool about a lot of stuff, so I guess it all evens out." Not like Josie's parents.

"I mean, I'm going to UMass Lowell in the fall, but I'm not really interested in college. My boss wants me to take on this big project at work—this greenhouse for year-round local produce—and I really want to do it. It was partly my idea, even. And..."

And I can't say what I really want to. I mean, how can I admit Astrid does sometimes cramp my style right in front of her and scar her for life? She doesn't deserve that. Her obsession with frogs isn't so different from my thing with gardening. It's kind-of neat that she loves frogs that much. Maybe she'll grow up to be a herpetologist or something.

"Kirsten, can you describe for me how you and your parents dealt with Monday's events that evening?"

I shrug. "I guess we were still processing it all. We didn't talk much."

Mom looks at me and Astrid, as if suddenly aware of her failure. Beside her, Dad looks smaller, somehow, than he really is.

"If you had talked, what do you think you would have said?"

"About what? The shooting?" I ask.

"That, or the losses your family experienced," says Jamaica.

Loss. She means *loss*, not losses. Because we only lost Uncle Nick. I shrug and play with my charm bracelet. Everything was so crazy, Monday, Astrid forgot to give me the charm she picked out. And I forgot to ask her about it yesterday.

Wait. I did ask her. She just giggled and....what? I don't remember. But I think I looked under the couch. Or was it under her bed?

"Kirsten?" Dad's voice cuts into my thoughts.

"Sorry... what?"

"If we'd talked, Monday, instead of... well, if we'd talked. What do you think you would have said?"

"I don't know." I look at the dusty plants, the row of self-help books (two on the bottom shelf are green), the empty coat-hook on the closed door—anything except for Dad, Mom, or Jamaica. Then I accidentally look at Jamaica. Is she watching me? I think she's watching me. Why is she watching me?

"People handle trauma in many ways, Kirsten," she says. "It's similar to the way we handle grief. Do you know the five stages of grief?"

No. "Like how you get over it when someone dies?"

"We grieve when someone dies, yes. But there are other types of loss, as well. People who experience trauma often feel a sense of loss afterward. And whenever we experience loss, we grieve."

I consider Luther. "My friend's brother... he was injured. They couldn't save his eye. You mean loss like that?"

"Sure," Jamaica says, making a note. "Your friend's brother will mourn the loss of his eye, and the experience of being fully sighted. But even people who weren't physically harmed may experience grief over Monday's events. We don't have to be present at a terrible event to feel the shock of it or a sense of loss because of it."

I stare at her for a minute, but can't meet her gaze. Instead, I study her outfit. She's wearing wide-cut, flowy, tan pants and a cocoa-brown tank top beneath a lavender summer cardigan. Her sandals are strappy and the polish on her fingers and toes is wearing at the tips. It matches her cardigan and her shim-mery lipstick.

I take a deep breath and shake my head. Stare at her laven-der-painted toes.

"I don't want to think about it."

She nods. "It's certainly a difficult thing to think about."

"Yeah."

Jamaica makes another note, then sets her notepad face-down on the desk. "Unfortunately, we need to stop for today," she says, leaning forward. "Shall we meet again in a week?"

Not me. She means well, but I don't need help, and she didn't even talk to Astrid. Maybe that will happen next time? What do I do until then, to help Astrid understand she's safe?

We all stand. Mom and Dad shake hands with Jamaica, so I do, too.

"In the meantime," says Jamaica, looking at me, "Remember the grounding exercise we did. You can do that on your own, Kirsten, whenever you feel overwhelmed. Mom and Dad, you can remind Kirsten of the exercise, or initiate it, when you notice her feeling anxious. And please call if anything comes up before we meet again. Here's my card. This number..." she points to one corner of the business card "is our emergency number. There's always someone on call."

"Thank you," mumbles Dad, taking the card as Mom opens the door.

Astrid and I zip through it and return to the waiting room. Behind us, Jamaica stalls Mom and Dad, probably with an insurance question.

Back in the waiting room, Brent is already there, his head down and his hands in his lap. He doesn't even have his phone out. His long, dark hair is a curtain around his face.

I sit beside him and let Astrid start up a game of Tic-Tac-Toe against herself on my phone.

I nudge him. "You okay?"

He snorts. "Not. Really."

"Wanna play Tic-Tac-Toe with Astrid?"

"No." The word hits me like a slap. Before I can do more than register his anger, though, he gets up and turns toward the door. "Tell your parents I'm waiting at the car."

He's gone before I can say anything else, the door slamming behind him so hard the receptionist startles behind her glass window.

"He misses Uncle Nick," I tell Astrid, but she's not paying attention.

A man sitting across from us stares openly, his brow pulled into a scowl.

I pull Astrid onto my lap and he turns away.

Astrid places a winning X in the bottom left corner of the screen. She grins, oblivious to the rude guy, who's already back to staring at us.

In the car, nobody says anything all the way home. We're all on our own tiny islands, and none of us has a boat to reach the others.

If I try to swim for it, I'll drown.

8

WEDNESDAY, MIDDAY

Cushcushcushcush.

Years ago, I worked out a one-mile route through the neighborhood. Right now, I'm finishing my second lap and coming up on the news vans lined up outside our house. They have the decency to not jump all over me in the middle of my run, and they're not bothering Astrid, who is on the front porch step, in a pair of green shorts and a blue shirt with green polka-dots. She's wearing her frog boots and there's a watering can beside her. I'll have to explain a tree needs more water than that.

Last night, she slept in her own bed and I was the one who couldn't sleep. I must have given up at some point and gone to Astrid's room, curling up in my quilt on her floor. Listening to Astrid's snores are proof that everything will be okay in the end.

"Kyurp! When-you're-done-can-you-help-me-give-my-tree-a-drink?" she shouts as I jog past.

"One more lap!" I throw over my shoulder. I head up the hill and around the curve, toward the Broderick's. News vans lie in wait there, too. I turn right at the end of the block and slow to a walk as I round the last corner and home comes into view. Josie's ratty Honda pulls into our driveway. It idles for a minute, then she cuts the engine and climbs out.

Panting a bit from the midday run, I gesture for her to join me, and continue up the walkway. When I reach the porch, I take a few huge gulps of water from the sports bottle I left out.

"Now?" asks Astrid.

"Gimmie a minute, Frog Breath," I say, watching Josie amble up the front walk.

"Hey," says Josie.

"Hey."

"I thought I'd check and see how you're doing."

I glance at Astrid, still sitting on the steps. "I promised Astrid I'd help her water the willow. Wanna join us?"

"Oh..." Josie smiles weakly and runs a hand through her hair. She glances at the news vans behind her. "Okay."

Astrid jumps up, leaving the watering can on the porch, and tears around the corner toward the back yard. I follow Astrid and Josie follows me, slowly. Untangling the hose and unkinking it as I drag it downhill, I nestle the open end inside the stone ring Astrid made on her birthday. I should really just leave it in place, at least until Dad needs to mow the lawn.

"Okay, turn it on real slow," I call.

She wrestles with the spigot knob, but nothing happens. I trudge up the hill, scanning for missed kinks along the way, and reach Astrid's station beneath the kitchen window-box. She's turned the knob righty-tighty.

I get the knob loosened again and use the intensity of the faucet leak to gauge how much water trickles its way through the hose to Astrid's willow. Taking her hand in mine, together we troop down the hill and check my effort. It's a little light, but that's okay; we'll just leave it on longer.

Josie stands in the middle of the yard, watching, that weird, watery smile still on her face.

Astrid tugs on my shirt until I lean down. "Can she help us do the fairy dance?"

"Ask and maybe she'll say *yes*."

But Astrid shakes her head and slips behind me. She didn't use to be this shy, and it's a little annoying, but I guess it's understandable. The district hasn't even decided yet what to do about the rest of the school year for the elementary kids. It's only been a few days, so the school is still closed. Still… there's only a few weeks left until summer break. There's not really enough time to even help the kids realize everything can get back to normal. And what does it mean to get back to normal? Should we even want to? Would that mean pretending nothing ever happened?

I do know that normal doesn't include hordes of counselors set up in temporary offices in case we need someone to talk to. If the conversation I had with Jamaica this morning was normal, I'm not sure anyone will ever get used to it.

Normal doesn't include Astrid ducking for cover every time she hears a car backfire, Mr. O'Meara's motorcycle roar to life, or the table saw in Mrs. Bacon's garage workshop. Or a fucking cookie sheet warping in the oven, like last night.

Normal doesn't include Astrid seeming to appear out of thin air like a ghost, or Mom and Dad stumbling through everything robotically. And it's not as if Brent will someday not miss his dad. Or, like Luther will someday not remember what it was like to have two functioning eyes. And Lexie will always…

Always what? My mind hits a wall of fog.

Shaking my head to clear it, I realize Astrid is clinging to my arm. I'm her life-preserver.

"She wants to know if you'd like to help do the fairy dance," I tell Josie. "It's this thing I taught her, to help the tree grow." I wink at her, and she nods, her eyes flicking toward the tree.

"How about if I just watch?"

I take Astrid's hand, but she pulls free. "The tree fairies don't like your dance," she reports, holding her arms by her sides and going up on her toes. "The tree fairies said a willow needs a water dance."

She breaks into one of her routines from Irish Step class, her arms straight as fence-posts and her loose rain boots slapping out a ragged rhythm. It looks more like she's trying to ride a broom-stick horse than anything, the way she clomps around the tree, slipping a little in the mud that's blooming on the lower side of the slope.

I laugh and move to stand beside Josie. I want to reach out and hold her hand again, but she's crossed her arms. She glances between me and Astrid. I can't read her face.

Astrid keeps going, spattering mud up the sides of her boots and along the edges of her shorts. I guess maybe it's better that the rain boots prevent her kicks from reaching anywhere near her butt, for all the mess she's making at ground level.

"Astrid…" I say, and glance toward the house, half-expecting to see Mom scowling at me through the kitchen window. But she's probably taking a nap. I heard her last night, walking the halls.

When I turn back, Astrid is crouched beside the creek, peering toward the mossy rocks. "Hey, creek-fairies. Are you awake yet? Did you like my new dance?"

The delicate lavender irises bob in the breeze that tickles their sunlit patch, prompting Astrid to scramble up the bank and grab my hands. She jumps up and down. "They liked it, Kyurp! Did you see? They answered and said they liked my dance!" She goes skipping up the lawn and into the house, singing, "my dance is better than Kyurp's dance…"

I shake my head and smile at Josie. "I never thought I'd have so much patience for her," I say. "But after Monday…"

She nods, linking her arm through mine. It sends a shiver through me. We climb the hill slowly; I don't want her to have an excuse to let go.

"How are you really?" she asks. "Are you all…getting through it okay?"

Her words are tentative, as if she's stepping on water-slicked stones and doesn't know which ones will shift beneath her weight and wrench an ankle.

I nod. I'm okay—I think—except for this itch in my head that says I'm not really. Plus, everyone seems to stop talking whenever I walk into the room. What does that mean?

Mom and Dad said Jamaica wasn't worried about Astrid. I looked it up on the internet when we got home and found an article on WebPsych that said stuff like nightmares and panic attacks are common after a traumatic experience. That PTSD is when it lasts for a lot longer. But If Astrid's still having nightmares by the time I start at UMass in the fall, I'm going to make Mom take her back to Jamaica's office.

Mom's putting on a brave face for Dad's sake, and Dad is just numb. He's hardly said anything at all today, and I don't think he's showered since Monday. He wore his Celtics cap when we went to Jamaica's office, and Mom drove.

Mom never drives when we're all together.

Josie stops before we reach the deck, and faces me. "Kirsten? If you want to talk… or anything…" She's crying. Why is she crying? She didn't lose anyone. None of her close friends lost anyone.

She grabs both of my hands in hers.

"I just… I want you to know I'm here for whatever you need."

I should want this moment to last for hours, and I can't explain why I don't, but I sososo do not want this moment to last. Tugging my hands free, I look away. "I know. Everything's cool. Cool enough, anyway." I nod toward the house. "I gotta go make Astrid lunch. I'm trying to keep her out of everyone's hair. Want to come in? Have a sandwich or something?"

She puffs her cheeks out, then blows the air out in a loud rush. "Yeah. Yeah, okay. I guess…"

I lead the way onto the deck and around to the side door. It's like our PDA breakthrough on Monday has taken some bizarre turn off the road and our relationship GPS is sending us to the middle of a field or a lake or something.

Or maybe it's me. Maybe somewhere deep inside, I expected everything to be rainbows and unicorns between us, now that she'll hold my hand in public. I forgot she still has to deal with her don't-ask-don't-tell parents, at least until she's done with college.

"Hang on while I change," I say, and Josie sits sideways on the booth seat. I head for my room, passing the closed den door. It sounds like Brent is on the phone. Astrid is nowhere obvious, but her door is closed, too, so she's probably in there playing again.

Leaving my sweaty workout gear on the floor, I pull on a pair of shorts and an Emily Snow shirt, then slide my feet into a pair of sandals before returning to the kitchen.

Josie sees my shirt and says, "Ohhhh. The concert is Friday… I guess you probably can't go."

I'd forgotten about the concert. Would it be weird, or insensitive, or too soon to take a breath of normalcy? Maybe it would do us all some good.

"I don't know—I guess we can still go, if Oakley's mom doesn't need her help with Luther." Something nags at the back of my consciousness, something I've forgotten that might make going to the show a selfish move. I should probably check with Mom and Dad.

I open the fridge to grab some deli slices, but the shelves are packed with quiches, lasagnas, casseroles, and I don't even know what else. Mom must be collecting the stuff everyone brings for Brent. I really want that ham and gouda quiche, but pull the deli drawer open like I'd originally planned.

"Turkey, swiss, and avocado? Guacamole, actually."

"Sure." Josie is beside me now, pulling a pair of plates from the cabinet.

"Don't forget Astrid," I say. Josie pauses in the middle of closing the cabinet door, then retrieves a third plate, setting them all on the booth table. I hand her a pitcher of iced tea and she pours three glasses.

I slap together three sandwiches (no lettuce, guac, or yucky crusts on Astrid's) and am about to call her in when I catch the tightness on Josie's face. I leave Astrid's lunch on the counter and slide into the booth across from Josie. She's obviously got something on her mind.

I do, too.

Sitting across from Josie over sandwiches reminds me of the first time she came over. It was a snow day in late January, and Winslow had already called enough snow days that all three principals had declared this one, our fifth, a Blizzard Bag day. If enough students turned in the assignments our teachers posted online, it would count as a regular school day. Josie dug her car out and rattled over so we could work on our Civics assignment together.

Mom and Dad had left me technically in charge of Astrid, but she was over at Lexie's grandma's. They were probably turning the whole place into a replica of Lost Pond Shores from *Lily's Pad*. Lexie's grandma is a pushover like that.

Josie and I ate some leftover lasagna—like the tray in our fridge now, for Brent—and then headed back to my room.

The Civics assignment was up on my laptop but the screensaver had kicked in. Josie's Chromebook was in her backpack, which was leaning against my dresser… all the way across the room.

We lay spooning on my bed, my arm slung over her, talking about how to celebrate one month together.

"How about if we go into Boston?" I asked. I wanted to do something other than watch a movie with Oakley or Brent in the next seat as our disguise. Even after only a month, it was tiresome.

"That'd be so expensive," she countered.

"It doesn't have to be expensive. We could do a museum or the aquarium or, I don't know, get hot chocolate and go skating at the Frog Pond…"

Josie rolled over and faced me, her face beautifully full of her smile. "Can we see the ducklings? I've never seen them."

I met her eyes and lost myself.

"Sure we can," I said, smiling back. Our faces were so close, our noses almost touched, and the sprinkling of freckles across the bridge of her nose was even more adorable than usual. I disappeared the tiny distance and gave her a soft kiss. "We can do whatever you want. I just wanna be with you."

She kissed me back, and my whole body warmed with the touch of her lips. My breath caught in my throat, then released in a sigh; I ran my hand along her body, memorizing the slight curve of her hips.

"I wanna be with you, too," she murmured. "I just get nervous, you know? I'm not ready for everyone to know."

"I know. I've been there…"

She traced a finger along my jaw, making me shiver. "And your parents are just so cool about it. I don't think my mom would understand at all, despite my Uncle Stu…"

Her uncle—her dad's brother—had just gotten married in December to his boyfriend of four years. From what Josie told me, her mom had refused to attend the wedding. It wasn't that her mom was opposed to gay people in general—just the idea of people in her family being gay. So Josie and her dad had gone to the wedding without her.

"Let's not talk about that. It's fine for now. I'm not out to the whole school or anything."

She lowered her eyes. "Yeah, but you're out to enough people that someone could figure us out. I don't even have the guts to tell my best friend."

I kissed her again. "It doesn't matter. Skating, then the Public Garden? I'll even take a picture of you on Mrs. Mallard…"

She smiled. "Promise?"

"Cross my heart," I said, pulling her on top of me.

Now, thinking about the photo I took of her, bundled against the Massachusetts winter and sitting on Mrs. Mallard, one arm wrapped around the metal duck's neck and blowing me a kiss with her free hand, it feels like more than just five months ago. It feels like five years ago. It feels like maybe it never even happened.

I take a bite of my turkey sandwich and wish I could rewind time. Live either of those days again, instead of this one.

"You sure your parents will be cool with you going anyway on Friday?" she asks. "What about…you know, funerals and stuff?" It feels like she's dancing around something, trying to say something without saying it.

"I don't know—I guess, if Nick's funeral is then, I do that instead." I glance at the microwave display. One o'clock. "But I think it's tomorrow. Mom and Dad have a thing at the funeral home in a while, so I'll know for sure later today."

Visibly relaxing as our conversation slides into negotiating routines and schedules, Josie nods, chews and swallows, and says, "Do you think you'll go to any of the other funerals?"

Before I can answer, Astrid enters, crouched on the floor and hopping like a frog. "Ribbit, ribbit…"

"Finally," I say, standing and retrieving her plate. "Want to eat in front of the TV? I'll put on whatever episode you want."

Astrid turns and frog-hops out toward the living room. I follow her, leave her plate on the floor in front of her usual spot, pull up the requested *Lily's Pad* episode (the one where

Lily and Shelley meet a new friend, Zippy Dragonfly) and return to the kitchen.

Brent is there, sitting across from Josie, in my spot. Josie flashes me a wide smile that looks more like Oakley's than her own. It's too big for her face. Brent slides out of the booth and opens the fridge. "Any more turkey and guac?" he asks.

What were they talking about? I glance between them. Josie stands, clearing her plate and shifting awkwardly from one foot to the other. She pulls out her keys.

"I've got... um..." she starts, then seems to change her mind. "Want me to arrange everything with Oakley? For Friday?"

"Yeah, sure," I say.

Is she leaving because she doesn't know how to act around Brent now that Nick's gone? She seemed fine yesterday.

And anyway, what's to know? Brent's still a total geek whose jokes I don't get. He's still the only reason I passed chemistry. He's still the one who cut his gaming night short one Saturday night in the fall of our Junior year, when my first girlfriend ever dumped me in the parking lot at the Burlington Mall. He drove down Route 3 to get me, then took me to Cocina Santiago and helped me pull myself together over queso dip and guacamole. And Brent is still the one who convinced me, this past September, to take the risk and ask Josie out.

We were sitting on the footbridge between our back yards. "You can't let last year be what you expect all your relationships to be like," he said, giving me a shoulder-bump. "I know it seems easier, but only at first. After a while, it's hard to never trust."

Underneath the trauma, Brent is still Brent.

After Josie leaves, Brent takes his sandwich and a glass of water outside and sits at the table on the deck. I follow him and lean against the deck railing.

He chews silently for a minute, staring toward the footbridge where we've had most of our deep conversations. Finally, he sighs and puts his sandwich down. "I'm not ready for this. For tomorrow." He glances at me and I pull out the seat beside him and sit.

"I don't think you're supposed to be. I mean, it's impossible. Right?"

This weird look of… is it relief?… washes over his face and he shakes his head. "I guess so. I feel like everyone expects me to not just say a few words, but to say something profound. Something that encapsulates all this. But what I want is for it to not be happening." He looks at me again, squints a little, and nods his head, as if we've agreed on something secret.

I don't know what we've agreed on.

"And if I can't have that," he continues, "I'd at least like it to be done with."

"Are you going to say something?"

He shrugs. "I guess. I mean, I want to. But how do I know if I'm saying the right thing?"

With one finger, I trace the delicate open-weave pattern of the circular, metal cafe table. "I don't think there's any one right way to eulogize someone. I think whatever you say will be perfect."

"That's a cop-out."

"It's not," I say, meeting his eyes. "If it's from your heart, if it's true to your relationship and the way you want to remember Nick, it'll be perfect."

Brent considers this, then jerks his head toward the house. "Mind if I finish this in the den? I should get some stuff down while my head's in the right space."

"We don't have a den, but maybe you can work in your room."

He nods slowly, picks up his lunch, and heads inside.

Moving to the deck steps, I watch Astrid. She must have snuck out when I wasn't looking, because she's splashing around in her rain boots along a shallow spot in the creek, tadpole hunting. I watch until the neighborhood noises— barking dogs, Mrs. Martin's wind chimes, and kids playing zombie-tag in the woods further down the creek—fade away.

Why are you out here all by yourself?

I'm just sitting, Frog Breath.

Can I sit with you?

Sure.

Kyurp? Are you sad?

No.
I mean, I guess I'm sad for Brent.
I'm sad Uncle Nick is dead.

Uncle Nick died, too?

Yeah. You know that.

I didn't know. I was in the cafeteria.

Why aren't you sad for yourself?

Maybe I am, I guess. I'll miss Uncle Nick.

Oh. What about me?

You'll miss him, too.
It'll be weird, not seeing him ever again.

But won't you miss me?

Stop it.
You're not going anywhere, Frog Breath.

Don't say that. It's a lie.

What do you mean?

You know. Kyurp, you know.

I don't.
I know you're probably really scared.
Do you want to talk about it?

I want you to.

I can't, Astrid. I… I wasn't there.
But I can let you talk.

You weren't there.

But you're not here, either.

I don't know how to make you be here.

When I head inside again, some time after Astrid does, she's sprawled out on the living room floor again, in front of the blank TV. I start another *Lily's Pad* episode for her, then head for my room.

Mom and Dad are shut up in the master bedroom, shouting at each other. I pause at the sound of Mom's clipped, insistent voice.

"All I'm saying, Erik, is that nobody expects you to act like nothing's happened. They're covering my hours at the library. Your boss told you to take some time. So use it instead of staring at the wall. Go back and see Jamaica, or someone else, on your own."

"I don't want any time. What am I supposed to do with time? I can't think about it, can't stand to be here with..."

"With who? With me?"

"That's not what I meant, Maren."

"That's what you said."

"That's not what I said. You didn't let me finish."

"So finish."

Dad sighs. He's probably doing that thing where he rubs his face with his hands. He mutters something that sounds like *telling Brent what Jamaica said...* but it's low. So low I can't trust my ears.

Mom stabs out a laugh. "You think seeing her like this is easy for me? Jamaica said she's okay for now. Things like this aren't supposed to happen, but it did. It happened to our family. But you can't check out mentally and emotionally, and leave me here all alone....What am I supposed to do?"

There's a long pause as Dad mutters something that clearly pisses Mom off even more.

"What? Wearing lipstick doesn't mean I'm not a mess. That's bullshit and you know it. I'm wearing lipstick because I don't know what the fuck else to do. How I look is the only thing left I can control. I'm showered and dressed, but I'm *not* okay. I don't have it in me to go through this without you." Mom's voice sounds choked and tight. "Pull yourself together, Erik. Soon. Before I fall apart." The door jerks open and before I can scurry away, Mom storms out and pulls the door shut with a slam. I'm caught in the middle of the hallway, in a sort of trapped-animal crouch. We lock eyes for a moment. Mom's face is tear-streaked and blotchy, her eyes swollen.

Through the closed door, Dad throws a string of cusses at Mom.

"Kirsten," Mom's voice is instantly soft as she reaches a hand toward me.

I shake my head and back away.

"Kirsten," she says again.

But I turn and flee the last few yards to my room. I lock the door and curl up on my bed, an explosion building inside me. Taking deep breaths, I press against my closed eyes with the heels of my hands, pushing the threat downdowndown until it's in my feet.

I need to run.

Is that wrong?

Cushcushcushcushcushcushcushcush.

My feet crunch in the gravel and slip in the leftover piles of leaves along the roadside, but I runrunrunrun until there's a stitch in my side. Even then, I only slow enough to keep a hand pressed against my spasming muscle. Pebbles and gravel, trapped in my sandals, stab at my heels and the balls of my feet. I run through the pain.

Ahead, a car pulls over. Someone rockets from the driver's side and runs awkwardly toward me, grabbing hold of my arm and tugging me to a stop.

"Kirsten. What are you doing running on the road? Why aren't you on the trail?"

Oakley?

I look around and, as if stepping out of a fog, realize I'm on Route 113, headed toward Lowell. At this point on the road, the Merrimack Trail is still visible through the trees to my right. Oakley rubs my arm and looks around, like she's hoping to find an adult somewhere nearby. She's wearing the eggplant-purple dress she bought for graduation, and a pair of gold, strappy sandals with a low heel.

Are there funerals already?

I figured they'd have to do full autopsies on everyone who died. Or—maybe they did, and it doesn't take as long in real life as it does on TV.

I'm panting too hard to speak. Instead, I bend at the waist and extend one arm up and over my head, trying to stretch out the cramp in my side.

I focus on the *tic-tic-tic* of Oakley's phone as she texts someone while I'm cooling down. When I can breathe mostly normally again, she slides her hand into mine and leads me to her car. Once we're seated, she turns and looks at me. The last time Oakley and I were in a car together, I was in the driver's seat. I blink hard. I won't think about that day, about where my dinky little Ford took us.

"What are you doing on the main road, Kirsten?" She looks—afraid? Worried?

"Just running," I say.

She points to my sandals. "In those? You know better."

I shake my head. She's right about my shoes—but the thing is, I don't remember deciding to run. I don't even remember leaving the house—and I should. "I don't know… I just…" I can't admit, even to Oakley, that I don't remember how I got here.

She takes a deep breath. "Your mom is freaking out. Nobody knew where you were. Come on, I'll drive you home." She starts the car and a blast of icy air hits me from the AC.

I look out the front window. Just visible down the road is the white post-and-rail fence bordering the field where River's Edge Spa grazes its horses. How long have I been gone? Long enough to run almost three miles. "Yeah, okay…"

Oakley pulls onto the road, makes a uey, and drives back toward Winslow.

A rusty Buick turns onto the road ahead of us. It's going so slowly, we catch up to it quickly but can't pass, thanks to the stream of oncoming cars.

"Hey," says Oakley. "Isn't that the same car we saw on Monday? Mr. Good Sam Club?"

It is the same Buick, and we're stuck behind it again until the driver comes to a complete stop, then turns left into the parking lot near the playground. By then, we're at the edge of our neighborhood and there's no use in speeding up.

Instead of pulling into our driveway, Oakley parks where she did yesterday morning and we cut through the woods, avoiding the news crews again and entering my house through the side door. Mom is standing in the middle of the kitchen, looking at the pile of Astrid's gifts still waiting to be opened. She wraps me in a suffocating hug, addressing Oakley over my shoulder.

"I'll call you in a bit. Fill you in."

Fill her in about what? Probably Nick's funeral time or something. It's weird that she wouldn't call Mrs. Washington, instead, though.

Oakley gives my shoulders a squeeze and a few moments later, the door clicks shut behind her.

Mom won't let go of me. She's not crying, but I can tell from the way her breaths are coming—long and jagged—that she's only not crying because she's forcing herself to hold it in. She smooths the back of my hair like she used to when I was a little kid. "I know this is hard on you, Kirsten. I wish you didn't have to go through this. But I need you to let me know when you leave the house. I… I'm fragile right now."

"I'm sorry, Mom. I wasn't thinking." What else can I tell her? Not the truth. Not that I don't remember leaving.

I glance at the clock on the microwave display. Two o'clock.

On a normal Wednesday I'd be in the middle of Civics, counting the minutes until I could hit Callahan's with Oakley, Brent, and maybe Josie, to blow off the stress of the day until my phone reminder buzzed, telling me it was time to go pick up Astrid.

On a normal Wednesday, I'd pull out of the gravel parking lot at 3:15 and head toward the bridge, singing along at the top of my lungs to the Emily Snow playlist on my phone and running through my homework assignments in my head.

On a normal Wednesday... will there ever be any normal Wednesdays again?

I never unpacked my backpack on Monday. I don't even remember what we had for homework that night. When we go back next week, will the teachers pick up where we left off, like nothing ever happened? They'll probably know none of us did anything. They'll probably review. Or were we prepping for finals? They're supposed to run next week, for seniors.

Mom finally loosens her hold on me. She holds me at arm's length and tries to look me in the eye, but I turn my head and pretend to survey the counters. I can't help but notice all the plastic trays of muffins and coffee cakes.

I pull away, still not meeting her eyes. "I need to get some stuff done. Some review for finals. I forgot to do it Monday and I should probably do it before I forget again."

She sighs and steps aside. "Dad and I are leaving for the funeral home in a few minutes. You'll stay home until we get back?"

I nod and step around her.

When I reach my room, Astrid is standing beside my bed. Mr. Ribbit is propped on my pillow as if he's napping. "Can I stay with you?"

"Sure, Frog Breath."

I pull back the blankets and she climbs into my bed. She snuggles in and I lie on top of the blankets, wrapping an arm around her.

"They were yelling before," she says softly. "I don't like it when they yell."

"I know, it's scary."

"Are we still gonna be a family?"

"Ohhh, Frog Breath, sure we are." I pull her close. "Sometimes moms and dads fight. Just like sometimes, you and me fight."

Her mouth twitches. "It doesn't sound the same."

"Yeah… grownups can get loud."

"No, I mean, I think they're fighting about me."

"No, no, no. Dad's really sad about what happened. Mom, too. But they both have different ways of dealing with it. That's what they're fighting about."

"I'll never get to open my presents," she says, then closes her eyes, sucking on Mr. Ribbit's foot until she falls asleep.

She knows that's not true.

I keep forgetting to ask her where she hid my new charm. Fingering the existing charms on my bracelet, I grab my phone from my desk and check my Twitter feed, scrolling past tweet after tweet about the shooting without reading them. None of it seems real. This happens in other towns, not Winslow. To other people, not my best friends.

Not my family.

No—not my Dad.

Easing off the bed, I slip down the hall and into the kitchen. I take a few trips getting Astrid's presents relocated to her bedroom, but soon they're all spread out on her bed. When she wakes up, I'll make her a snack and help her open them.

For now, though, I climb back onto my bed and snuggle up to her. This won't last. Eventually, she'll get over the whole horrible event and go back to sleeping in her own bed. She'll stop clinging to me like her very existence depends on my presence.

I breathe in the reassuring scent of her small, sweaty body.

9

WEDNESDAY AFTERNOON

Later—maybe two hours, maybe longer—Mom does that thing where she knocks on my door, then opens it without waiting for my *Come in.*

"Kirsten? I'm leaving to pick up Grandma from the train station. I need you to take control of dinner."

She doesn't notice Astrid, still snuggled under my blankets despite the heat.

"But I was going to go running."

"Again? Kirsten…"

"Fine. I'll take care of dinner. What's involved?" Pocketing my phone, I follow her down the hall and into the kitchen.

There's a disposable aluminum tray of chicken marinating in barbecue sauce on the counter. She puts it into the fridge, then points to a box of Pastabilities. "Make a salad, please?"

"What time should I preheat the grill for Dad?" We're already over a month into grill season—we start as early as we can, in New England.

Mom sighs, and glances over her shoulder toward their bedroom. "Do it in the oven tonight."

"What? I'm not turning on the oven. It's hot enough in here."

"Then pan-fry it, Kirsten. I don't have time for this. You know what it's like heading to South Station during rush hour."

Grandma Villi—Mom's mom—had planned to visit from New York for my graduation, but after the shooting she changed her ticket so she could come early and help.

Whenever she visits, she never rents a car. It's more convenient, I guess, to have Mom pick her up from the hotel every morning and drive her back every evening. She won't stay with us, though—she says we need our space as a family. Which is true, but how much space do we have, as a family, if Mom has to keep driving back and forth between the Nashua Radisson and our house? When Grandma was over this past Christmas, I stepped in for Mom a lot. But instead of making things easier, all it did was lead to her nagging me instead of Mom. *Kirsten, are you sure you're studying enough? You spend so much time at this garden center job of yours and that's not where your future is. I worry you'll fall behind in your schoolwork. Your real job is school. You don't want colleges to accuse you of falling into a—what do they call it?—a senior slump.*

Explaining to her (several times) that my job at Dirty Knees was exactly what I wanted to do with the rest of my life didn't matter. Or that I agreed to attend college since it's covered because of Mom's job, but that Mom and Dad get how much gardening means to me. She kept coming back with *I just don't see how gardening is a career. Gardening is a lovely hobby dear, but if you really want to study plants, maybe you should become a horticulturist. That's a wonderful career.* So even though school is practically over, now, for me—at least until I start classes at UMass Lowell in the fall—Mom offered to go back to chauffeuring her.

I sigh. "Why can't you tell her to suck it up and rent a car?"

She takes a deep breath and looks around the room, her eyes resting on the height tick-marks in the doorway. The most recent entry, Astrid's, is from this past Sunday: *June 2, 43 1/4*. I marked it in Sharpie so it wouldn't wear off. Green Sharpie. Astrid made me draw a little frog beside it, only I can't draw, so it kind-of looks like a floppy green flower with bug-eyes.

"Kirsten, this isn't the time to fight that battle. I have to go. It's already four-thirty. Make the pasta salad. Cook the chicken. There's a platter of veggies from Market Basket. Brent will be here by six-thirty. Daddy is—he's asleep. His phone is on the counter. Just let it go to voice mail if anybody calls."

I haven't called him Daddy since I was seven.

"Who's going to call?"

Mom sighs. "I don't know."

"What were you guys fighting about before?"

"Kirsten..."

I pick up the box of pasta salad mix. "Okay, fine," I say. "I'll take care of dinner. I'll watch Astrid. Put on more *Lily's Pad* and maybe take her to the park or something."

Mom nods absently; she plucks her keys from the hooks near the back door, shoulders her purse, and pauses. "Please pull out a set of towels for Grandma."

"She's staying here? But Brent's using the futon."

Suddenly, Mom is hugging me tighttighttight and smoothing the back of my hair, even though it's probably fine. "Tell me something you see," she says.

"What?"

"Tell me something you see or something you feel. Please?"

"Fine. I feel you squeezing the life out of me. Okay?"

She deflates around me. Then she lets go and is gone, the screen door wheezing shut behind her.

I make the pasta salad, adding extra peas and chopped-up roasted red peppers to supplement the icky freeze-dried vegetables in the Pastabilities flavor packet.

As I'm finishing, Astrid comes in and starts picking out peas and eating them one by one, the way she used to eat Cheerios when she was a baby. Maybe if the first Dirty Knees greenhouse does well, Maura will build a second one for trellised plants. Winslow—and Astrid—can have fresh peas anytime.

"Hey," I say, grabbing the bowl and holding it out of her reach.

She makes a few half-hearted jumps, then sits at the booth, kicking her heels against the wooden base.

I stow the bowl of salad in the fridge and notice a Boston Cream pie from the grocery bakery. Mom never buys ready-made platters or desserts from the bakery, but now they're all over the counter and stacked up in the fridge. It's probably because she feels guilty for spending so much time helping everyone else, she doesn't have time to pull together dinner for us. Or else people are bringing them to us because they know Brent is here, now.

At least we get dessert again. Usually, we only have dessert on the weekends.

"Want me to pull up a fresh *Lily's Pad* episode?" I ask.

"I like the one that's on already," she says. "Can I have a snack while I watch?"

"Sure. I'll bring it in."

She wanders out of the room and when I enter the living room with her juice box and bowl of Cheezy Whalez, she's not there.

"Astrid?"

I set her snack down on one of the TV tables and restart the episode. Astrid enters, wearing her frog boots, and sits down, ignoring the crackers and juice. I leave the remote beside them and return to Mom's list: pull out the towels for Grandma, leave them in the bathroom, set the table (for six, now), make a pitcher of lemonade. When I'm finished, I join Astrid in the living room. It's not even five-thirty.

I probably should take her to the park or something, like I promised, but I don't want to move just yet, so I curl up on the couch to watch her watch her show.

My text alert buzzes.

> **Pussycat:** Hey…
> **GreenThumb:** Hey! What's going on?
> **Pussycat:** I just needed to see your avatar
> **GreenThumb:** :)
> **GreenThumb:** Everything okay?
> (pause)
> **Pussycat:** Oakley said she saw you out for a run a while ago. I'm just checking to make sure you're not pushing too hard. Like I said, I just needed to see your avatar. Bad timing, though, cuz now Mom's calling me. She's in a mood
> **GreenThumb:** :(Later?
> **Pussycat:** Yeah. Later

I stare at my phone for a while. That was weird.

When the *Lily's Pad* episode ends, I haul Astrid off the floor, promising to let her go on the merry-go-round as soon as we get to the park. To avoid the news vans, we cut through the yards until we reach that spot on Pinto Lane where Oakley keeps parking. As we near the park entrance, Lexie and her dad are just leaving.

Mr. Oh gives me an awkward hug while Lexie and Astrid just stand there like they've never met and aren't best friends.

"Hi, Lexie. How're you? Are you coming over for Astrid's party this weekend?" I mean, I guess we'll still have it. Right?

Lexie hides behind her dad, peeking out at me cautiously. It's weird; she hasn't done that since she was three.

I tilt my head to meet her gaze. "I think we're going to play Pin-the-Tail-on-the-Raccoon… and LeapFrog."

Her eyes go wide and she buries her face in the back of her dad's shirt. He offers a tense smile and picks her up like she really is three. "She's not… Lexie's having a hard time," he explains.

I recall her blood-caked pigtail, the brownish-red smear across her pink cotton dress, and nod, my eyes tearing up. With one hand, I find the back of Astrid's head and stroke her hair. "I understand. Astrid… it's like she's blocked whole chunks of it out."

Mr. Oh, his brow furrowed, rubs Lexie's back and steps away from us. "We… we need to get going. Lexie's getting hungry." He turns and hurries away, Lexie peering over his shoulder at me.

I shrug and turn Astrid loose in the park. Astrid calls it the Mixed-up Park because it's a weird combination of 80s and modern equipment. In a sunny spot at the edge of the meadow where party-goers set up volleyball nets, there's a new play area with tons of recycled-tire mulch, a well-stocked sandbox, and a trio of toddler-sized bucket swings. But mature trees shade most of the park, and the ground there is hard-packed dirt. Beneath the trees, the old equipment still beckons: a metal merry-go-round, the belt swings on their ten-foot-high steel A-frame, and the big, shiny metal slide that stands eight feet high at the top. The maintenance crew tries to keep the old equipment surrounded by pine mulch, but somehow it always ends up scattered and brushed away. Mom says the old equipment is the kind she grew up playing on, and that a good scraped knee is an important part of childhood.

Astrid climbs on the merry-go-round; I grab one of the vertical bars and race around and around and around, revving it as fast as I can before letting go and veering off a few paces to watch it rock on its post as it spins. Astrid screeches with glee. A trio of boys—older than Astrid by a few years but not as old as Oakley's brother Luther—lope over and as the ride slows, two hop on and one revs it up again before joining his friends. Astrid, tucked as close to the center as she can get, continues to shriek and giggle. The older kids take turns speeding it up every time it slows down. Eventually, Astrid starts whining.

"Kyurp, my stomach hurts," she calls.

The trio keeps the merry-go-round spinning, spinning, spinning until I step in and grab a vertical bar, dragging the ride to a halt.

"Why'd you do that?" grumbles the last kid to rev it up, as Astrid clambers off and wobbles about.

I wrap a steady arm around Astrid's shoulder and glare at the boys. "Because you're making her dizzy. Do you want her to spew all over the place?"

I lead her to the pair of benches near the street edge of the trees.

"What a freak," one kid says. The other two laugh, but I let it go. I don't know what they're dealing with. Maybe they lost a sibling or a friend. Maybe a teacher.

I sit down, and Astrid climbs into my lap and lays her head on my shoulder. I stroke her hair, waiting for her stomach to settle enough for the walk home. Mrs. Martin shows up with Jeremiah. He heads straight for the tall slide, charging up the slick surface in defiance of a girl just reaching the ladder's crest. Mrs. Martin smiles and shakes her head as she walks toward the benches, aiming for the one Astrid and I are on. As she gets closer, she recognizes me. At first, she slows and veers toward the other bench, then squares her shoulders and turns abruptly, joining us.

"What're you doing?" she asks, miming my hair-petting.

"What do you mean?" I respond. It's obvious what I'm doing. She frowns and scrunches up her mouth.

We sit silently, while Jeremiah reaches the slide's platform and stands there—king of the playground—arguing with the girl who's using the equipment the right way.

I think of Luther, how he'd climb up behind the girl and join her cause, citing safety and general fairness until Jeremiah relented and wandered off to bully the sandbox toys away from toddlers.

Astrid leans close to my ear and whispers, "He does that to me every time. It makes me want to push him off."

I nod. "We should probably head home now. Want to piggyback?"

Next June, I probably won't be able to piggyback her even five feet, but for now I can manage long enough to get us away from Mrs. Martin.

Astrid climbs on and I stand, wobbling a little. As I lean forward for balance and start toward the gate, Mrs. Martin calls my name. I plaster on a polite smile and turn. "Yes?"

She's left the bench and is standing right here, too close.

"I'm so sorry. We're all… we're all so, so sorry." Then she's rubbing my arm and tearing up as she murmurs something about how God gives and God takes away. It's supposed to make people feel better, I guess, but not me. Instead, it stabs me in the gut and twists, and I don't know why. It's hard to keep the smile fixed on my face, but I do. I nod and smile, as if she's making a difference. Astrid gets heavier the longer I stand here.

Behind his mom, Jeremiah reaches the bottom of the slide, then turns around and scrambles right back up the wrong way. The girl, still waiting at the top, shakes her head and starts down the ladder.

I side-step toward the gate. "I really should get Astrid home."

Mrs. Martin's face twitches, her smile faltering.

I turn and head for the sidewalk, where I make Astrid slide down. She holds my hand all the way home, even when we cut through the back yards.

The hose is still in place from today's earlier watering, so we turn on the spigot together and let the water trickle. I sit on the edge of the weathered, wooden footbridge, watching as Astrid does her fairy dance.

We're still outside when Brent steps out of his house, cutting through his back yard and meeting me on the footbridge.

Astrid continues her Irish Step-inspired water dance, oblivious to Brent's arrival. He sits beside me, letting the backpack slung over one shoulder fall to his side.

"Is it six-thirty already?" I ask.

He shakes his head. "I had to get out of there. I kept looking at the clock, like Dad was out at the grocery store, or working late, or... someplace he could come home from."

I think about that: the idea of waiting for someone to come home. Knowing they're going to walk in the door any minute, even though they never will again.

Eventually, Brent breaks the silence. "Why are you out here, anyway?"

I nod toward Astrid and her tree. "Watering the tree again. I know I shouldn't do it twice in one day, but I'm trying to keep her occupied and clean enough to get scooped up by Grandma."

He looks over at me but says nothing. We're never this quiet, on the footbridge. Ever since that first summer, when he was still Nick's foster kid, it's been where we tell each other everything. Like freshman year, after he helped me put up the collapsible greenhouse I got for Christmas.

Mom and Astrid were at Lexie's birthday party, a few streets over; Dad and Nick had left early for the game at Fenway. Regretting my decision to try setting up the greenhouse on my own, I was trying to figure out how to steady the structure and pound in the stakes at the same time, when Brent cut through the yard on his way home from either Tomás's or Sean's house.

"Need help?" he asked, pausing.

"Apparently, I do. Hold this?"

Brent held the greenhouse securely as I pounded in the stakes one by one, leaving the cords a little loose until everything was in place. Once we were done—the cords tightened until the house was square and stable—I zipped the doorway shut and we walked downhill together to the footbridge.

We sat for a few minutes, watching the creek rushing over the pebbles and rocks. Finally, he nudged me and grinned. "This feels really middle school, but I promised Tomás I would test the situation. He's wondering, if he asked you out, if you would say *Yes*."

I closed my eyes. I think I maybe even hung my head.

"You don't like him like that," said Brent.

I laughed a sort of snorty laugh and rubbed my eyes. "God, Brent, it's…" The words spilled out faster than I'd ever thought possible. "Tomás is a nice guy, he really is, and it's cool hanging out with him sometimes and all but I don't really like any guy like that because I'm pretty sure I'm totally gay."

He didn't say anything.

I opened my eyes and glanced up at him.

He was nodding his head. "Yeah, I thought so. I tried to steer him away from you without actually saying anything, but…"

"You knew? How could you know?"

He shrugged. "I'm really good at reading people, I guess. I kind-of had to be, before Nick adopted me."

"Oh."

After a minute, he asked, "Does anybody else know?"

I shook my head *No* and let out another nervous laugh. "It's not exactly the same as telling everyone your favorite book, you know."

He nodded, then glanced at me. "Listen, I'll just tell Tomás you're interested in somebody else, but wouldn't say who."

"Seriously? You'd do that for me?"

He mock-shoved me. "God, Kirsten. You're like a sister. Of course I'll do that for you. No question."

I leaned into him. "Thanks, Brent."

"But," he continued, "I think your parents would be awesome about it. And Oakley. I think you should tell them all."

I shrugged.

"I'm serious," he said. "Like I said, I'm a good judge of character."

And he was right—they were all unsurprised and totally supportive.

Why can't I be supportive like that for him now? What's wrong with me? I don't even know what to say. *I'm sorry your whole family is dead?* Because Brent is totally alone. Uncle Nick grew up a foster kid, too, and never got married. But he wanted a kid so bad, he adopted Brent.

When I think about Brent's life now, I'm an open wound. Tears rush in, filling my vision before I can hold myself in check. Without a word—because if I try to speak, I'll give myself away—I stand and stumble up the hill, not even waiting for Astrid.

Inside, I scramble down the basement stairs and sit in the dark on the cold, cement floor. *You're okay. Astrid's all right.*

Am I, Kyurp? Am I all right?

Yes. You're fine, Frog Breath.
This isn't like the time when you were almost three

and I was changing your pull-up
and you reached out

and touched the bare, blazing bulb in my goose-neck lamp.

I remember that.

How can you remember that?

I don't know. But I do.
I remember the light, and how bright and warm it was,
and wanting to hold it like it was a fairy or something.
And I remember my palm hurting.

I didn't mean to let it happen.
I mean, I was right there, and before I knew it
you had your hand wrapped around the bulb.

Did you take me to the doctor?

I was only fifteen, Frog Breath—
I couldn't drive, and Mom and Dad were at work.
I called Mrs. Martin and she came over
and looked at it and told me to
keep a bag of frozen peas on it until Mom got home.

And then I went to the doctor?

It was just a first-degree burn.
When Mom got home, she called the doctor,
then put some aloe vera on it and a bandage.

I remember I made you put frog stickers
all over the bandage.

You know, it's weird.

> *In my mind, the whole thing happens in slow-motion,*
> *and when you touch the bulb, you just keep your hand there*
> *until I pull it off.*
> *But it can't have happened that way.*
> *You must have pulled back in an instant.*

Sometimes your mind tricks you.

> *Stop it.*

I'm still downstairs when Mom gets back with Grandma. They bustle in through the side door, the suitcase banging up the stairs and thunking onto the kitchen floor, then thundering away through the dining room and down the hall.

"Down here!" I call, then turn back to the open plastic bin in front of me. I don't remember opening it or pulling out the remnants of the Lily Frog Halloween costume I helped Astrid with two years ago. We used cardboard, felt, and way too much glue to make a pair of frog legs, which we duct-taped to the sides of her green sweatpants. She made the cardboard-and-felt mask by herself, but the eye-holes were too far apart and she refused to let me help her with a new mask. There were tantrums from Astrid because she couldn't see out the eye-holes—and eventually, tantrums from me and Mom over Astrid's refusal to re-do the mask.

Halloween afternoon, the three of us were in the living room, awaiting Lexie's arrival.

"I can't see out," Astrid whined.

"Oh, for the love of Pete…" grumbled Mom.

"Lily!" Lexie shouted, banging on the storm door. "Lily! It's me, Shelley!"

Astrid shoved the frog mask up and answered the door. Lexie, with one of those plastic disc sleds painted to look like a turtle's shell and strapped to her back, couldn't get through with the sled on.

"Lexie, why don't you leave the shell out here?" suggested Mr. Oh.

Lexie scowled. "I'm Shelley. I'm a turtle. I can't take my shell off. It's part of my body."

Mr. Oh rolled his eyes and smiled. "How 'bout you turn sideways, then?"

Lexie did, then she and Astrid jumped up and down in the foyer. Astrid's mask fell off, and I snatched it up before it got trampled. If she'd used a paper plate, like I'd suggested, it would've curved easily around her nose and the eyes would've been fine.

Hmmm.

I held the mask to my face.

Mom and Mr. Oh were negotiating pick-up time for Lexie, so I ducked into the kitchen and used the edge of the booth to add a slight crease between the eye-holes. I held the mask to my face again. Closer. After a few more adjustments to the depth of the crease, the holes were too close together for me—probably perfect for Astrid. I headed back into the foyer.

Mom was on the couch, tugging on her sneakers. "There you are, Kirsten. Are you sure you don't mind staying in for candy duty?"

"It's fun to guess who everyone is. Anyway, Oakley promised to come help—we're going to watch a movie."

"Just don't forget to answer the door," Mom said, shaking her head. I handed her the adjusted mask and her flashlight, and she ushered Astrid and Lexie outside.

Astrid strapped her mask on and squealed, "You fixed it! You're the best mommy ever!"

Mom turned and mouthed a *Thank You!* before speed-walking down the path to catch up with Astrid and Lexie.

I turned on the porch light, plugged in the light-up pumpkins and our skeleton, Jack, then stole a pack of Skittles from the candy bowl. Oakley was bringing over *The Cabin in the Woods*.

Now, sitting in the still-cool basement, I run one finger along the mask's flattened-out crease, then stow it and the frog legs in the bin before snapping the lid back on. The basement shelves are stocked with plastic bins full of all the stuff Mom wanted to save from our childhood. *Someday you girls will bring my grandchildren over and I want to read them your favorite stories or let them play with your favorite toys.*

I shove the bin back onto the shelf, then head upstairs. Mom and Grandma are sitting across from each other in the booth. Grandma's hair is just barely more salt than pepper, and held back like always with a fancied-up headband. She barely fits into the booth, but she's leaning forward, holding one of Mom's hands.

"I don't know if I can handle it," says Mom, her voice choked the way it was when she and Dad were fighting earlier.

"Handle what?" I ask. "Is this about Dad?" Thinking about Dad makes me think about how we're not grilling the chicken, which makes me realize it's actually already dinnertime. I preheat the oven.

Mom doesn't say anything, just glances at Grandma. Grandma pats Mom's hand.

I open the fridge and pull out the chicken, popping it right into the still-warming-up oven. "That therapist—Jamaica? She said everyone processes grief their own way. Give Dad some time. Uncle Nick was his best friend." I lean against the counter, opposite the booth.

"Kirsten," says Grandma softly, letting go of Mom's hand and reaching out toward me.

Mom stares at the booth table and shakes her head. "Mom—don't."

"I'm helping out," I say. "Taking care of Astrid, so Mom can take care of Dad and Brent and—you know—whoever else needs it."

"Oh, baby," murmurs Grandma. She pushes up from the booth and wraps her arms around me, rubbing my back with one hand. "Oh, sweetheart...it's okay to let it out."

I lean against her soft, warm body and breathe in the scent of the Bengay she rubs into her shoulder like three times a day.

I could let it out.

I could break down and sob and sob and sob for all that's happened to our family and my friends' families. But if I start, I won't stop.

It's better to hold it in and keep going like nothing's changed. For me, at least, it's mostly true.

The oven's temperature signal beeps. Slipping away from Grandma, I set the kitchen timer for 30 minutes, then retrieve the pasta salad and veggie tray from the fridge and set them in the middle of the dining room table before heading down the hall to check on Astrid.

Brent and Dad are in the den, sitting on the futon. Dad's hair is still a mess.

"I don't know," says Brent. "I want to say something—I really do—and I spent the afternoon writing some stuff down. But what if I lose it up there?"

"It's okay if you do," says Dad.

"Will you look at what I wrote?" asks Brent. "Make sure it's not stupid or anything?"

I round the corner and open Astrid's door. She's on the floor, surrounded by *Lily's Pad* action figures.

Grandma's suitcase is on Astrid's bed.

Rage surges inside me from someplace fathoms deeper than the Marianas Trench. I have to hold on to the door frame and count to ten... twenty... fifty... one hundred. It takes forever. Then it's okay.

It has to be.

But when I look at Grandma's suitcase again, it's not okay, and I don't know why.

I yank the suitcase off Astrid's bed and roll it down the hall, dumping it by the front door, then storming into the kitchen.

"You can't take Astrid's room."

Grandma stares at me, mouth open.

Mom sighs. "I need you on board with this, Mom."

Grandma gives the tiniest nod and looks away, blinking back tears. "Maybe a hotel would be best this time. Maybe I can rent a car, too."

I over-baked the chicken. Dad's been chewing the same piece for what seems like five minutes. My own piece looks like a rock coated in barbecue sauce in the center of my plate. It's almost the same shape and color as the boulder I dug out of the willow's hole on Sunday.

The rock was huge—it took me a good three hours, at least, to find the borders and use the crowbars to ease it up an inch at a time. When I finally tipped the boulder from the hole, its thud reverberated through my shoes and rocketed through my body.

If I eat the chicken on my plate, will it sit as heavy as that boulder in my stomach?

I pull Astrid's meal toward me. "Here, Frog Breath. I'll cut your chicken for you."

Mom and Grandma glance back and forth between each other, me, and Astrid. I saw at the chicken until it's a pile of bite-sized chunks, then push the plate toward Astrid.

"Kirsten," says Mom. "Could you…" she looks at Dad, but he just takes another bite of chicken. She turns back to me. "Could you…share what you see on the table?"

"What?"

"I mean… look around the room where we are right now and…"

"You want me to look around the dining room? Why?"

"This is delicious," interrupts Grandma.

Mom gets this defeated, helpless look on her face, plucks a piece of raw cauliflower from her plate, and chews it like it's as overcooked as the chicken.

"You're doing it wrong," says Dad. He takes a huge gulp from his beer, then grunts. He hates baked meat. He's one of those hard-core grillers who dig out the grill after every snowstorm.

"At least I'm trying," says Mom.

Grandma frowns and tries to catch Mom's eye, but Mom just shakes her head.

Beside Dad, Brent shovels more pasta salad onto his plate. He keeps his head down, focusing on the food like he did last night.

We all fall back into ourselves, the only sounds the scrape of silverware against ceramic and the squelchy sound of our chewing.

Dad finishes his beer and starts a second.

Once we're all done, I send Astrid off to her room, then help clear the dishes before taking up my nightly station at the sink. I scrape, rinse, and load, dumping the contents of Astrid's full plate right into the garbage alongside the bits and crumbs from everyone else's. Even her milk is untouched.

The house phone rings and someone—probably Dad—picks up an extension.

Mom and Grandma scurry back and forth, putting leftovers into plastic containers and stowing them in the fridge. Grandma pulls out a bunch of Astrid's juice boxes and leaves them on the counter to make room.

Dad and Brent hustle through the kitchen and out the back door; a minute later, Dad's car rumbles to life, the noise fading as they retreat down the driveway.

"Where are Dad and Brent going?"

Mom crouches down to rearrange the drawer of plastic containers. Grandma never re-nests things the way Mom likes. "The funeral home. Or the church. Probably finalizing something for Nick's service tomorrow."

Astrid appears in the doorway. "I'm hungry."

Mom would normally jump on this opportunity to say something like *Maybe next time you'll eat the meal that's served* before sighing and handing over a yogurt or a cheese stick. Tonight she just keeps tidying the drawer of plastic containers.

So I say it, then tell Astrid to grab a cereal bar. "You can eat it in the living room, but throw away the wrapper when you're done."

Mom slams the drawer shut and rushes out of the room.

Grandma sets the empty disposable pan beside the sink, then follows Mom out, leaving me to finish up on my own. "Maren..."

Down the hall, a door bangs shut.

It's like we're all adrift in the same sea, but hanging onto different bits of shipwreck. We can't reach each other. And I don't see a lifeboat anywhere.

FUGUE

10

THURSDAY MORNING

I'M SITTING on my bed, wearing a simple, dark dress and heeled sandals. I don't remember showering or getting dressed, but I'm awake now. The dress is the one I picked out for graduation last year, but I don't remember the ceremony. Did we even have it? We must have—though I can't find any photos from the day on my phone. The idea that Oakley and I didn't take a ton of selfies together is unfathomable, but maybe they're all on her phone?

My running shorts, sneakers, and an old tee are in the duffel by my bedroom door. I don't remember packing them, but I know they're there, waiting for me. I also know it's nice out today, and that after Nick's service, Oakley's parents are hosting a lunchtime reception in his honor. Did Oakley tell me to bring clothes in case we can sneak off for a run? She must have.

I close my eyes and take a deep breath, gathering my courage for Nick's memorial.

When I open them, Astrid's here, scowling. Her hair is still tangled from sleep. She tugs at the waistband of her white tights with one hand. "Can't I wear my green birthday dress?"

"From last year? It's way too small. And anyway, I can't find it. I looked last night."

I opened bin after bin in the basement until Mom came down and made me stop.

"Go upstairs, sweetie," she said. "It's after midnight."

"Astrid needs something to wear to Nick's one-year memorial. I promise I'll put it all back the way you had it," I replied, but she sat on the bottom step and looked at me like I was a puzzle without a picture on the box.

"I don't know what to do," she said.

"About what?"

She squared her shoulders and looked at me, determined. "Tell me five things you see here."

"Seriously? That exercise Jamaica told us about last year? We haven't done that in ages."

"Just humor me." She extended a hand toward me, but I didn't take it.

"Fine." I rolled my eyes, then looked at the mess I'd made looking for Astrid's 6-year birthday dress. "One blue bin, two blue bins, three blue bins, four blue bins. One of my old dresses."

I grabbed the outgrown dress from the top of the nearest bin, squeezed past Mom and bolted up the stairs.

Behind me, she made a weird, fretful noise and started tidying up the bins.

Astrid's wearing the dress now: a ruffled, puffy-sleeved dress that's even itchier than it looks. I had to wear it for a great-aunt's funeral down in New York when I was eight, just like Astrid. Wait—is she eight? No—she's seven. I'm certain.

I ironed away all the creases last night before finally going to bed, but the dress still smells like the basement: stale, cold, and a little damp.

"This dress is stupid," Astrid says, as I reach for my hairbrush. I yank the brush through her hair and she leans further away from me with every tug.

"That reminds me. Why are your presents still piled up in the kitchen? You know last year was an unusual situation."

Why can't I remember this year's party? She must have at least had Lexie over…

"I don't have birthdays anymore," she says.

"Don't say that. Everybody has birthdays." I divide her hair into three sections and braid it tightly, securing it with an elastic from my stash.

She bolts from the room. I sling my purse and duffel over one shoulder and follow, latching my charm bracelet on as I go. For some reason, last year's charm and this year's are both missing—from the bracelet and from my memory.

Mom's standing in the middle of the living room, putting in her earrings. Her gaze darts around like she's a lone deer in a field. "Where's your father?"

I look around, as if he's just sitting on the couch and Mom has simply overlooked him. "Maybe he's still in your room?"

"Help me get stuff to the car," she mutters. "We should have left ten minutes ago."

"What stuff?"

"Grandma's already moved it out to the porch." When I wouldn't let Grandma stay in Astrid's room last year, she moved to a hotel—one of those places with a little kitchenette —and never left. She comes over for dinner every evening, though. I don't understand why she hasn't bothered to settle in, if she's staying.

Mom furrows her brow, then shakes her head slowly, as if she's pondering something.

Outside, Brent's old car chugs to life and he pulls out of the driveway. As we open the front door, a few of the news vans pull away from the curb and follow Brent—they can't let the one-year anniversary pass by without trying to get a story, I guess.

Dad wanted Brent to ride with us today, but he refused.

"I need to get used to doing it all on my own," he said, as if he hasn't been doing it all on his own for the past year.

I follow Mom to the porch and pick up one of the canvas totes from where Grandma has lined them up against the side of the house. Grandma takes another, and Mom takes the last two. The handles of my tote strain a little under the weight of whatever.

"What's in these?" I ask, wobbling in my heels on the uneven slate walkway.

"Photos for a project we're working on," says Mom.

At the same time, Grandma says, "Never you mind."

Trying really hard to ignore the remaining news vans, I walk to the SUV, which is backed into the driveway for easy trunk-access, and set the tote on the ground before reaching for my door. Mom tugs open the hatch. She gasps.

"Erik?"

Mom skitters around the car and yanks open the driver's door.

Dad's in the driver's seat, already belted, the keys in his hand and sweat beading on his brow from sitting in the hot car. He's staring at the dash and startles when Mom says his name.

"Maren. I didn't see you."

"Erik, I've been looking all over the house. What are you doing sitting out here?"

Dad shrugs.

Mom shoots him an intense look, like he's a lost little boy. Like she's about to tell him we don't have to go. That we can head back inside and he can pull the shades and crawl back into bed the way he has almost every day for the past year.

But he smiles—tight, toothy, and self-conscious, more like pain than a smile. He smiles this aching smile at Mom and reaches for her hand. "I'm sorry I scared you. I… are we ready to go? Where's Brent?"

"He wanted to drive himself, remember?"

Dad frowns and shakes his head. "I shouldn't have let him do that."

Mom eases the keys from his hand. "Erik? Maybe I should drive."

He unbuckles and climbs out, then walks slowly around and gets into the front passenger seat. Grandma, Astrid, and I climb into the back and buckle up as Mom adjusts the driver's seat and mirrors. I'm stuck in the middle with almost no room, thanks to Astrid's booster seat.

"Maren?" says Grandma. "Why don't you wait a minute while I put the booster seat on the porch?"

"Not today, Mom."

"But we would have so much more room…"

Mom whips her head around. "Mom. I'm not ready."

Grandma looks down, her lips pursed, a blush rising in her cheeks. I don't know why it's such a big deal—so Mom's just following the guidelines. And so Grandma didn't know them. Anyway, Astrid hasn't grown any more than her willow has. She—and it—are still the same size as the day we planted it by the creek. Maybe I should give the willow an extra feeding this year.

Oakley's family sits right behind us for Nick's service—First Unitarian is their church, too. Luther is here today, his eye bandaged. I don't remember Oakley mentioning any upcoming surgeries, but that must be it. Maybe the doctors figured out a way to give him some of his sight back. Sean and Tomás are here too, with their families, a couple of rows behind us. Even Tomás's sister, Xiomara, is here, her right arm in a sling. Isn't that the one that she got shot in? She must have hurt it again.

The service begins, and the minister talks about the way Nick was always around to help with the youth group, and how he'd work the clothing drive every winter, bringing heaps of "old coats" with him that she suspected he'd bought specifically to donate.

When Dad gets up to say a few words, I feel Oakley's hand on my shoulder. I lean back into her one-armed hug.

"You good, K?" she whispers. I nod.

Up at the pulpit, Dad is talking.

"I met Nick Broderick the first day of ninth grade," he says. "He was the new kid, and super-shy, but I'd seen him at the batting cages at Max's Mini-Golf over the summer. I was determined to convince him to try out for the school team."

I smile—I know this story. Dad dogged Nick for over two weeks until Nick agreed to try out in the spring.

By the end of that two weeks, Nick ate dinner over at Dad's house more often than not and, to hear Nick tell it, had more than one friend for the first time in his life, thanks to Dad introducing him around.

I let my mind wander.

The last time we all headed to the Washingtons' house for a party—though today it won't be a party—was their annual End-of-Summer Blowout before senior year. Astrid was five. I can't remember last year's party; I think maybe they skipped it, after the shooting. But I don't really remember anything from last summer.

The year Astrid was five, though, she was super-bored because Lexie hadn't arrived yet and Luther and his friends were all playing zombie-tag. Astrid was afraid of the zombie part. Plus, Oakley and I were off doing our own thing down in the far corner of the yard, hiding behind the cluster of forsythia with a few contraband beers.

When Astrid started crying, though—just standing there in the middle of the zombie-tag game, blubbering about the undead—Oakley and I relented, and coaxed her over to join us.

While I calmed Astrid down, Oakley made a run to restock our provisions, returning with the bowl of pretzels, two more beers, and a lemonade for Astrid.

"This is our special big-kid party hideout," said Oakley, as we settled our backs against the fence. "And there's only one rule: what happens in the hideout, stays in the hideout. Understand?"

Astrid nodded solemnly.

"You have to toast to the hideout to prove you'll keep the secret," I said. Oakley and I raised our beers. "Bump drinks with me and Oakley."

Not the right thing to do, teaching a five-year-old to keep secrets—but it's not like we let her have beer or anything.

Eventually, Lexie and her dad arrived, and Astrid flew out of the hideout. "Shelley!"

The party kicked into gear as evening approached. When Mrs. Washington lit all the citronella torches, Oakley and I stayed where we were, putting up with the bugs in exchange for our privacy.

Up near the house, Mr. Washington had fired up the grill and the smoking egg he'd just gotten. He, Dad, Nick, Mr. Oh and most of the rest of the men clustered around the meat machines, discussing the optimal order of operations so loud and full of alcohol, we could hear them all the way in our little secret corner.

Most of the women sat in camp chairs or plastic Adirondacks, resting their feet on the brick wall of the fire pit. Their voices rose with every new round of beer, hard lemonade, or cider.

Lexie and Astrid had joined a bunch of other younger kids in a squirt-gun fight. Astrid dashed across the yard, squirting wide and wild, her finger heavy on the trigger and her soggy braids flopping like wet cotton.

Eventually, Mr. Washington shouted, "Burgers, chicken, and dogs are done!" and all the little kids squealed and raced for the table where everything was out on platters.

Oakley and I ventured out, piling our plates with chicken and burgers, baked beans, and Mr. Oh's fancy mac-and-cheese. We also snagged a pair of hard lemonades.

Brent, Sean, and Tomás joined us in the hideout with their own plates. They'd brought enough beers for the lot of us, plus a bag of Doritos.

"A toast," said Oakley, holding up her lemonade. "To the best damn school year ever. To Senior Year!"

Clinking bottles, we let out a chorus of hoorays. Even full of barbecue, beans and pasta, and chips and pretzels, Oakley and I were pretty much drunk by the time that round was done.

As evening deepened, the 80s and 90s hits kicked on and the volume cranked up.

"God save us all," I muttered.

"Nobody's even paying attention," reported Brent. "We could go grab another round…"

At the fire pit, Nick and Dad were jumping around, air-guitaring and singing along to another 80s song with an insanely danceable beat while Oakley's dad stood on the wall of the fire pit, beat-boxing a complementary rhythm.

I blink back to attention. Brent is up at the pulpit.

"…I used to figure I'd end up juggling two or three jobs in retail or fast food and that would be my life, but Nick changed everything when he became my dad. Because of the home he gave me, and all his love and encouragement, I got into a good college. I have a chance to do something I'm really excited about. And I hope, someday, to do the same thing he did, and adopt some kid—some older kid who's given up—and help them reach for the future they deserve. Thanks, Nick—Dad—for teaching me to believe in myself."

He steps down from the lectern, folding up the paper with his speech on it as he returns to our row. Sitting on the other side of Dad, he fiddles with the paper.

Dad wraps an arm around him, leans in close, and whispers, "I love you, too. You won't be all alone."

11

THURSDAY AFTERNOON

As I CLIMB out of our car at Oakley's, Luther wanders past, toward the enormous oak in the front yard. Brent, Sean, and Tomás follow him.

They climb easily into the oak, Brent and Tomás sitting in the broad fork between two sturdy, low branches. Luther leads Sean to his usual spot about halfway up, but he moves tentatively, like he's afraid he's going to fall.

Mom and Grandma head toward the house with most of the bags. Dad is already inside. I smile and wave at Brent. He waves back and says something to Luther, who's reached his favorite branch and settled with his back against the trunk. I can just see them through the leaves.

I tug at Astrid, who won't get out of the car. After two more tugs, I leave the door ajar, grab my workout bag and the one Mom left for me to carry, and head down the flagstone path toward the house. By the time my hand is on the knob, Astrid is beside me, clutching my arm with both her hands. My bags bump between us. The open car door chimes and I run back to shut it.

"Why'd you leave me?" she asks when I return to the front stoop. There's a whimper in her voice I'm not used to hearing. I take her hands in mine and duck my head just enough to meet her eyes.

"Hey. You're safe, here. It's the Washingtons' house."

"But you left me. I was waiting."

"Waiting for what?"

"For you." She scrunches up her eyes against the forming tears.

I sigh and pull her to me, stroking her thick hair as much as I can without messing it up. I know what she's thinking. She's thinking about the shooting. Even though it's been a year—or maybe *because* it's been a year. She's thinking, if I'd been on time, she might have been closer to the gunman. She might not be here.

I think that sometimes, too.

Last year, Jamaica Knox said that when the symptoms of trauma stick around, it becomes PTSD. Is that what this is? Because if it is, she should go back to Jamaica's—for more than a single appointment, this time.

"I know, Frog Breath. It's scary. I don't want to think about it, either. But you're okay."

"But..."

I crouch down and meet her gaze full-on. Squeeze her hands almost too tightly. "No. No buts. You're safe. You're here. You get to grow up."

Her chin trembles a bit and she flings herself at me, sobbing. "Who says?"

"I do. I say you get to grow up."

Forcing back my own tears at what might have been, I hold her and rub her back and let her sob all over my shirt until she's all sobbed out. Then I dab at her eyes awkwardly with the edge of my sleeve, take her hand, and lead her inside, where in no time, she'll be raiding the spread Mrs. Washington's probably got all laid out in the sunroom.

A little while later, Oakley and I are sprawled across her bed. The Washingtons' house is a Cape, and except for a huge cedar-lined closet on one side where Mrs. Washington stores all her handmade quilts, Oakley has almost the whole attic to herself. Her dad even had a bathroom put in with a shower and everything. Oakley shows me the new playlist she made for the drive to this year's Emily Snow concert when the door opens. It's Josie. She shuts the door behind her, leans against it, and groans.

"Where are you going? What time will you be back? Do I know this Oakley? How come I've never met her? Maybe I should talk to her parents..." Josie mimics her mom.

"Driving you crazy, huh?" says Oakley. "That your gear?"

Josie nods, plunking her bag to the floor.

I bite my lip. Even though Josie and I are still seeing each other, and she's a little braver about holding hands or kissing in public, she still hasn't come out to her parents.

At least, I think she hasn't.

The shooting brought things into focus for a lot of people, including Josie. But sometimes—for me, at least—it feels like things got fuzzier. I find myself in rooms I don't remember walking into. Or I'm holding something that doesn't make sense, like baby toys Astrid stopped playing with ages ago.

I'm probably just stressed from homeschooling Astrid and keeping up with my own classes at UMass Lowell. What did I even take, this past year? My memory is a swirling sinkhole, and the number of things I'm not sure of keeps growing.

The three of us change into our running gear, then stretch a little in the back yard. Dad and Mr. Washington are sitting over by the fire pit, talking quietly. We spring off onto the hard-packed, backyard trail meandering through the neighborhood, toward the park and the paved trail along the Merrimack.

We only run two miles, maybe three, but it takes a while for us to work up a sweat. June in New England is hot and cold and everything in-between, including rainy. By now, though, the trees are well-leaved, and give enough shade to keep us comfortable. The early afternoon light filtering through the forest is refreshing and green. We run silently, the crunch of our sneakered feet on the path the only sound above our breath.

Cushcushcushcush.

Astrid is only seven, now—no. She's eight. It's been two years, and she won't go back to school. But someday, she and I will lie beneath her willow and look up at the long, ropey branches above us to see light shifting and dancing just like this. We'll remember the day I taught her the fairy dance and we'll laugh together at how kids will believe anything. Beyond our oasis, our own kids will roll down the slope, splash through the creek, and climb the rocks on the far side of the gully—until we call them for the picnic lunch we've set up in the sheltered hollow beneath the branches of the willow.

The sparrows and nuthatches nesting in the trees beyond the gully will cluster around the well-filled feeders, squawking and threatening with their wings as they compete for fresh seed.

After lunch, we'll pull out the shovels, the mulch, and the compost. We'll roll and heave and lug the tree delivered that morning by Merrimack Nurseries. An oak. Or a birch. Maybe a hemlock. Or a maple.

Then we'll dig. It'll take all afternoon, and we'll unearth two basketball-sized rocks before we're done.

When we're done—when the tree is planted—we'll teach our kids the fairy dance if they're young enough. The bright afternoon sky will soften to an indigo close, the birds flitting to lower branches and watching us with round, black eyes.

Now, on the Merrimack trail, Josie runs beside me, matching my easy pace as Oakley surges ahead.

"You okay?" Josie asks.

"Yeah…"

"I apologized to Brent already, but sorry I couldn't make it to the service. My mom is… well, things are weird right now."

"It's fine. It was just a memorial service. I mean, it's been three years."

She trips up on a thick, fallen stick and goes sprawling to the ground.

I turn and hold out a hand, but she waves me off, her face red but her expression as noncommittal as she can make it. "I'm fine. I should watch where the hell I'm going."

She rises, brushes the grit from her knees and palms, kicks the stick off the trail, and nods. "Let's go."

I feel like I said something wrong, but I don't know what. We jog the rest of the way in silence.

As soon as we get back, we stretch, then find Oakley in the almost-too-warm sunroom. She's pouring three huge tumblers of water. We grab seats and take huge gulps.

In the kitchen, Mom, Grandma, and Mrs. Washington sit around the table, paging through what looks—from here—like photo albums. They're making little piles.

Watching them sort through photographs reminds me of this assignment Oakley and I did together for ninth grade Spanish. We had to do a labelled poster of a bunch of items along a specific theme, and ours was El Supermercado. We spent hours one Saturday at Market Basket, taking pictures of mangoes, tomatoes, ground beef, and everything else we thought we had a chance of accurately translating, then uploaded all the photos to the pharmacy photo service and ordered prints. When we'd finished gluing everything to the poster board and labelling it en español, I left it on the dining room table for the glue to finish drying.

"Remember fall of freshman year, when Astrid cut up that photo-collage we had to do for Spanish?"

Oakley nods. "Who knew safety scissors could do so much damage?"

"Then I had to explain it in Spanish, so I was all 'Lo siento, Profe Ruggerio… mi hermanita…' and I didn't know how to say 'destroyed our entire project with her stupid safety scissors' so I mimed cutting stuff up…"

Luther enters through the sunroom door and joins the moms at the table, resting his head in his arms. Mrs. Washington rubs his back.

Ever since the shooting, I've noticed things that nobody else seems to. Things like the way the kids who were in the cafeteria haven't moved on—but in the weirdest ways. It's like time stopped for them. The rest of us keep going, but they don't grow, don't change, don't move on. Luther is no exception: the cuts near his eye haven't healed. Instead, there are fresh, delicate scabs on Luther's face where there should be shiny scars.

Oakley smiles, but it doesn't reach her eyes. She watches Luther for a minute, until he gets up and heads across the hall to his room, shutting the door behind him. She shakes her head. "Damn, this sucks."

We're refilling our waters when Josie gets a call. Oakley and I can hear her mom shouting at her through the receiver. Josie shouts back.

"Mom, I told you. Oakley's house." She flushes. "Just a friend. From school." She must mean high school, because Josie's at Framingham State, and Oakley's at the University of New Hampshire.

"We met in the fall, through my friend Kirsten." She stands and steps out the back door, pulling the sliding door closed behind her.

A few minutes after that, from somewhere in the back yard, she calls for us.

"What's wrong?" asks Mrs. Washington, looking up from the photo albums.

"We'll check, Mom," says Oakley.

Outside, Brent and Tomás are crouched over something beneath the cluster of hemlocks at the north edge of the yard. Sean and Josie are behind them, Josie still holding her phone. Silently, Luther joins us. Astrid stands off to one side.

"It's dying," says Brent, as we get nearer. His voice sounds weird—tight, but like he's about to explode. Tomás rests a hand on Brent's shoulder.

"Poor thing," Tomás says.

Josie is all teary. She pockets her phone. "Can't we do something? Can't we help it? It must be so scared."

Luther leans in a little, then pulls back and shakes his head. "It's okay. It must've fallen from the nest."

Josie shakes her head *No* and flaps her hands a little, like she's trying to take flight herself.

Oakley steps forward but I hang back, glancing at Astrid. She seems calm, undisturbed. She nods.

Oakley looks around. "Where's the nest? It must be nearby." We peer into the branches of the nearby trees until Josie finds the nest.

"There!" she points into the shadows of the largest hemlock, just a few feet away. "What do we do? Won't the parents abandon it if we touch it?"

Brent shakes his head. "That's just a myth," he says. "Only people abandon their kids."

"Brent..." Sean says, but Brent is already stepping onto a wide, low branch to check out the nest.

"Good," he says. "It's still in decent shape. There's another nestling up here, too."

Josie whimpers.

Returning to the ground, Brent squats over the fallen nestling and moves to pick it up.

"Can I do it?" asks Josie.

Brent stands and takes a step back.

Josie crouches and gently lifts the fallen nestling. When she stands, I see it for the first time. It looks naked, like a plucked chicken, but so much more fragile. A slap would kill it. If it hadn't fallen into the fluff of dropped needles and forest mulch, it would have never survived. Cupping the tiny nestling in one hand, Josie climbs into the hemlock—she needs two branches where Brent only needed one—and tips the bird into the nest.

Once back on the ground, she glances at me and flashes a smile of relief. "Its little heart was beating so fast..."

Oakley and Luther turn back toward the house. "Let's tell Mom to keep an eye on that nest," she says. "Get it? An eye?"

He responds with a playful punch, and Oakley pulls him into a rowdy, one-armed hug.

Brent and his friends drift off toward the forsythia hideout. By the trees, Astrid stands like a sentry—but I can't really see her for some reason. Everything is blurry. Am I crying?

Why am I crying? Birds fall from nests all the time. So we saved one. What about all the nestlings that nobody finds?

12

THURSDAY EVENING

TIME PASSES TOO FAST—AND takes forever at the same time. Four years—five years—what's the difference? Sometimes I blink and it feels like everything came crashing down five minutes ago.

Josie, Oakley, and I go running every morning.

Grandma is still here all the time—she sold her condo in New York, and even leased a car, but three years later she's still in the hotel with the kitchenette. She's always over at our house, even though I'm already here, old enough to help. I'm not sure why I'm not good enough in Grandma's eyes—it's like nobody trusts me to be aware of what's going on. I'm aware enough to know that living in a hotel for six years is stupid-expensive, and it's not like she's rich or anything. It makes no sense. Why doesn't she buy a condo or a town house here, and settle in?

After the shooting, the elementary school stayed closed for the rest of the school year. It was only two weeks, so I guess it's okay. It's not like it will keep anyone out of Harvard or MIT in the long run.

The superintendent issued a press release the day of Nick's funeral, saying Winslow Elementary would remain closed "indefinitely" and that in the fall, kids would attend classes in the old Riverview Elementary, on our side of the river.

They spent the summer cleaning Riverview up and repainting the inside. But when the first day of school came, Astrid freaked out and wouldn't even get in the car for me to drive her in.

Halfway through week two of Astrid hiding under the bed every morning, I persuaded Mom to let me homeschool her.

We check out tons of books from the library and read them and talk about it all. We watch nature shows and history shows and go for long walks along the creek and through the woods, looking for frogs. I dropped my course load to two classes, and cut my hours at Dirty Knees to part-time, but whenever I leave Mom in charge of Astrid's education, I'm pretty sure she lets Astrid do whatever while she and Grandma sit in the kitchen, sucking down coffee and staring at each other.

Right now, Astrid is sprawled on the floor, bundled in her flannel pajamas and winter bathrobe, watching *Lily's Pad* again, even though she's getting kind-of old for it. She's been here all afternoon. I sit beside her on the floor. In front of us is a stack of her favorite picture books about frogs, bats and turtles. I open *All Along the Creek* and flip through it idly.

The frog thing started when Astrid was three, back when Mrs. Martin watched her during the day. I picked her up from next door every afternoon. One Friday, while Astrid was pulling on her shoes, Mrs. Martin said, "She's been talking about frogs again all day. I put on a nature show, but that wasn't enough. I'm just warning you." She shook her head as if she wouldn't wish frogs on anyone.

I nodded. "She heard them in the creek last weekend, and got it in her head that she can catch one and keep it as a pet." Astrid handed me her jacket and I helped her into it. Her shoes were on the wrong feet.

"Frogs are coated in mucous, not slime," she said. "That was on the TV today."

"See you next week, Astrid," Mrs. Martin said, and Astrid called *Bye* over her shoulder as she hopped down the porch steps. She hop-jumped down the sidewalk, then up our front walk.

I fixed her a snack—corn chips and a lump of guacamole with two bits of red pepper for eyes and four celery-stick legs—and pulled up an episode of some random kids' show to keep her busy while I sped through my Spanish homework. Afterwards, I shut the TV off and held out her jacket. "How about we go frog hunting?"

She scrambled up and into her shoes, bolting outside before I've even pulled out the mesh net I'd picked up at the garden center. I stuck the handle in my back pocket and started down the hill.

"Now, what do you know about catching frogs?"

"You hafta be quiet. Listen for splashes. And prob'ly you'll get wet."

"And be careful on the slippery rocks, okay?"

"But you'll catch me if I fall. Right?"

"I will always catch you," I said. It was an impossible promise.

I let her search the creek for a few minutes, listening for splashes and lunging after several frogs before almost getting one.

Then I held out the net. "Maybe this will help?"

"Yeah! Yeah!" She examined it and turned back to her task, capturing a frog after a few more tries.

I took the net from her, holding it so the frog, barely two inches long, was nestled into the mesh but visible if I arranged the opening just right.

I crouched beside the creek.

Astrid reached out and stroked it with one finger, tracing a line from its green head to its muddy brown tail. It sat rock-still but for breathing. "Can I keep him?"

I shook my head, even though she wasn't looking at me. "Sorry, Frog Breath. Wild animals belong in nature."

She stroked it again. "Wild animals belong in nature. Yeah."

"I'm going to call him Greeny," she said, petting him a few more times. Carefully turning the net over, I let Greeny out onto the dirt at the edge of the creek. He sat for a moment, then leapt back into the water—*plip*!

"Maybe I can catch Greeny every day with my net and we can be friends."

"Maybe," I said, laughing.

"Bye, Greeny! I'll see you again tomorrow!"

Now, standing in the foyer beside Grandma, Mom is crying. "Kirsten, please. Put on something else. Better yet, turn it off already. I can't take it anymore."

Grandma is holding what looks like a bunch of scrapbooks or photo albums. She shifts her grip on them and wraps one arm around Mom.

Mom doesn't know I hear her walking the halls all night. She also doesn't know I don't remember turning the TV on, or even walking into the living room. How long have I been sitting on the floor with Astrid and her books?

"Sorry," I mumble, and flick off the AV setup. "Astrid, let's go outside and take care of your willow." Her willow is feeble. I honestly can't tell if it's grown at all. I've done online searches several times for advice on soil amendments, fertilizer, and food—even broke down and asked my boss, Maura, what to do. She came over and looked—she said it seemed fine to her. That I'm doing everything right. When I pressed the subject, she just smiled and said, "Kirsten, Hon, just trust me and leave it alone for a while." She's never not helped me, before.

"Is Lexie in school?" Astrid asks as we step out onto the deck. The hose is still in place from our last watering.

"Lexie's on summer break."

"What about Jerky Jeremiah?"

I have to crack a smile over our secret name for the little shit. "Yes, Jerky Jeremiah, too."

"What about… what about Hunter?"

Hunter, whose dad started this whole thing. How much does Astrid remember? Mom never took her back to Jamaica Knox; I've suggested it once or twice, but Mom responds by asking me to name five blue things, or five things I smell, or whatever. Finally, last night, I offered to drive Astrid myself.

We were in the kitchen, and Mom was loading the dishwasher. I finished stacking leftovers from Mrs. Washington into the fridge. I'm not sure why Mrs. Washington is still taking care of us—it's been years. Maybe it's because she knows Brent is part of our family, now.

"What do you mean?" said Mom. "You're not getting behind the wheel. Not now."

"I've been driving with Astrid for years. Why are you suddenly worried?"

She stood there, holding a scrub-brush in one hand and a plate in the other, staring into the sink as the faucet ran.

"Mom? Why are you suddenly worried about me driving Astrid around? Don't ask me to name five whatevers. That's bullshit. I can take her. It's no big deal. I've taken her to the dentist before, and I took her to the Urgent Care that one time last year when she had an earache."

"You've never… she doesn't have an earache, Kirsten," Mom said, her voice tight and choked.

"I know. I'm just saying…"

She whipped around. "Astrid doesn't have an earache! She… she's…"

Something broke inside her, splintering across her face like spider-web cracks across a windshield. She flung the dish in her hand, smashing it on the floor, and dropped to her knees, scrabbling through the slivers and chunks.

I knelt and started helping her gather the pieces.

But she was dragging a large, pointed shard down her forearm, over and over and over again, screaming. Screaming in this guttural, primitive way and carving herself up. Huge welts rose on her arm, bits of skin poking through the long, ragged wounds.

"Mom! Oh, my god, Mom!" I grabbed for the shard but she twisted away, still screaming and shredding herself to pieces. "Mom, stop!"

She stopped slicing and just sat there on the kitchen floor, clutching the shard like a life preserver, her screams devolving into gasping, fragmented sobs.

I grabbed a clean dish towel from the drawer and pressed it against her arm.

"Maren?" Dad's voice behind me made me cry, too. He dropped to the floor beside us, reaching for Mom's arm, and I seize the chance to flee to the basement. Behind me, Dad murmurs, "I'm here, now… I'm here… I'm sorry, Maren. I'm here…"

I don't remember what I did in the basement. I just remember voices in the kitchen above me—Dad, Mom, Grandma—shoutingshoutingshouting at each other. The next thing I remember is Grandma sitting on the floor with me in the basement, holding my hands and telling me stories from times I visited her as a little kid. "…then Grandpa took you down to the garden center. You picked out a packet of four o'clocks, because you wanted to see them wake up every afternoon at four. We sent you home with that flower pot and a little watering can, and you made your mom video-call us every day so we could watch the sprouts grow…"

I remember that. The next year, I begged Mom and Dad to let me plant a tree in our yard. I chose the apple tree that's now in the sunny side yard between our house and the Martins'. That fall, I planted iris bulbs in the sunny patch on Uncle Nick's side of the creek, because Mom and Dad weren't ready to commit to letting me landscape the front yard. It was the right decision—I was only seven, and driven by a desire to plant every purple flower I could, with no understanding of different plants' needs.

When Grandma finally coaxed me upstairs last night, the kitchen was spotless—the floor washed, the dishwasher chugging away. I glanced out the kitchen window, and Astrid was in the back yard with a flashlight, doing her fairy dance around the willow. She probably never heard a thing.

"No," I tell Astrid, now. "Hunter's not in school, either."

"His dad wasn't supposed to be there. His dad wasn't allowed to pick Hunter up from school anymore."

"I remember, Frog Breath."

"Maybe Hunter's being homeschooled like me."

Hunter's not being homeschooled. Hunter never survived his father's rampage.

"Maybe," I say.

We turn the water on at a trickle and she heads down the hill to do her fairy dance. Dad is sitting in the grass, maybe a yard above the willow. Astrid is so small—no taller than she was the day we planted the willow. Why hasn't she grown? Why hasn't the willow? It's been six years almost exactly—her tenth birthday is today. Is this going to be like last year? And the year before? And every year since the shooting? Are her gifts going to stay piled against the wall in the kitchen? This year, I've already moved them to her bedroom and piled them on her bed. I don't remember what we've done all those other years. I just remember the gifts piled up, waiting.

I waited for you.

I plod down the slope and sit beside Dad, fingering the frog charm—the one from Astrid's fourth birthday. Mom was still helping her hide them, then.

We hid it in the shed, in the watering can.

I know.

You were lucky I didn't need to water the hanging plants.

I would've sogified the box.

No, we weren't lucky.
Me and Mom planned it that way.
She said to hide it

right before it was time to look for it.
And we paid Dad in extra cake to keep you busy.

> *Oh, is that why he got like half the cake that year?*

It wasn't half.

> *I think it was half.*

"Dad, you remember that year you ate like half Astrid's birthday cake?"

He doesn't respond.

"She's out here every day doing her fairy dance," I say. "I wish I knew what was wrong with the willow—why it's hardly grown in four years. I keep expecting her to ask why the fairy dance isn't working." Four years? Actually, it's been seven, but I don't correct myself out loud.

The corners of his mouth turn down.

Astrid abandons her dance and picks her way down the slippery creek bank. Across the water, on Brent's side, the lights in the kitchen blaze on.

"Fairies don't exist, Kirsten." His voice is quiet. Tired.

"I know that. I'm just having fun with her."

He closes his eyes for a long moment before speaking. "You're having fun."

"Yeah. I'm sure she knows it's just a game. She's nine." Ten. Eleven. Twelve.

He nods. Astrid steps from rock to rock in the low, cold creek.

"But really—what if she asks why it's not growing? I mean, it's not diseased. Not that I can tell, at any rate. It's just...not growing. It should be...I don't know, twenty feet tall by now. Maybe more, given where I planted it. Weeping willows grow fast."

"I guess..." he shakes his head like he's clearing water from his ears. "I guess everybody deals with it differently."

I frown at him, but he doesn't notice. We sit there for a while, in silence but for the frog-song—*gao, gao... gao, gao*—while Astrid goofs around on the rocks. Why doesn't she act her age? I get up. "Astrid, I keep telling you—the fairies won't come if you pester them. They're shy. Why don't you go inside and get ready for your birthday?"

She grins and hops across the creek to our yard. Her rain boots flop as she double-times it up the hill ahead of me and scrambles onto the deck. Dad re-stained it the week before Astrid was six. You can't tell the stain-job is that old, though —for some reason, it hasn't weathered at all.

"Boots off outside!" I call. She only still fits in them because she's as peaked as her willow. Isn't that a medical thing, when kids don't grow? Don't thrive? Doesn't it have something to do with food allergies or something? She ignores me.

By the time I'm inside, she's already holed up in her room. Mom and Grandma are in the living room, arguing again. Mom's wearing a cardigan that hides her sliced-and-bandaged arm.

"Just put it all away someplace," says Grandma. She's holding the books that Astrid and I left out.

"I can't, Mom."

"It's not healthy. She needs to focus on the world around her."

The doorbell chimes. I open it, and Mrs. Martin is standing there with Jeremiah. He's finally stopped biting Astrid every time she's in the yard, but the pinched look on his face reveals that his mother has forced him to accompany her. He's chewing on his hand again. Mrs. Martin is holding a box from Dunks.

"Hi," I say.

"Kirsten." She's smiling, but there's this terrified look in her eyes. It weirds me out, and I look at her ear so I don't have to meet her gaze. She has two holes in her right ear, but no earrings. Mrs. Martin thrusts the Dunk's box toward me, but I don't take it. I switch to staring at her left ear. Three holes—also no earrings. Mrs. Martin doesn't seem like someone who would have three piercings. She's too straight-laced, in her mom-jeans and tucked-in, button-down blouse, to have ever chosen the extra piercings. Her outfits remind me of Barb from that show *Stranger Things* more than anyone else.

"We thought… just a little something to have on hand."

I look down at Mrs. Martin's hands; she's still holding the box out.

Suddenly, Mom and Grandma are beside me. Grandma wraps an arm around me. "Come on. Let's go sit in here." She leads me into the kitchen.

Behind us, Mom says, "Geraldine. Thank you so much…"

Grandma sits me in Dad's spot in the booth. The kitchen, with its butter-yellow walls and light wood cabinets, is too bright after the dusky, early-evening sky. The open window over the sink lets in a cool breeze, full of the spicy scent of my window-box peonies. I can just hear the *gao, gao… gao, gao* mingling with cricket-chirps. Grandma bustles about, making me a mug of peppermint tea. She sits across from me, in Mom's spot, cupping one hand around her own mug.

The booth seems smaller than it used to, especially with all Astrid's gifts piled up. Didn't I move these to her room earlier? It's her tenth birthday tomorrow. No, wait—her eleventh. How could I forget that? And how was there ever space in the booth for two people on a side? We never use it anymore. With Grandma and Brent added to the family, we eat in the dining room every night, now.

"I'm worried about you, sweetheart," says Grandma. "You're spending a lot of time alone in your room."

"Sure," I say, shrugging. "I've got studying. I'm in a summer session. My professors assign a lot of reading. And anyway, I'm not alone. Astrid comes in sometimes and does her work in there, on my bed."

She stares at her mug.

Mom comes in and sets the box of doughnuts on the counter. She looks at me, then Grandma. "Mom?"

Grandma stands, dumping her still-hot drink into the sink. "Kirsten was telling me about her college classes."

I take a sip of tea. "Grandma thinks I'm spending too much time in my room. I told her I have a lot of homework. College isn't like high school. I don't get retakes on tests or anything. Right, Mom?"

Mom plops a tea bag into her own mug and pours the hot water, then slides into the booth on her side. Grandma leans against the counter and looks at me like I'm an injured bird.

"It's not like I'm a recluse or anything," I continue. Why do I have to justify my behavior? "I have my job at Dirty Knees. And I go running every morning."

"That's another thing I worry about, sweetie," Grandma says. "Are you sure you're not running too much? Pushing yourself in a bad way?"

"There's nothing wrong with a few miles a day. Some people even run these things called marathons, you know." I meet her gaze and hold it until she looks away, turning to Mom. I'm not sure why I'm so defensive, but I'm ready to dig in and win, no matter what. I'm not giving up my running.

"I even did a half-marathon with Oakley a few years ago to help raise money for the new school playground." I'm not sure where the money went, though, because I don't think it ever got built. Not after…

Something inside tells me giving up running would be like giving up breathing.

Grandma frowns. "Years ago? I thought that was just last…"

Mom slaps the table with one hand. "Mother."

Still looking at Mom, Grandma folds her arms and changes her angle of attack. "I think Kirsten should spend a little more time out here helping you with preparations for Sunday. Maybe she could design the program on the computer? Give you time to handle other things? She can't hide forever."

"I'm not hiding," I say. "And preparations for what? What happens on Sunday?"

Mom prods the tea bag with a spoon and sighs. Her eyes are bloodshot, with dark bags beneath them. "Mom… please… I've already asked you to leave it alone."

Grandma sets her lips in a thin line and shakes her head. Just as I think she's about to get into it with Mom, she pushes off the counter. "It's getting late. I'm heading out. You two sit. Talk. Do something together. You need to communicate." She leaves through the side door.

Mom throws a frown over her shoulder. "Don't tell me what I need to do," she mutters. Then she stands, dumps her untouched tea, and stomps out the side door. I hear her join

Dad on the back deck. Their voices drift through the open window.

"I know she's putting the scrapbook together for Brent, and she means well, but honestly, I'm glad she's staying in a hotel," says Mom. "I wish I'd suggested it, myself instead of… well…" her voice drops to a level that renders it nothing more than murmurs to me.

My tea is almost cold, but I keep holding onto the mug. My parents' voices become an undercurrent, prodding me toward something unknown. Something I don't want, but cannot escape.

After some unknown amount of time, Dad calls through the window, "Kirsten? Come on out?"

I join them outside, taking my usual seat at the round, four-person outdoor dinette table. The metal cross-braces that hold up the top surface are rusting.

"How are you doing, honey?" he asks.

"I'm cool."

"I know Grandma can overreact a little. Mom and I are concerned, though, about whether you're pushing yourself in ways that may do more harm than good."

"Like what?"

He pauses. "We… well, we want you to know… it's hard for all of us. Dealing with this… this… tragedy. If you want to talk to us—or to someone else, like Jamaica Knox…"

"You think I'm crazy? What am I doing that's crazy?" The powdery orange rust beneath the black, open-weave pattern of the table surface reminds me of Halloween, and the time, before she was obsessed with frogs, Astrid trick-or-treated as a princess-frog-ballerina-scientist-pirate. Grandma was the one who pulled that costume together, with a lab coat that ended in a green tulle skirt, a rhinestone-encrusted tri-point hat, and matching eyepatch. That was crazy. I'm not crazy.

"Nobody's crazy," Dad says.

"Then why do you guys want me to talk to Jamaica again?"

Mom sighs. "Kirsten, the shooting was…"

"Ages ago," I say. "And Astrid's okay—mostly. If anyone should see a therapist, it's you guys. I'm pretty sure 'home-schooling' doesn't mean 'let your kid lie around and watch cartoons all day while you sit in the kitchen, ignoring her.' I'm not the one carving myself up, Mom."

She glances at her sleeve, where there are a few blood spots seeping through from one of the deeper gashes.

"And Dad, you're going to get fired if you don't pull it together. You are both so detached from reality. I know Nick was your best friend, Dad. But he was Brent's father, and Brent hasn't gone off the deep end. The reason Grandma stayed here instead of going home to New York is because you two have bottomed out. She put her life on hold for you, and so did I. If it weren't for me and Grandma, the laundry wouldn't get done. Neither would the vacuuming, or cleaning the bathrooms, or dinner."

Mom takes Dad's hand in hers and reaches for me with the other one. "Sweetie…"

I stand, shaking my head. "Yeah. I'm having a hard time. I'm —" how old am I, if Astrid is eleven? My brain seizes up on the math. "I'm her sister, not her parent. Same goes for Grandma. I mean, you two can't even give Astrid a decent birthday."

Storming back inside, I pause to survey the pile of gifts, running my finger along the edges of a medium-sized package that rattles a little when I pick it up. I set it back in place and retreat to my room.

There, curled up beneath the fern-printed quilt Grandma gave me for Christmas my senior year in high school, I stare out the window. Dusk creeps toward night like a vine across a brick wall. I guess I doze off for a few minutes, because the next thing I know, Astrid is crawling into my bed.

"What time is it?" I ask.

Not answering, she snuggles against me. She's freezing.

"What'd you do? Hide in the basement?"

"No."

"Where, then?"

"I'm cold."

I wrap my arms around her and within minutes, she's asleep.

I slide out of bed and head down the hall in search of something for dinner.

What are you doing out here?

Out where?

In your garden.

In my garden? I'm… gardening.

It's too dark to garden.
And anyway, that's not what I mean.

What, then?

Why aren't you helping Mom and Dad?

Helping them with what?

Helping them get ready for Sunday.

What happens Sunday?

Sunday, we say goodbye.

I'm awake.

I'm awake, and outside, kneeling in the dirt between the bell peppers and the bush beans. I'm in my pajama shorts and an old tee. The soil and the plants are wet, and my clothes are damp where I've brushed against the plants.

What was I doing? Why did I come out here? I'm wearing my running headlamp, and a can of soapy water sits solidly in the dirt beside the bush beans.

It's way too dark to pest-pick.

I can't let Mom and Dad know I'm out here pest-picking in the middle of the night—and, worse, that I don't remember coming out. Leaving the soapy water by the corner of the garden fence, I turn off my headlamp and creep, in darkness, through the wet grass. When I reach the deck steps, I try to wipe my bare feet off a bit on the opposite calf, so I don't track mud and bits of grass inside.

Once inside, I wipe my feet and calves—and my knees—off more thoroughly on a kitchen towel, then clean up the evidence of my footsteps and toss the towel down the stairs to the laundry pile.

When I reach my room, I find Astrid starfished across my bed. Leaving my headlamp on my desk and grabbing my phone, I retreat to her room and crawl into her bed. As I pull the covers up, a noise in the hall catches my attention.

The door clicks open and Dad creeps in, still wearing the sweatpants and t-shirt he had on this evening. I can just see him in the dim light of Astrid's night-light. He looks over at the bed and takes a deep breath, letting it out super-slow, before stumbling over, pulling out Astrid's chair, and sitting. Does he know I was outside?

Astrid's room is unsettling. It's not that it's unfamiliar—more like the opposite. Though she's starting high school level subjects in the fall, she won't let me help her update anything. Her walls are still the same pale green she chose when she was four. Her bookshelves still hold all those easy-readers and picture books about bugs and frogs and other wildlife— and her *Lily's Pad* toys. I think she plays with them from time to time, because there are usually a few pieces scattered across the floor or arranged on her too-small desk, as if she'd just stepped away to get a snack.

"Kyurp?" Dad whispers. "Are you awake?"

"Only Astrid gets to call me that," I murmur.

He nods. "I thought I heard you in the hall. Did the rain wake you up, too?"

Rain? That must be why the ground was so wet—not dew, but rain.

"I guess so."

I lie there, in the dark corner, in Astrid's bed, and watch him at her desk. He fiddles with some of the toys she left set up. I wait for him to press me about why I was outside in the garden, but he says nothing for a long time.

Slowly, my mind crawls toward sleep. Just before I drift off, Dad clears his throat.

"It's harder than I thought it would be," he says, his voice slurred.

"What is?" I ask, my eyes still closed. I know he means Uncle Nick. He always does.

"Moving on, when there's a hole so big nothing can ever fill it."

"I know," I say. It's what I'm supposed to say, and it's a lot better than something like *He's in a better place, now.*

And anyway, why are we still talking about a loss that happened eight years ago? Not that Dad should be over Nick's death—because how do you even do that?—but isn't there a point when Dad won't be a mess, anymore? When he won't leave the house for hours at a time and go—I don't know. Driving around? Out to O'Hara's Pub, only without Nick? I don't even know where I go, sometimes. How can I know where he goes?

He's in a better place. What could be a better place than being with everyone and everything you love? Oakley said, once, that when she was little and her Grandma was dying of cancer, her great-aunt told her people in heaven are so happy to be with God that nothing else matters. They don't miss anyone they left behind.

To me, that sounds like hell. Or at least dementia—which is hell for everyone you love. Why would anyone wish for that?

"It's like trying to flood the Grand Canyon," Dad continues. "Can you imagine trying to flood the Grand Canyon? No matter how much water you pour in, it'll never reach the rim. There's a river at the bottom, flowing in and out again. You'd have to dam up the ends. Can you imagine damming up the

Grand Canyon? Where would you find that much rock? How would you transport it to the Canyon? Fit it into place so there were no leaks? And wouldn't the pressure of the water eventually be too much? I think it would be too much. I don't think anyone could ever flood the Grand Canyon."

"Uh-huh," I say, to let him know I'm still awake.

He makes a noise. At first I think it's a sneeze, but his shoulders heave and he curls into himself and clutches a toy from Astrid's desk—probably the one that's her favorite figure of Lily—and keeps making that sneezy, breaking noise.

I get out of bed and shuffle over to where he sits. I put a hand on his shoulder. Slowly, he pulls together, until finally he wipes his eyes with the hem of his t-shirt. After one final, huge sniffle, he lets out a short laugh, the reek of booze hitting me full-on. I wrinkle my nose, then hope he didn't see. It's not entirely his fault.

"So if you could never flood the Grand Canyon," he says, "why would anyone think they could fill this kind of hole? I don't have words for how deep it is. And I'm trapped at the bottom. But I can't find the river that flows in and out again. There's got to be a way out. Right?"

"I don't know."

He sighs. "I shouldn't even be talking to you about this. It's not fair. I'm supposed to be the parent. I'm supposed to be there for you and help you make sense of the big stuff. Not the other way around."

"Shit, Dad. It's okay."

And in this moment, it is. I can be here for him; I'm not a kid anymore, or even a teenager. I'm only still living here because Mom and Dad need me. And because *they're* still so torn up, Astrid needs me.

He shakes his head, takes a deep breath, and stands. "No, Kirsten. It's really not okay. I should lean on your mother, or call one of those therapists, so you can lean on the both of us." He takes another deep breath and squares his shoulders, then pulls me into a hug. "I'm sorry. This has been tough for you, too. I promise I'll do better."

What's been tough for me is having to act like Astrid's parent instead of just getting to be her sister.

He steps over to Astrid's bed and pulls aside the quilt so I can climb back in.

I climb back in.

He pulls the quilt up and folds it over a little at the top, then dots my nose with his finger, like when I was a little kid.

Bending down, he kisses me on the forehead.

"I'm sorry I woke you. Try to get a few more hours."

His hand is already on the doorknob when I say, "Dad?"

"Yes?"

"I love you."

"I love you too, Kirsten."

But what I really want to say is: sometimes I feel like I'm stuck at the bottom of a canyon, too. Only I don't know why.

13

FRIDAY, MIDMORNING

My phone alarm goes off and I fumble for it, confused for a few seconds about where it is, until I remember I'm in Astrid's room again.

In the hallway, there's a murmur of mixed voices outside the bedroom door. It sounds like Mom, Dad, and Grandma arguing about a dress for Astrid, but I don't hear Astrid's voice.

Just Dad, his voice rising to a shout. "It doesn't matter what dress they put her in. Everything's going to be closed."

"I don't care that it'll be closed," Mom says, matching his volume. "I'll know. I'll know what she's wearing."

Dad mutters something, then his footsteps recede and the front door slams.

"I'm not being stupid, Mom… am I?" Mom asks Grandma. Her voice sounds… dependent. I've never heard her sound like she needed her own mom before, but that's exactly what she sounds like. The idea of Mom needing Grandma scares me. Who do I turn to if something bad happens, and my mom can't handle it because of whatever's going on between her and Dad?

I guess I just figure it out by myself.

They're still in the hallway, and Grandma consoles Mom. "Of course not, dear. It's important to control the things you can. But let's go through the closet after Kirsten's awake."

Mom lets out a harsh *Ha!* "If we haven't woken her up already…"

Their voices fade as they move toward the kitchen.

Once I'm sure they're gone, I climb out of Astrid's bed and return to my room, where I dress for a run. There's no sign of Astrid, but maybe that's a good thing. Maybe she went for a walk, or agreed to let Mom and Grandma take her shopping for whatever dress they're talking about. She hardly ever leaves the house anymore—unless she's watering the willow or walking along the edge of the creek, looking for frogs. I understand. The only things I want to do, besides my daily run, are spend all day out in my garden and increase my hours at Dirty Knees. The local produce greenhouse project has hit some zoning snags, but the change was finally approved and Maura thinks the permits will come through with no more major issues. Managing the greenhouse is more my speed than anything I can get from college… which is probably why it's taken me eight years and I'm still not done with my degree. Do college credits have an expiration date? I bet I'm going to get a letter, any day now, that says, *Finish up, already!* Or, *Too late! Start over!*

I'm not starting over.

Josie graduated years ago and got a position as a counselor with the Lowell Girls and Boys club—she's still living at home, too, and we're still keeping reality a secret from her parents.

Reality doesn't like being a secret.

Wedging in my earbuds, I step outside and warm up with a brisk walk, cutting through the back yards and coming out one down from Brent's house, where the news vans wait like crouched big cats. Every year, they mark the anniversary of the shooting by trying for interviews. Hanging a left on Morgan, I slow as I pass Oakley's house. The good car is in the driveway and Luther is racing a remote control car up and down the front walk. Wait—that can't be Luther. He's in Los Angeles for the summer, interning at the District Attorney's office. Maybe he's a younger cousin? He sure looks like Luther from here, though. Exactly like Luther—he's even wearing an eye-patch like Luther had to when he was fresh out of fifth grade and one of the heroes of the Winslow Elementary shooting.

Luther never wanted to be a hero. He just wanted to keep his friends safe.

I push the volume up a little and settle into my pace as I reach the bike trail that snakes in and out of the thin strip of woods along the Merrimack.

Cushcushcushcush.

The comfortable, damp scent of leafy mulch beside the trail rises to greet me and wraps around me like a blanket. The Merrimack trail is my favorite: cool and shady during the day thanks to the trees on the left side of the path, and with a clear view of the water where the bank drops away to the right.

Today the edges of the trail are still wet from an early summer storm that flashed through overnight. You wouldn't know it to look at the sky, but there's more rain forecast for tonight and tomorrow. Now, though, sunlight shines through the trees, and the air is cool. It almost feels like early spring. The world is mixed-up, I think. Confused. Like me.

Cushcushcushcush.

Maybe I run here, by the river, so some of the clear view will wash the confusion from my mind—because sometimes it's as if I wake up from a dream and look around, and nothing is what I thought it was. I feel like I'm looking for something and I can't find it anywhere.

Sometimes I wake up in the basement—well, I don't really wake up, I just come out of a fog, or something—and I'm looking through baby boxes or cleaning up the stuff Mom's got stored on the shelves for when she's a grandma. I'm trapped in a nightmare where my hands are sieves and everything real slips through the holes. No matter how hard I try to hold on, reality keeps leaking out of my grasp.

Except, the reality from my dream isn't the actual reality.

In my dreams, life is a river with rapids leading to a waterfall and I've been thrown from a capsized boat. I'm trapped beneath the surface of the water, unable to find my way up and out. The river churns and froths around me, tossing me about like an old rag doll, and just as I smash my head against a submerged boulder, I wake up.

Or I'm hiking along a cliffside path and it gives way beneath my feet and I fall and fall and fall, scrabbling my hands raw against rock as I try to grab onto something—anything—but my fingers come away bloody and broken, and just before I dash to pieces against the rocks below, I wake up.

I think I'm losing my mind.

I can't let anyone find out.

Running is real, though. My feet hit the ground in regular, rhythmic strides. I move forward, always forward, even though I'm not running toward anything specific. Like we move forward—always forward—in life, sometimes knowing where we're going, but most of the time trusting that our decisions, minute by minute, will lead someplace that makes sense.

Cushcushcushcush.

Running is real.

I breathe in through my nose, out through my mouth. Cold, crisp air during the fall and winter and spring. Warm, thick air during the summer. It fills me. Buoys me. Calms me.

Breathing is real.

Sweat clings to my hairline and trickles down my neck. It beads up between my breasts and dampens my bra.

Sweat is real.

Cushcushcushcush.

I'm startled back to the river path by the sense of a runner coming up behind me. Glancing around, I find I don't know where I am; I've never been this far along the trail before. Trying to keep my breath and pace steady, and my mind from assuming I'm about to be kidnapped, I peer through the trees on the roadside, searching for signs of houses across the street. There's a single house-like building, with no lights on —maybe a shop that went out of business. The Entering Lowell sign is just up ahead.

Edging to the right and slowing to let the runner pass, I tug out one earbud.

Brent pulls up beside me, chugging along like he's about to die.

I stop, bouncing in place.

"Holy shit," says Brent, gasping for breath. He looks pale and like he wants to throw up.

"Since when do you run?" I ask.

"I… don't. But I… thought… you seem so… into it… maybe I should… try."

I laugh a little. "What's the verdict?"

"It sucks."

I laugh louder. "You can't go so far and so fast on your first try. You gotta build up to a long run. Especially someone as out of shape as you."

He rolls his eyes at me, then jerks a thumb toward home. "Finish together?"

"Yeah, sure. Astrid's probably wondering where I am—I told her I'd be back in a flash."

Brent squints at me for a minute, then nods.

"Yeah, well… let's go, then." He turns and I follow.

Cushcushcushcush.

I set an easy pace since he's struggling so much. We jog in silence until we're about a half mile from our street. I can tell he's about to drop, so I slow to a walk.

"You okay? You look like shit."

"I feel like shit," he says, after he's caught his breath again.

I frown. "What's wrong?"

"Last night—I got wasted."

I don't answer right off—I guess it makes sense, Brent getting drunk. He's held it together for years, even better than my dad, who constantly picks fights with Mom and sometimes doesn't bother going to work. Whenever I ask when he's going back, Dad says, *When I'm ready, Kirsten. I need a little more time.*

Brent couldn't swing college at Rensselaer without Uncle Nick's help, so he's working his way through school at UMass Lowell. I mean, *worked*. Like Josie and Oakley, he's already graduated. I don't know what he does now—some sort of computer job. But he never drinks, and he never stays out late.

"So, any special reason you suddenly got wasted, then topped it off by running three miles?" I ask, as we cut through a yard to follow the creek the rest of the way to our footbridge.

Brent sucks in a deep breath. "Don't be a bitch," he says, almost under his breath. "I was thinking about Dad."

Oh.

"I'm sorry," I say. It sounds so lame. Of course Brent was thinking about Uncle Nick—he owns the house, after all—though I don't know how he makes the payments. And even though he hasn't cleaned out any of Nick's stuff, I'm sure it comes to mind. Probably every day. When do you move on—and how? Is it getting rid of their stuff that does it? Or do you have to be ready before you get rid of someone's stuff? How soon is too soon? And how long is too long?

We're wrestling with that, too.

Mom and Grandma fight about it all the time. Then either Grandma leaves, crying, or Mom goes on some imaginary errand to get out of the house and away from Grandma. Grandma is always right there whenever Mom turns around. *Helping,* she says. But always on top of Mom, or in the middle of stuff that's private family stuff.

I caught her in Astrid's room yesterday, tidying up.

Putting Astrid's books back on the shelf, all in the wrong order. Astrid doesn't alphabetize them. She files them by subject. Frog books on the top shelf. Turtle books on the middle shelf, on the left. Bat books on the middle shelf, on the right. Bug books on the bottom shelf, on the left, stacked up. Beside the bug books, her old *Lily's Pad* toys.

It's not helping if I have to go behind Grandma and fix it.

That's what Mom says, too. *It's not helping, Mom, if I have to follow behind you and fix it. It's not helping if you're making more work for me.*

Grandma puts her hands on her hips. *How can I be making more work for you? I'm doing the laundry. Washing the dishes. Dusting.*

You're not doing it the way I do. Please just leave it, Mom.

Brent and I reach the footbridge and stop.

He glances at his back door and fishes the key from his pocket. "I should probably take care of a few things."

"Yeah, me too," I say. "Astrid wants to hang for a while before I go out this evening."

He looks like he wants to throw up even more now.

"What the fuck is your problem?" he says, grabbing my arm. His face is fixed in a sneering grimace, like he can't decide if he's pissed or on the verge of crying.

I yank my arm from his grip easily.

"What the fuck is *my* problem? What the fuck is *yours*?"

"Can't you—don't you—"

He gives in to both the anger and the crying. "When are you going to stop? When are you going to stop playing this game or whatever it is?"

"What game?"

He's crying so hard he can barely talk. "…Astrid…" he manages.

What?

We stand there for a moment, me not knowing what he's talking about and him just crying until his face is all blotchy.

"What about Astrid?" I finally ask.

"Just… *fuck you*," he says, choking on his spit and tears. He turns back toward his house, stumbling a bit as he goes.

Maybe I was wrong. Maybe he hasn't held it together better than Dad. Maybe I should tell them that Brent needs help.

Inside, Mom and Grandma are in the living room, arguing again; I forget all about Brent.

"I put them back again. Somebody needs to…" Grandma says, cutting her words off as I enter.

She's sitting in my spot on the couch, holding a cup of tea in both hands. Mom's got the ironing board out in the middle of the room, where Astrid usually sits to watch TV, and she's ironing one of Dad's dress shirts. The old gashes on her left forearm are still hidden by the sleeve of her cardigan—I don't know why, but like the scabs on Oakley's brother's face, Mom's gashes haven't really healed. Sometimes, if I brush against that arm the wrong way, she winces like they're still fresh wounds.

Draped across the arm of the leather easy chair is a dress I recognize as one of Mom's serious-occasion dresses—black with a white collar and French cuffs—plus the dark blue dress she sometimes lets me wear when we go into Boston for a play. Hanging on the door of the coat closet is Grandma's maroon dress suit and a light pink blouse with a froufy bow at the collar.

Who died? I want to ask—but that's crass. I settle for, "What's going on?"

There's more silence.

I glance at Grandma. She's giving Mom a pointed look with wide-open eyes and raised eyebrows. I turn and face Mom, who's giving Grandma the don't-push-it scowl. Done with the sleeves, she arranges Dad's shirt on the board and presses out the shoulder area.

"Okaaaay," I say.

"Your grandmother and I are having a difference of opinion," says Mom. There's a bite to her voice that I'm sure is directed at Grandma.

Grandmas mutters something and sets her tea down on the side table.

Maybe it's best to ignore the whole thing, but it's not like I'm a little kid anymore. It's not like they need to protect me from anything. I move the pile of un-ironed clothes to the couch, beside Grandma, and slump into Dad's chair. Sitting beside Grandma would seem like taking her side against Mom, and I'm not taking sides until I know what's going on.

"Aaaand?" I prod, glancing back and forth between them, trying to read their faces.

They answer by glaring at each other.

Sometimes if I get them talking about something else, the real issue leaks out, so I gesture toward the ironing board.

"What's the occasion?"

Mom gets this weird look on her face—a series of looks, really, all melting into each other. Her eyebrows go up, then furrow lines form across her forehead. Her mouth is a thin line, then turns down, then up into a laugh-cry sort of smile. "I—We—Ha! Have… Have you… seen…? I was writing… working on…"

She looks over at Grandma and her chin quivers.

Grandma doesn't say anything. Worse, she doesn't move to hug Mom.

So I edge around the ironing board, gently take the iron from Mom's hand, and wrap my arms around her. We're almost the same height, I realize, as I hold her.

"Seriously, Mom… is everything okay?"

"No," Mom manages, then the tears begin. "No, Kirsten, everything is not okay. But I can't… I can't talk to you about it. Not right now, at least. Maybe in a little while."

I hold my mother and let her cry. Grandma gets up, takes her mug into the kitchen, and doesn't come back.

Ever since Grandma moved up here, she and Mom have done nothing but fight. I wish she hadn't sold the condo. I wish she could move back to New York and leave us in peace.

"What are you and Grandma fighting about?" I ask, quietly.

Mom's tears ease up, and she pulls away, sniffling. She takes my hands in hers. "Oh, Kirsten… sometimes mothers and daughters don't see eye-to-eye about things. That's all."

Don't I know it? I'd give her an eye-roll, but she'll get on me for acting like a teenager.

How many times in the past eleven years have we fought about the super-lax way she's homeschooling Astrid? Or the way she lets Astrid stay holed up in the house? More than I can count.

And after every fight, I get this feeling like I should crawl back to her and apologize—though I'm not sure why. Also after every fight, I find Astrid curled up in bed, blankets pulled over her head, whimpering. Or crouched in a corner, head tucked beneath her arms—or in her closet, hidden behind the clothes. Always crying, even now, at sixteen.

Wait—seventeen.

And when I try to console her, try to coax her out, Astrid says, *It's not supposed to be like this.*

I know, I say, *Fighting sucks. But that doesn't mean we don't love you. That's why we're fighting, I guess. Because we all love you. We just don't agree on what's best for you.*

That's not what I mean, she says. *I mean, you have to stop coming into my room. You can't sleep in here anymore.*

I don't understand why. I mean, I'd sleep in my own bed if Astrid would do the same, but I keep finding her sprawled in mine. What other choice do I have, besides the floor?

I give Mom's hands a squeeze, then turn toward the kitchen. Suddenly, I want to surround myself with something that makes sense. Something easy.

"Where are you going?" asks Mom, following me.

In the kitchen, Grandma sits in my spot in the booth, holding her probably-cold tea with both hands and crying.

"The basement," I answer.

"What's in the basement?"

I shrug, but pause. "Dunno. Stuff. I thought I'd look through the baby boxes. You know, just... relive stuff."

I'm waiting near the top of the stairs, expecting her to say something about how you can't move backward in time or recapture the past. Instead, after a beat, she sits across from Grandma and says, "Just put things back when you're done."

I nod and thud down the stairs into the darkness, snicking the light on with a yank of the chain.

Astrid is sitting cross-legged in the dark, at the foot of the shelves. She's staring up at the boxes I was going to look through.

"Frog Breath?"

She jerks her head up and scowls at me. "Stop it."

"Sorry." I sit beside her. "I keep forgetting you're growing up. But it's just a nickname."

She snorts and drags a finger through the dust on the smooth concrete floor, but it doesn't leave a clean streak behind. Weird.

"It's not the nickname. It's…"

"What? Growing up?"

"Yeah. I mean… I guess it's everything. Everything is messed up."

"What, specifically?"

She doesn't answer.

After a few minutes of silence, I give in and let her own her sulkiness. I stand and drag a plastic storage box from an upper shelf, setting it on the floor where we can sit on either side of it and explore.

I peel up the lid, revealing a yellow cotton blanket folded across the top. Astrid shifts onto her knees, leans over, and peers inside.

"That one's all baby blankets. Most of the rest of them are outgrown clothing and stained bibs and stuff."

I let my shoulders slump. "Well, that's depressing. Why'd she save that junk? Why doesn't she put your old toys down here?"

Astrid shrugs. "Maybe she's not ready to put them away yet. There hasn't been enough time."

"Time? What is she waiting for—Senior Prom?"

Astrid gives me a weird look—like I'm mocking her or something—and lowers her eyes. "Stop it. You know I'm never going to a prom."

"I only mean there should be at least a box of wooden blocks, and some picture books, and maybe Tinker Toys or Lincoln Logs or something. You know, stuff we can pull out when we come visit with our own kids someday."

"I'm not going to have any kids."

"Well, whatever. She can pull it out and embarrass you in front of your Significant Other."

"I'm not going to have a Significant Other."

"Astrid, I get it. You're your own person. But you don't have to be so goddamn hostile about everything. There's nothing wrong with falling in love. Nothing wrong with having kids —or not," I add, raising my hands in surrender as she starts to object again. "But you never do anything. You won't even take any on-campus classes. The campus isn't big—it's right downtown in Lowell. I could drop you off and pick you up. You need to get out, meet people, join a club or a team, go out for pizza or coffee after class. Normal stuff. You can't spend your life holed up in this house—or worse, in your room."

"How do you know what I do? You're always out running. Maybe you should take care of your own issues before you go telling me how to fix mine. You have no idea what's going on with me."

"Then tell me, Frog Breath."

She scrambles to her feet. "I said, *Stop it.* You can't call me that anymore. You have to let that shit go."

Thumping up the stairs, she leaves me sitting on the cold floor, staring at the box of baby blankets. I pull the box toward me and flip through it, anyway. Beneath the yellow one is a pair of green-and-yellow crocheted ones made by Grandma Madsen. I set all three on the lid to keep them from getting dusty on the floor. Next are a few flannel ones decorated with frogs, rabbits, and bluebirds. There's a small version of one of those fleece tie-edge blankets—pink on one side and blue on the other. I made it before we knew Astrid would be a girl. At the bottom are three hospital-issue infant blankets—the kind with the red and blue stripes running down the center. Loose at the bottom are two green hospital binkies and Astrid's hospital ID bracelet.

Replacing everything in order and checking for dust or bits of dirt, I seal the bin back up and cram it into place on the shelf. Should I go through the rest? Why aren't any of them labeled? Well—some of them are. The bin with my old dolls is labeled. And the one with all my elementary school projects. I guess it's like what people say about kids and pictures: tons of picture of your first kid, a few of your second, and then nothing. Mom kept all my childhood stuff, and none of Astrid's. It's even worse—Astrid's old toys are still in her bedroom. It's like Mom can't even bring herself to gather them up.

And Astrid's probably right about what's in the unlabeled boxes. If I go through them and she finds out, she'll accuse me of not believing her. Of thinking she doesn't know what she's talking about.

But she doesn't, sometimes. She's only fifteen. Sixteen. No—seventeen—and there's a lot more to come before she's grown.

She's still just a kid, I think, climbing the stairs.

But what if I'm wrong? What if she *does* know what she's doing? What if I should let go of trying to fix her issues? Maybe *I'm* the one who doesn't know anything.

As I round the corner and step into the kitchen, Mom, still in the booth with Grandma, says, "I've said it already, just stay out of it. It's none of your business. You're not helping."

Grandma scowls. "I'm just looking out for you. Can't I look out for my daughter?"

"Not when it gets in the way of me looking out for mine."

Then Grandma catches sight of me and gets this *oh you poor child* look on her face.

"Why are you looking at me like I'm broken?" I ask.

She doesn't respond, except to open her mouth, glance at Mom, then close it again.

I shake my head. "Okay, then. I'm hitting the shower. Plans with Oakley and Josie tonight."

Last year, you gave me the ghillie charm. Remember?

Uh-huh. Me and Mom got it at the dance studio.

Remember where you hid it?

That's not where your new charm is.

Come on, Frog Breath. Just a hint?

I can't.
Kyurp?
Remember the time Lexie came to Irish Step with me,
and Hunter was late?

Friendship Day, right?
I tied his ghillies for him.

And his mom wearing those giant sunglasses
that made her look like she had
bug-eyes?
And she didn't take them off even inside?

I remember, Astrid.
I also remember the way your arms
flopped all over the place
at the beginning of the year.

I was less floppy by recital time.
Hunter stopped coming after Friendship Day.
I asked him why in school and he said
it was stupid and boring and girly. But
I know he liked it, because he always
smiled and joked around and was nice
there.

Is that different from the way he was other times?

Yeah.
Other times he was always quiet.
Except in Irish Step and in art.

You know,
I made you a thing in art.

I know.

I wish you got to see it.

Me, too.

I sink to the floor of the tub. *Me, too. Me, too.*

I'm crying, the water streaming over me, mixing with my tears and running hothothot down my face.

Me, too. Me, too.

A knock at the door. "Kirsten?" Mom.

Me, too. Me, too.

The knob rattles. "Kirsten? Sweetie? Are you okay?" Pause. "Mom, get the lock-pick-thing. It's on my dresser. In the shell."

Rattle.

Clatter.

Click.

The light and air cool as the door swings open. "Kirsten, sweetie?"

I can't answer except to keep crying. *Me, too.*

The curtain slides open and Mom is here, on the edge of the tub like when I was little and she's leaning into the shower gettingsoakedgettingsoaked and she pulls me close and holds my head to her chest. The water streams over us both and I just keep crying *me, too* until I can't tell if maybe she's crying too.

"Honey, sweetie, Kirsten. I know. I know." She strokes my hair and I cry harderharderharder, not even making words anymore. "Oh, honey. I'd go through it for you if I could. I'd go through it a million times…"

"What's going on?" Dad. In the hallway.

"Maren's got her." Grandma. The door clicks closed, the air warming again. "Maren? I brought fresh towels." She waitswaitswaits on the other side of the curtain.

Mom brushes my bangs off my face and Idontfixthem. The water drags them back down.

"Sweetie? Can you take a deep breath in, then out? Can you do that for me, nice and slow?"

My breath is ragged, hitching. But I inhale, then let it out to Mom's ten-count. We do that a few more times, until my tears are gone and all there is is the water, getting cooler.

"Honey? Can we turn the water off? Can you get out and dry off?"

Still curled into her arms, I nod.

She leans over and swivels the shower control off. Drapes a towel over me before either of us even stands. Wraps another around me and helps me out of the tub. Together, Mom and Grandma dry me and bundle me up in softsoft towels and blot the water from my hair.

"I'm sorry," I mumble. "I don't know why I was crying. I just couldn't stop…"

"It's okay," murmurs Grandma, rubbing my hands with her own. "We're here."

"Can you…" Mom's voice falters. "Can you name three things in here that are pink?"

It's that exercise Jamaica taught us all those years ago. "Um… the wall."

"And?"

I look around. The wall was easy. "The flamingoes on the shower curtain. And the toothbrush holder."

"That was good, sweetie." She combs out my hair for me. "You're going to be okay. Are you sure you want to go, tonight?"

"Go where?"

"Out with Oakley and Josie. To the concert. You don't have to, if you don't want to. They'll understand."

Grandma opens my bathrobe and slips it over my shoulders. I worm my arms through and tie it closed, letting the towels drop to the floor.

"Yeah," I say, automatically. Then I remember—it's Emily Snow. We've been planning this for ages. "Yeah," I say again. "I want to go."

Mom stoops over, retrieves the towels and holds them in a bundle. Grandma opens the door. "Why don't you put something comfy on and we'll bring you some tea?"

"No, thanks. I've got to get ready." Grandma follows me to my bedroom, where I sit on the edge of the bed and try to remember, again, what I'm getting ready for. She kisses me on the cheek, then leaves, the door shutting with a soft click behind her.

14

FRIDAY, LATE AFTERNOON

Beside me, Astrid is flopped across the bed. "Do you have to go? Just stay home with me. I'll let you take me someplace…"

Weaving my hair into a pair of low, loose, damp braids, I laugh. "'Stay home and I'll let you take me someplace'? That doesn't make sense, Frog Breath."

She ignores my use of her old nickname, and sits up. "Just… stay. Don't leave me. I hate it when you go out."

I shake my head, and dress for the show in shorts, sandals, and the Emily Snow tee Josie gave me for my birthday senior year. I'm not sure how, but it's still in like-new shape. Tonight was Oakley's idea, I think. I keep expecting Mom and Dad to say they need me here this evening, but they seem eager for me to go out. It'll be just like high school, when Oakley used to come along as our disguise… especially since it's another Emily Snow concert. I don't remember the one we went to at the end of senior year, but I know we went. "I haven't hung with Oakley in forever, and you know Josie and I are together. Or, as together as we can be, living separately."

Astrid sighs. "It's just that… when you're not here, nobody pays attention to me." She stares out the window above the bed. Outside, the sky is grey and heavy, full of a building storm. "It's like…"

"Like what?"

She doesn't finish the thought. Instead, she asks, "How come my willow never grew? It looks like it's frozen in time, the same size as when we planted it."

"I'm doing everything I can for it. I fed it again this morning. It's just…" I shake my head and shrug.

With a sigh, she curls back up on the bed, holding Mr. Ribbit tighttighttight like she did when she was four.

"It's just one night out with my friends, Frog Breath. I promise."

She nods.

I sling my purse over my shoulder and head down the hall, passing Mom and Grandma tidying up the bathroom. It's a mess in there, and looks like Astrid used every towel we own for something.

In the living room, Dad's in his easy chair, wearing that pained smile I just can't get used to, even after ten years. Twelve.

"…something normal…" he's saying.

Oakley, perched on the sofa, is nodding at Dad but still holding her car keys. Seeing me, she stands and bounces on the balls of her feet. "Hey, K. I told Josie we'd pick her up early and find someplace to eat in Foxboro. I'm not eating stadium nachos for dinner."

I fiddle with my charm bracelet, hoping it will call subtle attention to Astrid, but Dad doesn't seem to notice. Instead, he stands and pulls me close, holding me tighttighttight like I'm going to break if he lets go. But he does let go. "Have a good time, Kirsten."

I take a few steps toward the door. "Let's go, then. Before rush hour kicks in."

Ten minutes later, Oakley pulls up to the curb outside Josie's house and beeps out a double-toot. When two minutes pass and the door hasn't opened, she honks again.

Another minute passes. "Let me run up," I say. When I reach the front door, I don't want to ring the bell—don't want to get in the middle of the shouting match inside—but it's not like Josie's not expecting us. We've had these plans for months.

So I ring the bell, then try the door. It's unlocked.

I ease it open and peek in. Josie's in the living room, sobbing and shouting at her mother, who is also sobbing. They're tugging back and forth on one of those nice, fake-leather notebooks.

"You bought it with my money, so it's mine."

Josie struggles to strengthen her grip. "Give it back—you had no right to read my private thoughts!"

"There's no lock. And I'm glad I read it. Now I have proof of the bad choices you're making. I won't allow that in my house."

"It's not a choice. You think I would choose something that would make you hate me?"

Josie's mom gives one last, ferocious tug on the notebook and wins it. Josie loses her balance and steps backward, tripping over her lacrosse duffel and backpack.

I scramble over and help her up.

"And you," says Josie's mom, seeing me and pointing. "You're the one who put these ideas into her head. You made her confused." She glares at me. "It's not natural, what you made her do. You tricked her into doing wrong."

"Kirsten didn't make me do anything! I was gay before I ever met her. And why is it okay for Uncle Stu but not me?" Josie grabs her duffel and a small suitcase I didn't see earlier. I pick up the backpack. We make for the still-open door.

"I never said it was okay for Uncle Stu." Her mom notices the suitcase and turns back to Josie. "You can't leave. Where will you go? You can't leave!"

Like she has a say in who her twenty-eight-year-old daughter hangs out with. Twenty-nine? Thirty?

In the doorway, Josie turns and faces her mom. "And newsflash, Mom—Kirsten's not my friend. She's my *girlfriend.*"

Whoa. What?

Before I can react, Josie slams the door behind us and we half-run to the car. Oakley's already climbing out of the front seat and holding the trunk open.

"What happened? Is that your stuff? Josie?"

We cram everything into the trunk, already half-filled with Oakley's workout bag, several towels, and the giant subwoofer her dad installed.

As we pull away from Josie's house, she bursts into fresh, cracking sobs. "That was just the end. We've been fighting all week. She read my journal yesterday. Fucking went through my room and my computer and all my social media... and figured it all out."

"She kicked you out?" asks Oakley, glancing in the rearview mirror.

"Essentially," mumbles Josie.

I start crying, too. I reach back for her hand and splutter out a lame-ass, "I'm sorry."

I keep saying it, over and over—*I'm sorry, I'm sorry*—like I don't know what else to say.

I guess I don't.

I mean, I've read stories online about people who came out to their families and got kicked out, or sent to one of those torture-conversion camps, but... like the shooting, I never imagined it happening to someone I know.

Someone I love.

My parents would probably let her stay with us, but Brent is still in the den and I don't think they're ready to let me share my room with my girlfriend—at least, not with Astrid still being in high school.

Oakley puts a hand on my arm. "Kirsten..."

I'm still saying it.

I stop.

We round the corner and head across the bridge toward Route 3. Oakley angles her head a little toward the back seat. "You can stay at my place tonight."

"Are you sure?"

Oakley nods. "My parents will be cool with it. I'll text when we stop for dinner and let them know you're coming. My room in the attic gets kinda warm in summer, but I've got a window AC and there's plenty of space for an air mattress."

Josie runs a hand through her hair, which she still wears short, and her crying slows. "Thanks, Oakley. I'll call my

Uncle Stu tomorrow. Maybe I can move in with him and Keith long-term."

"What'd your Dad say?" I finally think to ask.

Josie shakes her head. "Dad's out of town. He'll probably be sort of okay with it. At least, he wouldn't kick me out, or refuse to help me pay for college."

Is she going back to school? I need to remember to ask her about that later.

There's a silence that lasts for two exits. Finally, Josie says, "I didn't even have time to grab the shirt I wanted to wear tonight."

I turn and look at what she's wearing: long cut-offs and her red Winslow townie tee.

"It'll be okay. You can change into whatever shirt you buy."

"That's it. No more sulking. Let's get ready for an awesome night!" shouts Oakley, punching AUDIO on the car's touch-screen and pulling up a playlist. One of her favorite Emily Snow songs blasts on: "Psychedelic Sunset." She pulls into the left lane and speeds up, singing along. Some songs just need to be played super-loud, while you're driving super-fast. Oakley calls them Highway Songs, and this playlist is full of them. This one is trippy, from Emily's I-Wish-I-Was-Born-A-Hippie phase. Josie and I jump right in and soon, we're all singing at the top of our lungs.

...so high I'll become one with the clouds,
so high I'll never need to come down...

It usually only takes about ninety minutes to get down to Foxboro, but it's a good thing we left early because before we even reach Route 2, traffic slows to a near-crawl. Oakley merges into the middle lane, which is moving a little faster—

for now. After almost three miles, police lights become visible in the breakdown lane. I tense up a little. Two Mass State Police SUVs—one on each side of the divide—face each other with about ten feet between them.

Perched on the Jersey barrier—aimed toward our side of the highway—is a turkey.

Oakley and I bust out laughing.

"What?" Josie shouts over the blaring music. Oakley turns it down a little and Josie pokes her head between the front seats. "Holy shit!"

There are four troopers standing on this side of the barrier, beside the far vehicle, staring at the turkey.

Even from our spot, and even though we're still maybe ten car-lengths away, I can tell it's huge, probably close to thirty pounds. Some asshole up ahead in the left lane honks and the turkey startles, spreading its wings and hopping off the barrier. The troopers fan out, one of them shouting at the idiot who honked, motioning the driver over.

"Ha!" says Oakley. "Serves him right."

That trooper heads over to the honking driver while the other three try to steer the turkey back onto the barrier—or at least keep it out of traffic.

It darts toward the road, then veers off to its right.

It stops again, turning toward the cars.

We're still a few car-lengths away, but it's even bigger than I thought—close to four feet tall with its tail feathers fanned out.

"Come on, Pot Pie," says Oakley. "Back up on the barrier. Be a good turkey."

Josie cracks up. I hit Oakley on the shoulder. "You can't name a turkey Pot Pie!"

"Why not?" she asks.

"What about Butterball?" asks Josie, still laughing. "Is that better, Kirsten?"

"No! Give it a bird name, like—I don't know, like..."

But it's hopeless. I can't think of anything off the cuff and the two of them are shouting horrible names over the music, their laughter growing wilder with each suggestion.

"Drumstick," from Josie.

"Wishbone," offers Oakley.

"Stuffing."

"You people are sick," I say, watching as the turkey spreads its wings and hop-flies along the breakdown lane, the troopers trying to stay between it and the traffic—without backing into the left lane, themselves.

"Green Bean Casserole," replies Oakley, slapping her thigh with her hand. She's laughing so hard, I'm not sure how she's still in control of the car.

"I think nothing beats Pot Pie," says Josie. I turn and give her the stink-eye. She grins at me, then leans forward and gives me a quick kiss and a shy smile. "What the hell, right? I'm already kicked out."

Just as we pull past the scene, the turkey hops back onto the jersey barrier and settles into a fluffy lump.

The three of us erupt into cheers. "Yay," says Josie. "Way to go, Pot Pie! You get to live another year!"

Oakley snorts. "Thanksgiving's in five months."

Instead of stopping for food on the way, we head straight to Foxboro in case there's another slowdown. Josie pulls out her phone and finds a bunch of restaurants in the complex around the stadium. We settle on a local pizza place, Antonio's, that has decent reviews.

There's a TV on in the corner playing *Extreme Close-Up*, a game show where contestants have to guess what a commonplace object is from an extremely magnified image. The further out the camera pans, the less money the contestants win for guessing right. At least the volume is pretty low— though the girl behind the counter doesn't seem to realize we can hear her as she offers her own guesses. *Mildew. Oil. Moss —no wait, that's fuzzy...*

The real contestant guesses *toad*, and she's right.

We order a large pie with pepperoni, bacon, and extra cheese, plus a round of large sodas with free refills, and the counter-girl stares at Josie's townie shirt. She opens her mouth, then closes it without saying anything, and bites her lip instead. Josie ducks into the bathroom, returning with her shirt turned inside-out.

We fill our to-go cups and grab a booth, Josie and I sliding into the same side. Josie's thigh is warm against mine, igniting the tingle I usually get from holding her hand. I feel careless and carefree, like we're back in high school.

Across from us, Oakley stretches her legs out into the wide aisle. She texts back and forth with her mom for a few minutes, then pockets her phone. "Mom said she'll have the inflate-a-bed ready for you by the time we get home. And she said there's no rush; you can stay as long as you like. I can take you to get your car and more of your stuff tomorrow. We can ask my dad to come, if you want."

Josie sighs and leans back in the booth. She nods.

The girl from behind the counter strides out and slides our pizza and a bunch of paper plates onto the table, then returns to her post, where she leans on the counter and resumes shouting her guesses at the TV as if the game show host can hear her. *An eraser. Craft felt.*

Oakley doses her slices with tons of red pepper and parmesan. I stick with the parmesan only. Josie picks off all the bacon before eating, and Oakley plucks Josie's bacon rejects from her plate and adds them to her slice.

On the TV, they're showing a running track—obviously—and as the show goes to commercial, a special news bulletin graphic appears on-screen. The reporter is still fussing with her mic and clothing as the camera cuts to her.

We've just been informed that Kevin Adams, the man responsible for the Winslow Elementary shooting...

"Hey," shouts a man in another booth. "Turn it up!"

The girl behind the counter aims the remote and raises the volume.

...being transported to the Middlesex Jail in Billerica, where he will remain as he awaits trial. According to a source inside the jail, Adams will be placed in protective custody.

Here at Boston News Center Four, we will keep you informed as details become available. And our hearts go out, of course, to the families affected by the Winslow Elementary shooting. Such a tragedy, in our own backyard.

"He doesn't deserve protective custody," says the man. "Put him in with the rest of them and let him get shanked. Would be good riddance."

The girl behind the counter mutes the TV and ducks into the kitchen.

I'm not sure what fresh charges they've brought against Adams—maybe he shot someone else and they just found out about it?—or why he's moving to the county jail from whatever actual prison he's been in. But the man in the other booth keeps going on, louder and louder, about how people in Winslow ought to have never let Adams live long enough to end up in custody. How if he'd been there, he'd have taken him out himself. How it serves Adams right that his own kid died in the shooting.

Oakley and I knew Hunter. We were on his mom's babysitter list, and he was in Astrid's dance class for Irish Step for a while.

Hunter was a cute kid. A little shy, a little skittish, but he never gave me any trouble when I sat for him. All he ever wanted to do was draw or play with his finger paints. Mrs. Adams practically papered the kitchen cabinets with his art.

What happened to her, after the shooting? I don't know if she's still in Winslow. How do you move past being married to a mass shooter? Even if you had filed a restraining order and moved out before it happened? I remember the bruises she tried to hide with those giant sunglasses Astrid called bug-eye glasses.

It's always the same story, isn't it? I don't think it will ever matter to the people who can change the story, though.

Conversation at the other booths picks back up, though a few people keep glancing at the ranting man. Josie covers some of her inside-out shirt with her free hand. In the booth behind us, a little boy asks his mom why the man is yelling, and his mom shushes him.

Between us, there's nothing to say. We shrink into the booth, as if we could become invisible. Oakley's hand shakes as she reaches for another slice. She pulls her hand back without taking it. The three of us sit there, staring at our cups, our plates, the half-eaten pizza between us—anything but each other.

Playing with my bracelet, I think back to the day after the shooting: the way the three of us went running and were all there for each other. The way we stretched out on the field and held hands and touched each other. *Reached* each other. We're still hanging on, but it feels tenuous these days. Like we're all losing our hold. Even my bracelet is all wrong. I never take it off, but Astrid and I just stopped adding charms. She doesn't even remember where she hid the one from her sixth birthday.

The manager comes out and asks the guy to cut it out or get out. The ranter gets up, makes a big thing about refilling his to-go cup, then leaves.

We keep sitting here, staring at the pizza but not eating it.

The counter girl comes out, wipes down his table, and stops by our booth on the way back to the register. "Want this boxed up?"

Oakley shakes her head *No*.

The girl shifts from one foot to the other. "Was it okay? I can have them make you a new one if something's messed up."

"It was fine," says Josie. "We're just not as hungry as we thought."

"It's no trouble," says the girl. "I'm sorry about that guy from before. I... I have a cousin who's in fifth grade at Winslow Elementary. She's okay. A classmate pushed her into the bathroom. But... I mean... I'm really sorry."

Oakley stares at her. "What?"

"My cousin," says the counter-girl. "A boy in her class pushed her into the bathroom when the shooting started. So my cousin's okay. I think the boy got hurt, though."

"That was my brother," says Oakley, her voice flat. "My brother pushed a bunch of kids into the bathroom."

"Holy shit. Is he okay?" The girl tucks her rag into the back of her apron and leans toward Oakley, like she wants to grab her hands or something.

Oakley tilts her head. "Yeah… mostly. Kinda. He lost an eye to shrapnel."

"Can you tell him thank you from Lauren's cousin? She said he was so brave. He jumped up and went right for the door, holding it open for as many kids as he could."

Oakley glances at me, then back at the counter-girl, nodding. "Lauren. Yeah, I'll tell him." She slides out of the booth, making the counter-girl step back a bit. Josie and I follow, clearing the leftovers.

"Listen, we gotta go. But I'll tell him."

Counter-girl murmurs her understanding. We dump our trash and head for the door. "I'm sorry again about that guy," she says.

I keep trying to remember how this show compares to the one from our senior year, not long after the shooting, but it's like my mind has erased it. I don't even remember Emily Snow coming out with anything new since our senior year. Anyway, security is extra-tight tonight. Once we're inside the stadium, though, the event staff hand out these battery-operated glow stick bracelets that light up in different colors during parts of the show. It's better than our phone flashlights. We all pull on our concert tees, squirm out of our other shirts and tie them around our purse-straps. Finding our seats, we take in the crowd around us and the clash of pot smoke and sickening-sweet fruity vape scents hanging in the air.

After Emily's first two numbers, the screens behind her go black and all the stage lights cut off.

From the dark stage, she says, "Every day, families all over the United States are forever changed by gun violence."

One by one, dots of white light speckle the screens behind her.

"Each light represents a life lost to gun violence so far this year. I am donating the proceeds from tonight's performance to the Coalition to Stop Gun Violence."

Dots of light continue to appear on the screens, faster and faster, until the once-dark screens are blinding white. Oakley and Josie, on either side of me, each wrap an arm around me. I put my arms around them, too, and pull them in close.

Emily must be doing this since it's so close to the anniversary of the Winslow Elementary shooting. How many other people in the audience are from Winslow, or some other town where there's been a shooting? I just want to put the whole thing in the past, where it belongs, and move on—the attention at the pizza place was enough. I wish I could erase the whole damn nightmare from my mind.

"We may not all agree on the right way to address gun violence, but we must continue to work toward a solution. Everyone has a right to feel safe at school, at work, at home, and even in a crowd."

With the screens still blazing white-hot behind her, Emily accepts her acoustic guitar from a roadie and begins plucking out the opening chords to "Turn on a Dime," the song she wrote when her older brother died in that Pride festival shooting the summer after my freshman year of high school.

> *Yesterday morning when I said goodbye*
> *I never thought it would be the last time…*

It's just Emily and her guitar as she sings, the screens behind her displaying images of her and her brother growing up.

I'd forgotten how close gun violence is to her own life.

After she finishes, the lights come back up and she launches into a long string of fast songs that keep us dancing and forgetting that anything bad could ever happen.

For one song, Emily and her dancers are on this catwalk that reaches practically to the 50 yard line, and they pull a few people from the front row onto the stage. Josie, Oakley and I keep jumping, dancing, and screaming, our glow bracelets flashing in time to the beat. Nothing else matters except that moment we're sharing with over sixty thousand other people.

There's this one slow song Emily plays, after the sun's gone completely down, where the stage goes almost totally dark. In the audience, we're all swaying, waving our hands back and forth above our heads.

> *…I love everything about you,*
> *need everything about you —*
> *everything, everything, everything about you…*

Looking out into the rest of the stadium, the white glow bracelet lights twinkle in the velvety blackness. We're our own little universe. I wish I could stay here in it and never face reality again.

When she finally plays "Never, Never" though… that's when Josie and I reach for each other's hands. It's an old song—it came out our freshman year—but before I know it, Josie and I are holding each other and swaying back and forth in our little square of space as Emily sings like she's serenading just the two of us.

> *…asleep*
> *till a kiss from her love*
> *makes her heart complete.*
> *She will never, never, never wake up…*

I've wanted this for ages—the chance to be a couple in public, free of any looming fear of someone else's displeasure. And here we are, but it took Josie being thrown out with nothing more than what she could carry to make it happen. Do I laugh? Or do I cry?

I turn to Josie, and she meets my gaze. She pulls me toward her and gives me a long, soft kiss that makes me tingle so much I could levitate.

Emily ends the show with "Overdrive" and fireworks. Between the smoky air, the strobe of red-blue-yellow-green explosions booming in the skies above us, and the thundering of the crowd—I'm suddenly dizzy, the stadium tilting around me like we're on a shake table and I've got one foot each on platforms moving in opposite directions. I can't keep my balance. I have to sit.

Josie and Oakley don't notice, and I don't want to make them stop dancing, so I just sit there, trying to get control of myself.

But it's worse sitting down, with the crowd pressing in from all sides and the fireworks booming, flaring overhead. I hug myself, hunching over in my seat, my heart pounding, my breath coming fast and shallow. I want to leave but I can't move. Can't stand up and fight my way through all these people, even if the world weren't spinning.

Finally the music stops, the fireworks fading to pale grey smoke against the night sky.

The stadium lights come up, and I crash back to reality.

For a moment—a flash so short it must be a hallucination or one of those waking dreams—I want to sink to the floor and sob until I run out of tears.

Then it's gone, and all that's left is the ringing in my ears and Josie sitting beside me, holding my hand.

"Kirsten? Are you okay? Kirsten?"

A group of middle school kids and their middle-aged chaperone squeeze past us, half-shouting to compensate for their temporary(-ish) hearing loss.

Oakley pulls out her phone. "Want me to call your Mom or someone?"

"Sorry..." I say, embarrassed. "I just... I don't know, maybe I'm dehydrated or something. Maybe I got a whiff of too much pot smoke."

Oakley offers me what's left of her water. Though it's warm, it makes me feel a little better—or maybe it's that the air no longer feels so close, now that the rows above and below us are emptying.

Josie rests a hand on my shoulder; I reach up and hold it.

After a few more minutes, the exiting crowd even thinner, I stand up. My legs are steady and the stadium stays put when I look down toward the stage, where roadies are already breaking things down.

We make our way to the bathrooms, then back to the car, Oakley and Josie giving me worried looks and asking, "You sure you're okay?" no matter how many times I insist I'm fine.

"I was just dehydrated," I say, even though we all know I'm lying.

The night air is chillier than we expected, but after the heat of the packed stadium, it's refreshing. We roll the windows partway down and Oakley inches the car forward, obeying the event staff directing traffic with signal batons.

From the back seat, Josie leans forward and touches my arm. I reach my hand back and she holds it.

Her hand is warm and soft. It's a blanket.

We're still about ten minutes from the highway when it starts raining.

By the time we pass the outlet mall, the rain is so hard Oakley has the wipers on as fast as they can go. Conversation stalls as she peers ahead through the windshield, her hands at ten and two. She slows a bit more and moves to the right lane.

As we pass the exit for the Pike, Oakley tells me to put her Highway Songs playlist on. This time, we don't sing along. The ride home just doesn't have the same energy behind it as the ride out—we're exhausted by more than Josie's technical homelessness or the news report about Kevin Adams. I stare at the rain-spattered window, unable to make out more than smears of red and white light from the cars around us.

The music crashes around inside the car and my head—fast, cheerful music that's all wrong. It feels like somehow I'd be cheating, or a traitor, if I were happy.

Why was it okay on the way out to Foxboro?

I wish these things were simple—Josie's forced de-closeting, routine reports about a mass-murderer, even how to stay connected. I think maybe, that day on the football field, I had it wrong. Maybe we weren't a peace sign.

Maybe we were a cracked mirror.

Outside, the rain has stopped; we're coming up on Route 2—only a half-hour from home. In the back seat, Josie has let go of my hand and her breathing has grown soft and steady. I glance over at Oakley—she's still clutching the wheel at ten and two, but has relaxed a little into her seat.

Suddenly she cusses and hits the brakes. Even from the passenger side, I feel the antilock kick in and we only slip a little on the rain-slicked road. Ahead of us are three lanes of brake lights, stab-wounds in the darkness.

Josie startles awake. "What?"

"Probably an accident," I say.

Oakley inches us forward for about twenty minutes before the accident scene comes up on our right and we're forced to edge partway into the middle lane.

"Gape for me," she says.

On the shoulder, surrounded by police cars and an ambulance, is a small, white car, turned perpendicular to the highway. In the windshield—stuck like a sick version of one of those joke window-clings of a baseball surrounded by shattered glass—is an enormous turkey.

"Holy shit," murmurs Josie. "Oh, my God…"

I stare at the car as we creep past. The center of the windshield is completely blocked by the bird, the top of the glass buckling inward along with part of the roof. In the flashing lights, the warped glass looks semi-liquid. One of the turkey's feet points skyward, as if the bird was running, maybe taking off, when it slammed into the car.

Wet feathers stick to the windshield.

Even after we've passed the scene, and Oakley accelerates to normal highway speeds, the chaos of emergency lights strobe through my mind.

Like the elementary school.

Josie leans forward and rubs my arm. "Kirsten? You okay?"

I can't stop seeing wet turkey feathers clinging to the windshield, or the way smeared blood turned the hood into a Rorschach test.

Lexie had blood all over her dress. Blood in her hair.

"No—" I say, my voice choked and tight. "I mean, yeah," I say. "I'm good."

"You want me to stop?" asks Oakley.

"I'm good. I'm cool," I say, shaking my head to clear it. "It was just the concert. The heat and the smoke…" I shake my head again, realizing I'm talking about the wrong thing. I change the subject. "Anyone want to run in the morning?"

Oakley pulls onto the shoulder and parks, hitting her flashers. She looks at me and smiles, but it's thin and sad. She takes my hands. Josie reaches over and brushes away a tear. Why am I crying? It was just a turkey.

"You know it's going to be okay, right?"

Is Oakley talking about my weird panic attack? Or Josie getting kicked out? I nod. "Sure. Yeah. Okay."

Josie will move in with her uncle, no questions asked. And one panic attack doesn't mean I'm falling apart. Not like

Brent or Dad. If it happens again, I'll go back to Jamaica Knox for a session or two. But it won't happen. It was just the smoke and the heat from the crowd. I just got dehydrated.

15

SATURDAY MORNING, EARLY HOURS

Brent is in the living room, playing *War of Ages: Eleventh Hour*. After way too many years, he's finally hooked his gaming console up to our TV.

I perch on the armrest of Dad's leather easy chair and watch as he finishes the round. He's playing as his favorite avatar, a Zoot-suit-wearing, feline-human hybrid with grey tabby markings on their skin.

"Hey," he says, pausing the game.

"Were you waiting up for me?" I ask. It's just like him to want to make sure I got in okay.

"Yes and no," he responds. "I didn't want to sleep, so I played a few rounds. Then it occurred to me we could maybe go hit New Moon Diner when you got home." He glances at me, gauging my interest. "You up for that?"

"Coffee and deep-fried Oreos? Definitely. Give me five minutes?"

He nods, and I bolt for my room, where I check on Astrid—as usual, she's fast asleep in my bed.

When I return, the gaming system is off and Brent is in the kitchen doorway, keys in hand.

We climb into the old Volvo Nick bought him at the beginning of our senior year and ten minutes later, we're across the Rourke Bridge and weaving through the Highlands on our way toward downtown Lowell. The humidity outside makes the air stifling to breathe, so Brent keeps the AC on.

Ahead of us, an oncoming car jerks to a stop, then rockets past us. In Brent's headlights, a small white animal struggles to the side of the road. Brent slows as we pass the animal.

"Turn around," I say. "Is it okay?"

Brent is already making a uey. He pulls over and we climb out.

I crouch beside the cat, Brent standing over me. There's not a speck of blood on its fur, but it's panting, its eyes rolling against the pain. Is it in shock? I think this might be what shock looks like. But don't they always say, never approach a wounded animal?

I stroke the top of its head anyway, and it doesn't move except to jerk its head a little and let out a high-pitched cry that's swallowed by the hot, heavy air.

"You're okay, kitty," I lie.

"It's so thin," says Brent. "Probably stray."

He's right—I can see the cat's ribs through its patchy, matted fur.

"What do we do?" I ask, still petting the cat's head. "Do we call someone? Like the police? Maybe we should take it to a vet."

"What vet? Who's open this time of night? If we move it, we might hurt it more. What if its back is broken?"

I shake my head *No*. "We're not leaving it here to die all alone. Look around for something flat we can use as a stretcher." I pull out my phone and do an internet search for emergency vets near Lowell.

Brent comes back with a thick piece of cardboard. It's damp from the humidity, but not soggy, so it must have been put outside after the rain. It's sturdy enough, at least. The cat cries again and pants more heavily as we slide the cardboard beneath it carefully.

"There's a place in Westford, just off 495," I say. "The website says to call them on the way so they know we're coming."

Together, we ease the makeshift stretcher onto the back seat, and I climb in beside it. Brent punches the address into his GPS app and pulls away from the curb as I dial.

The woman on the other end of the phone tells me to ring the bell at the front door when we arrive, and they'll send someone out to help bring the cat in.

"It's okay, kitty. We're taking you to get help," I say, after hanging up with the vet's office.

Brent keeps the ride as smooth as he can, navigating through Lowell to the Connector and 495.

The cat looks at me warily—it must realize it has no choice but to trust me. Does it think we hit it? Or can it tell that we stopped specifically to help it? Does it even know why it's hurt? "Hang in there, kitty. You're gonna be all right." I'm not sure if I'm trying to reassure the cat, or myself.

After about twenty minutes, Brent exits the highway and, after a few right turns, pulls into the strip mall and parks at the curb right in front of the vet's office. He jumps out, presses the buzzer, and a vet tech comes out to carry the stretcher inside. Brent holds the door and I follow the tech inside.

"We saw the car that hit him, but it didn't stop. Is he going to be okay? Please tell me he's going to be okay."

"Wait out here," says the tech. "We need to take a look."

Brent comes in after he's parked the car and sits beside me on the hard plastic bench beneath the Cat Waiting Area sign. The receptionist comes over, handing me a clipboard of paperwork.

"I know you said he's a stray, but I need you to fill out as much as you can," she says. I nod and look down at the form. The first line says Pet's Name.

"Brent," I say. "He doesn't even have a name. What if he dies, and he's never had a name?"

"What do you mean?"

It's hard to push the tremor from my voice. "He's a stray. He doesn't have anyone to love him or even give him a name."

Brent looks down at his hands. "I know," he says, his voice flat. "You think I don't know?"

"No. I just… I think he deserves a name. One that someone gives some thought to."

"Come back to that question," he says.

I look at the rest of the form—the pet's age, gender, and coloring; my name and address; my credit card number…

It didn't occur to me I'd be the one paying to save his life. But it's obvious—if they can save him, I'll pay the bill, even if it takes me all summer. How can I not?

I pull the credit card Mom and Dad co-signed for me years ago, for emergencies, from my wallet. After I copy down the number, I return the paperwork to the receptionist. "He doesn't have a name," I say.

She nods. "He'll be Mr. Cat for now," she says, jotting in the name, then running a finger down the page until she sees my credit card number. She nods. "Have a seat. Someone will come out once they've finished assessing his injuries."

I rejoin Brent on the bench and lean against him. "So much for coffee."

He shrugs. "We'll go after. It's not like they'll let you take him home tonight."

"Should I think up a name for him now?"

Brent shrugs again, still staring at his hands.

"What's with you?" I ask, immediately regretting my choice of words.

In response, Brent scoots away from me, forcing me to sit up straight. He takes a deep breath and looks away from me.

"Sorry," I say. "That was crappy."

"Yeah."

I stand and step in front of him. "Really. I'm sorry. Tell me what's on your mind." Maybe it'll distract me from worrying about the cat. "Brennnnt." I lean over and touch my forehead to his. "Brennnnt. Come on, little brother."

He snorts, smiling reluctantly, and glances at me. "I'm not your little brother."

"Well, you practically are," I say. "You're a cousin, at least." It's hard to focus on him when our faces are this close, so I back up. "Talk to me."

He looks at me, squinting, and tilts his head a little. Then, nodding slowly, he says, "It's been... an extraordinary suckfest, this week. Everything I thought was set about my future is up in the air again. I mean, your parents are being great, and I'm glad I've got them to help me figure it all out. I'd be lost on my own. But…"

He pauses, and after a long break, finally says, "It's not the same as it was with me and Dad."

I'm not sure exactly what he's trying to figure out—maybe he's looking to change jobs, or go back to school—but I'm determined to not fuck this up the way I did our last conversation.

Wait—was that really just this morning? Or am I remembering some argument from years ago?

"I know," I say. It's the safest response until I know the details of Brent's suckfest.

He's still looking at me in that curious-dog pose. "I need to ask you something," he says, shifting away from me slightly and squaring his shoulders.

"Shoot," I say. Then, "Oh, fuck. I'm sorry. That was… that was…"

"I get it," he says, grimacing and glancing away. "Actually, though, that's what I'm talking about—the fact that you can still say 'shoot' without thinking first."

"I didn't mean to hurt you. It's just… it's a part of our culture, you know? Like, I'll bet they don't say that in Australia or Japan or… other places."

"Whatever." Brent rolls his eyes, and the grimace settles solidly onto his face. When he looks at me again, his eyes are cold. "Where are you, Kirsten?"

I laugh and bite my lip. "What? What do you mean? I'm…" I gesture toward the receptionist's desk and the door to the exam rooms. "I'm here with you, waiting to find out if a stray cat will live or die."

"Yeah, but what's going on in your life? What are you doing? Where are you?" He grabs my hands. "What's real, to you?"

I pull away, clenching one hand in the other. "I… I don't…" I can't think straight enough to answer what should be a stupid-easy question. Why can't I think? "What do you… why…? What do you think?"

"I have no idea."

"Then I have no idea how to answer that. Why would you ask me that? Do you think I'm crazy or something?" The receptionist clears her throat and I realize I'm practically shouting. I lower my voice. "I'm not crazy."

Brent sighs, and the coldness melts from his face. "I didn't say you were." He puts a hand on my arm. "I'm worried about you. You've been… a little out-of-touch, emotionally, since… the shooting."

Emotionally out-of-touch? Have I been so focused on Astrid that I've let down my friends?

"I'm worried about you. We all are."

Before I can respond, the vet comes out.

"He's got a broken hind leg and a lot of bruising, but I don't see any evidence of internal bleeding. Still, he's in poor shape from living on the streets. He's covered in fleas and ticks, and probably has worms, too. I'd like to keep him tonight, take care of his leg, push some IV fluids, and see if we can get him in better shape overall."

"But he's going to live?"

"I think he'll be fine. Are you…"

The vet has to break off because I start crying. Brent wraps an arm around my shoulder.

"Yeah, she's planning to keep him," he says. "Can't you tell?"

The two of them chuckle a little, which makes me start laugh-crying.

On the drive home, we barely talk. As Brent pulls out of the parking lot, I say, "I'm glad he'll be okay," and Brent replies, "yeah, me too." Then we lapse into the kind of silence that shoves you into thinking, *Is it weird that it's so quiet? Should I say something? I can't think of anything to say. Am I failing at holding up my end of the conversation? Or is this supposed to be a comfortable silence, and I'm the only one who's uncomfortable?*

What I don't want to do is talk—or think—about what Brent said about everyone being worried about me.

He's overreacting.

I'm fine.

We're at the light in the center of Chelmsford, Brent's left turn signal *ticka-ticka-ticking* as we stare up at the traffic signal, waiting for the green arrow.

When the light finally changes, Brent starts through the intersection, but a car roars up behind us. Music booming, it swerves around us, tires screeching as it takes the left turn way too fast before hurtling up the road past the fire station.

"Asshole," mutters Brent, finishing the turn and pulling over as a police cruiser, siren wailing, sails past us.

"I need to think of a name for the cat," I say. I should say something about the car—agree with Brent, or make a joke—but it took me ten minutes to think of naming the cat.

"Yeah," says Brent.

More silence.

Several miles up the road—past the rotary but before Zesty's—we see the rocket-car again. The cruiser caught up to it, and they're pulled over near the mill—the only spot with a decent enough shoulder. My heart quickens at the sight of the cruiser's lights until I recognize the rocket-car and start laughing. I roll the window down to get a look and there it is—the Good Sam sticker.

"That's the car Oakley and I keep seeing," I say. I turn to explain the whole thing to Brent, but he's cutting through Lowell to get to the bridge closest to our neighborhood.

"What car?"

"Never mind. You had to be there."

But I have to remember to tell Oakley that the rusted-out Buick actually has some zip in it, even after all these years.

When we get home, the master bedroom door is closed, and the low voices and clipped tones mean Mom and Dad are having another argument. Brent shuts himself in the den.

In my room, I find Astrid curled up beneath the covers, her knees bent so she kind-of looks like a question mark. Mr. Ribbit's foot is in her mouth, like she's still a little kid. It's late, but I turn on my desk lamp and give her shoulder a light shake. I want my own bed tonight.

"I made a thing for you," she mumbles, around Mr. Ribbit's foot.

"I got distracted," I say. It's the truth. And it leaves so much out.

"Do the fairy dance for me," she says, snuggling deeper into my blankets.

I give her shoulder another shake, but she doesn't respond.

I wish there really were such things as fairies. Maybe then I could blame the willow's poor growth on their failure instead of my own.

I turn off the lamp and nudge Astrid one more time. "Hey. Make room for me, Frog Breath."

She scoots a few inches over and I peel off my jeans and climb in, wearing just my concert tee. There's something comforting about snuggling with Astrid, even though we don't really fit in a twin bed together anymore. I'll probably move to her room later, but for now, I close my eyes and wrap one arm around her. Even bundled up beneath all these blankets, in June, she's freezing. I fall asleep trying to think of names for the cat Mom and Dad don't know I've adopted.

I wake suddenly, all the warmth in my muscles gone. Standing, shaking, I pull on my jeans, stuff my phone into the back pocket, and hobble into Astrid's room, my legs too tight to move properly.

Pulling her quilt up to my shoulders so I'm practically cocooned, I close my eyes and breathe in the scents that add up to my little sister: the damp mud of the creek, mint-chip ice cream, and her sour-apple, no-tears shampoo. Alone, each of these scents means nothing, but together, they will always equal Astrid, accidentally setting frogs loose in the living room. Astrid, waking me up by placing a turtle beside me on the pillow. Astrid, begging Mom and Dad, then Grandma, for a pet fruit bat. Astrid, reviewing her entire day with me, from morning drop-off clear through to whatever she and Lexie were doing right before I picked her up. That's not her, anymore. Ever since that day ten—twelve—years ago, she's

All I see is the white cat dragging himself to the side of the road and crumpling like an empty bag in the dirt. What if we hadn't stopped? What if he'd lain there, alone and hurt, until a bigger animal got him? Like the turkey and the car, there's always a bigger animal.

It's pitch-black in Astrid's room when I'm roused from sleep by shouting. What time is it? Is Astrid having another nightmare?

She needs to go back to Jamaica Knox. I'm almost thirty and if I'm going to live at home to keep helping Astrid, getting to sleep in my own bed all night by myself should be part of the ground rules. I've offered a half-dozen times to just officially swap rooms with Astrid, but she insists on this arrangement. Because it's not my room that she wants—it's me. So I put up with it, because it's Astrid.

I stumble out of bed and swing into my room to comfort her, but the room is dark and she's bundled beneath my covers, snoring.

At the other end of the hall, Mom's and Dad's door is open a few inches, the light blazing. I creep toward their room, stopping short of the bright, sharp angle of light. Brent stands in the darkness on the other side. I stuff my hands in my pockets and find my bracelet. When did I shove it there? For comfort, I pull it out and put it on, fingering the six lonely charms. Maybe we should start buying them again. Maybe if I asked, Astrid would leave the house for that.

"So, you get to freak the hell out and lose your shit, but I'm not allowed to?" Dad shouts.

Mom's voice is pointed. "I didn't say that. All I'm saying, Erik, is that I need you here, even if it hurts."

"What the hell am I supposed to do, Maren? How many times do you expect me to just smile and pretend it's all okay?" Dad's words are slurred again, but there's an odd edge to his voice. Something I've never heard before and don't want to ever hear again. It sends a jolt up my spine and makes me want to back away.

"How many times? Erik, as many times as it takes."

"I can't do it. I'm not going."

He must be talking about the memorial service for everyone who died at Winslow Elementary. They hold one every year on the anniversary of the shooting and we've never been before. But we're going this year. I guess someone told Mom and Dad it might be good for Astrid to face her demons.

"The hell you're not! I can't do it alone."

"They're in a better place, now," says Dad, his voice high-pitched as he mimics one of those things people say after someone dies.

"People are just trying to be nice." Mom's voice is softer now. "They don't know what to say."

"God always has a plan." Something heavy thuds to the floor.

"Erik..."

"The good Lord never gives you more than you can handle."

—*crash*—

Brent and I lock eyes. He raises his eyebrows and nods toward the door. I shake my head *No*. Not because I'm not scared—I am—but because even though Dad's tone makes me want to run, I can't. I'm rooted to this spot.

Dad hasn't been the same ever since Uncle Nick died, but I've never seen him like this. It was always Dad who held me when I had nightmares, Dad who rescued me when I climbed too high in the oak at the park, Dad who talked me through the geometry proofs that shredded my confidence sophomore year. There's never been a problem Dad couldn't help me get through, before.

So I know he'll get through this.

Then, when I have both my parents back to normal, we can all pull Astrid out of the well she's trapped in.

"They're at peace, now."

—*smash*—

"Erik, stop!"

"Watching over you." A grunt, then:

—*thud-thud-crack*—

"Erik, you're not the only person who lost someone. I don't care what you want, you're going tomorrow. She's going to need you. I can't do it all on my own."

Are they finally going to do something real to help Astrid? Their voices grow louder again.

Brent and I back away from the master bedroom until we can't see each other anymore. I linger in Astrid's doorway, invisible in the darkness.

"With the FUCKING ANGELS now."

—*crack-crack-crack*—

The door swings open. I take one more step back, into Astrid's room, before Mom speaks again, in a low, clipped tone.

"Get out. Go for a walk. A long walk. Get your head screwed on straight. Because when you come back, I need you sober and ready."

Dad stomps down the hall, past Brent's room, and a minute later, the front door slams. Mom cusses and closes their bedroom door.

Astrid lets out a snore I can hear from my position. How did she sleep through that? Once I'm sure the house is quiet again, I tiptoe into my room, grab my sneakers and running headlamp, and make my way to the kitchen, where Astrid's gifts sit, still-wrapped and forgotten. Dressed a little too warmly for the thick, impending-storm air, I step into the deck. But instead of stretching and running, I sit on the deck steps, peering out into the back yard. I can just make out the creek, swollen from the recent rain, the rushing water making me recall something Dad once said about the Grand Canyon. *Follow the creek out of the canyon*, I think. But I'm not in a canyon.

Just above the creek, the thin trunk of the willow rises from the shadows on the ground. It halts too, too soon. I stopped asking Maura for help with it years ago out of self preservation. All she ever said was, *Don't overfeed it, Kirsten. Too much of a good thing can have a negative effect.* If she finds out how pathetic my gardening skills really are, she'll demote me away from my greenhouse management position.

My chest gets tight the longer I look at the willow, but I can't look away. I'm not sure why.

Fog rolls in around me until I can't see past the edge of the bottom step. I slip my bracelet off and stuff it back into my pocket, shoving it down as far as it will go, and stare into the fog as if I can still see the willow and the creek.

All there is is a swirling whiteness. I let it claim me.

The soil beneath me is cool and wet from a rain shower earlier this morning, but not wet enough to make me get up from where I'm stretched out on my back beside the willow's sturdy trunk. My eyes are closed; sunlight reaches me through the green canopy above, creating swirling, shifting swatches of red-pink-orange-yellow behind my eyelids.

I love lying here, even now. I hide out beneath the willow and listen to the wind chimes outside Mrs. Martin's kitchen window and the mourning doves cry *woo-oo-oo-ooo, woo-oo-oo-ooo*. The breeze brings me the spicy scent of cut grass from one of the yards across the creek, and a pair of dogs bark. A lawnmower starts up somewhere down the block.

The deck gate bangs shut, and a trio of high-pitched voices spills toward me, cascading down the hill.

"Why can't we play in the creek before lunch?"

"Because lunch is ready now." Astrid answers. "Deck. Table. Sit. Now. Eat. Creek after."

"Will Aunty Kyurp let me help in the garden?"

"She used to let me help, so I'd say your chances are pretty good."

"Will we get to plant a tree, too?"

Astrid laughs. It's sharp and short, but not unpleasant. "Not this year. You have to be six."

"Why six?"

"Um… because the number six looks like a sprouting seed?"

"Hey, yeah!"

"It really does!"

"Is that really the reason?"

Astrid laughs again. "Well, that's what Aunty Kyurp told me when I was six. So it must be the reason. Now eat."

Their voices drop to a murmur, and the deck gate clicks open and shut again. Several moments later, the willow's long drooping branches rustle and the feel of the air shifts.

"Hey, Kyurp?" Astrid's voice is quiet.

I smile every time she uses her old childhood nickname for me. "Yeah, Frog Breath?"

She sits next to me and pokes me in the gut. "You better not call me that in front of the triplets. They've already got me outnumbered. I can't give them any real ammunition."

There's a short barrage of pop-pop-pops from some kids setting off contraband cherry bombs down the street; Astrid tenses beside me.

Blindly, I reach my hand out and she takes it. I give hers a squeeze. "You okay?"

She sucks a breath in and lets it out slow. She's counting to ten in her head like Jamaica Knox taught her to. Running through all the ways she's safe. All the things that are okay and good and beautiful in her life. "Yeah," she whispers. "Okay. Yeah."

She keeps hold of my hand for a few minutes, through a few more firecracker-volleys, only letting go when she's summoned from the deck.

"Mommy! The boys ate alllll the edamame!"

She parts the willow's curtain and leaves me hidden here as she climbs the slope. "Alllll the edamame? In the whole world? I see why you're upset."

She herds them back inside instead of turning them loose in the yard, and I'm left alone with the buzz of the lawnmower and the delicate tinkle of the wind chimes. I close my eyes.

The next thing I know I'm in the dark, lying in the wet grass beside a feeble tree that isn't dying but isn't growing either. The *gao, gao… gao, gao* of frog song reverberates through the still, early-morning air. *Gao, gao… gao, gao.* I stand and climb the hill. Climb the steps to the deck. Astrid is crouched in the corner between the cafe table and the deck rail, her hands over her ears and her eyes screwed shut.

The thick, humid air saps everything out of me.

Crouching beside her, I smooth her hair. "Astrid, come inside. Let's get you back to bed."

She lets out a squeak, but allows me to pull her up. "The deck, the doormat, Brent's car," I say, naming out all the red things I can see, like Jamaica taught me. Maybe it will help Astrid. "The poppies in the planter. Our bloodshot eyes if we don't get some sleep." I wrap an arm around her and guide her into the house.

I can't save Astrid's willow, and I can't save her, either.

16

SATURDAY MORNING, A LITTLE LATER

I give up.

I can't figure it out. I've tried every trick I know. I've even tried not doing anything.

It's time for Astrid's willow to go.

Maybe—this is stupid, but maybe Astrid is suffocating herself because the willow is weak. Maybe if I dig it up and throw it away, she'll have nothing strangling her. She'll be able to do things—everyday things—again.

I'll make it up to her somehow—let her pick two, or three, or an entire forest of trees.

It's still dark. I should really wait until morning, but the longer I wait, the more likely she'll see me and try to stop me.

It's for her own good—and mine, too.

I wait for my eyes to fully adjust to the overcast, pre-dawn sky before easing the shed door open and hauling out the tools I'll need. It takes three trips to get everything down the hill to the willow's plot, and I don't dare turn on my running headlamp until I'm ready to work. But when I do, it barely cuts through the fog.

First, I clear away the rocks that ring the berm. One by one, I heave up the stones that Astrid hauled from the rock pile at the edge of the creek the morning of her sixth birthday. They haven't been moved since, but they come up as easily as if they've just been placed. Now, I carry them back to the creek and pile them up. By the time I'm done, sweat dripping down my back, the rocks look like a cairn.

I can't leave them like that—a marker for the tree I'm about to kill—so I shift a bunch of them until they look more like part of a fieldstone farm-fence. So very New England. From the patch of irises across the creek, Astrid's old bird-watching frog statue watches me through its binoculars. If it could telegraph my actions to Astrid, it would.

I rake aside most of the mulch berm, dragging it through the grass until the soil beneath it is bare.

The spade slides in smoothly, with hardly any effort on my part. I loosen the soil, then reposition the spade a little to the right and slide it in again.

Loosen. Shift.

Slide. Loosen. Shift.

Slide. Loosen. Shift.

The humid air is heavy and hard to breathe. Rather than push and run out of energy, I slow down and pace myself, wiping the stinging sweat from my eyes as I work.

Once I've worked my way all around the tree, I switch directions, making a smaller circle of slices inside the first ring, facing away from the willow's trunk. This time, though, I lever the soil out and dump it into the wheelbarrow. I'll need it, plus more, to backfill the hole when the willow is gone. I'll have to get the "more" from Dirty Knees later today.

Slide. Loosen. Lever. Dump. Shift. Wipe sweat.

Soon I can feel the little island I've made shifting beneath my feet.

Why am I removing so much soil? Why didn't I just take the axe and hack my way into the roots as close to the trunk as I could? I'll need to cut the tree, anyway, if I'm going to get it out by myself. It took both me and Dad to position it when I planted it twelve years ago.

Even if it hasn't taken off the way it should have, I'm sure the root system is well-established.

How can it not be? The tree is still alive.

I toss the shovel aside and retrieve the axe from the shed.

It's heavy in my hand, and slightly unbalanced. The worn, wooden handle feels reassuring in my grip, though. As if the tree it came from knows what I'm about to do—and why—and doesn't judge me.

I set my feet shoulder-width apart.

I bend at the knees and swing the axe as high as feels right, then peer through the thick fog and take aim.

I bring it down.

Maybe six inches from the trunk, it sinks into the soft, rich soil. Too far away.

Swinging it up again, I adjust my position to bring it down much closer to the trunk—right where the trunk meets the soil, if I can. The trunk is only a few inches in diameter, so it's not like I'll need leverage to pull up the root ball.

"Kirsten."

I turn and lower the axe. Dad steps forward and places one hand on the long handle. Then both hands. Then he's taken the weight of it from me.

I let go, and he drops the axe to the ground. It thuds, an echo of the way the stone from the willow's hole thudded all those years ago.

"What are you doing?"

His voice is low and tight. There's a tremor to it that reminds me of the way he was yelling at Mom earlier... but it's not exactly the same. More like he pulled himself together like Mom told him to, and it wore him out.

"I'm digging up the willow. Or cutting it down. Whatever I have to do to get rid of it."

"Why? Why would you...?"

"Kyurp?" Astrid stumbles down the hill, wearing her fleece pajama bottoms and a long-sleeved tee. "What's going on? What are you doing to my tree?"

"It's for your own good, Astrid."

"Oh, for fuck's sake! I can't take this anymore," Dad shouts. He grabs me by the arm so tight I can't wrench away.

"Dad! Ow!"

But he's dragging me up the hill, onto the deck. My sneakers slip on the slick, dew-coated wood as he hauls me toward the house.

"Dad...Dad, stop."

Inside, the kitchen lights are on. He shoves me—hard—into the bench seat just as I scream, "Daddy, stop! You're hurting me—"

He lets go; I collapse into the seat and he backs away from me, breathing hard. Shaking his head. Staring at his hands. "No..." He clasps one hand in the other and holds them tight against his chest as he faces me.

"Kirsten... oh, God... Kirsten..."

Out of nowhere, Mom and Brent are here.

"Erik?" Mom looks at me first, then Dad.

But Brent's already kneeling in front of me, holding my hands. "Kirsten?"

I shake my head and scramble from the bench, pushing past him and dodging Mom. Racing for my room, I throw the still-blazing headlamp to the floor, grab my purse, and head back down the hall.

Mom meets me at the edge of the dining room. "Kirsten, your father didn't mean it... you know he would never..."

I raise my arm, the red-and-white welts from his grip still visible, a shadow of the damage she's done to her own arm. "Never what?"

She rockets her attention past me. "Erik!"

From the kitchen comes a cracking, sobbing noise that sends me sliding down into a Grand Canyon that's been dammed up at both ends.

I don't care that he's sorry.

He's been a mess for years—almost as bad as Astrid—while Mom and I have held everything together.

I don't care that he's falling apart.

I flounder in the rapidly rising water, scrabbling for something to grab hold of.

Astrid is sitting on the floor in the corner by the door, knees up and arms wrapped around them like a kid. She seems so small...

"Come on." Maybe I can save her. Maybe we can save each other.

"Where?" She looks up at me.

"Anywhere. We don't live here anymore."

Mom starts crying. "Kirsten, please... wait another day or two. Tomorrow is..."

"Where do we live?" Astrid asks.

"I don't know. Someplace else. I'll figure it out." I hold out a hand.

"You tried to dig up my tree."

"I'll plant you a new tree. An entire forest."

"I don't want an entire forest. I want my willow. Why'd you try to dig it up?"

"It's dead, Astrid. There's no other answer. I think it died a long time ago."

Mom makes a choky noise and turns, fleeing into the kitchen.

Astrid takes my hand and lets me pull her up. She follows me to my car.

Brent steps onto the front porch as I'm latching my seatbelt. I start the engine.

Astrid checks the back seat. "Where's our stuff?"

"I'll come back for it tomorrow."

Flipping on the wipers to combat the fog that's turning into an actual drizzle, I back out of the driveway, swinging wide to clear a bunch of vans parked all up and down the road. Barely visible in my headlights as I swing into the road, Brent darts down the driveway, toward the car, beckoning for me to wait.

I'm tired of waiting.

"What about me?" asks Astrid.

"What? I told you, you can stay with me."

"But..."

"I should have done this years ago."

I head toward Pawtucket, glancing into the rearview mirror just in time to see Brent in the street, waving at me to stop. The fog swallows him and we're on our way.

17

SATURDAY MORNING,
BEFORE DAWN

I SPEED UP PAWTUCKET, toward Lowell, the wipers on just fast enough to keep up with the misty rain.

"No," Astrid shakes her head. "I can't do this. Turn around. Take me back."

"Come on, Astrid. It's time to grow up. Rejoin the world. Face whatever it is you're afraid of."

"I'm not afraid of anything."

"Frog Breath," I say gently, "you were cowering in the corner not ten minutes ago."

"That's different," she says.

"It's not." I hit the gas and zip up the hill and around the corner as we come up to the UMass Lowell north campus.

She doesn't respond, just looks out the window at the nothing-she-can-see-through-the-fog. Even if she could see anything, it would only be the river and the falls. They're not really falls—just jagged rocks along a one-mile stretch of the river. I guess there is a drop in elevation, but mostly they're just cool to look at.

Okay, I'll play along if I can keep her here with me. "How is it different?"

"It just is. Can you take me home now? Please?"

"No. I'll find us an apartment. I promise. Just give me a chance."

"Kirsten, please. I don't belong out here." She doesn't sound like Astrid—she sounds older, somehow. Older and out of patience. As certain of who she is as I felt, myself, at eighteen.

We're past the campus. I approach the underpass, slowing down in case the cops are out in the speed trap beneath the rotary.

There they are.

Once we're around the bend, I speed back up, then hang a left and take the series of hairpin turns that lead up Christian Hill toward the reservoir. I'm not really paying attention to where we might end up. I'm just trying to move on after so many years of running in place. "What's up with you? Why are you still hiding in the house like the world is out to get you?"

"I'm here with you, now."

"You just said you wanted to go home. But, yeah, you are here now. If you can be here with me, you can get a job and go to college. Out to eat. Shopping. Normal stuff that everybody does."

"I'm not normal. I don't belong here."

"Mom and Dad have coddled you for the past twelve years—Grandma, too. That's what isn't normal. I think you just need a kick in the ass, and I'm going to do it for you."

"That won't help," she says.

"It'll help if you let it help."

Astrid doesn't respond for several minutes. The rain intensifies and I adjust the wipers. The headlights of the car behind me are blinding in my rearview mirror. Great, it keeps making all the same turns I do. If they're following me, they're out of luck—I have no idea where we are or where we're going. Squinting, I flip the mirror to its alternate position and keep driving aimlessly.

"Everything comes down to that with you," says Astrid. She's staring straight ahead, even though it's wicked foggy out and there's nothing to see past a yard or so in front of the car. Someone could jump out in front of us and I'd have no time to react. Like the car that hit the turkey, last year.

Last night.

Not that there's anywhere to go—the road is narrow and winding, without even enough shoulder for cyclists.

"Comes down to what?"

"What you think my life should look like."

"What do you expect? You're practically a shut-in. It's like something inside you is stuck."

Astrid folds her arms. "Maybe something is."

"What? Stuck?"

"Kind-of."

"Stuck where? And why?"

"You know where. "

I dig back through twelve years of memory, looking for something that makes sense, but there's only one thing. "The shooting?"

"The shooting," she repeats.

I sigh. "We live in the US. There've been hundreds of shoot-ings since then. Thousands. But it doesn't have to be the only thing that defines you, Astrid. You think you're the only person who was torn up by what happened? It doesn't have to be the end of your life."

"But it was. "

I pound one fist against the steering wheel. "But. It. Doesn't. Have. To. Be."

"You don't understand. You don't know what happened that day. You weren't there. You didn't see, and you refuse to admit…"

"Admit what? That I wasn't there? I know that. I do. But other kids were there. Lexie was there, and Jeremiah—"

Astrid grabs my arm. "Oh, God. Lexie." Her breath hitches. "Is Lexie okay? I was right next to her."

"What? She's…" She's what? Astrid is right, I don't really know. I haven't seen Lexie in years.

Days.

Blinking away the fog in my head, I dive back into my argu-ment. "This is about you, Astrid. You know you get to choose how you respond, right? How you live your own life?"

"You're wrong. I *don't* get to choose. All those choices were stolen from me."

There's no use arguing with her; she's got her mind made up that she's helpless in the face of the past. We fall silent as I navigate more winding roads. The car with annoying head-lights is still behind us. I think we're headed west again, through Dracut or the northern suburbs of Lowell, but I'm not positive. In the fog, nothing looks familiar. I should pull over and open up my GPS app, but the fog is so thick, by the time I see a driveway wide enough for me to turn around in, we're practically past it.

She sighs. "You think you know me but it's all in your head, this Astrid you've made up to fill some agenda that has nothing to do with the real me."

"What's that supposed to mean? 'The real you'? What have I made up?"

"Everything. Everything you think about me is part of some false reality you've invented."

I laugh because what else am I supposed to do when my sister calls me a nutcase? "Give me an example—one thing I think about you that's not real. I dare you."

She stares out at the fog obscuring the world as if it's a haze in her mind she's peering through.

"I'm cold," she says. "I'm always so fucking cold."

"You think twelve years of finding you bundled up to get warm hasn't clued me in to that reality? I mean, it's June. Do you really need fleece pajamas?"

A small animal darts to the edge of the road ahead of us, freezes, then turns and flees in the direction it came from. I swerve out of our lane to avoid it, regaining control as a dark pickup materializes in the oncoming lane, its horn low and long like a foghorn.

"Shit!" My hands are shaking. Suddenly there's this tightness in my chest, like I've just spent all afternoon running. But it's not cleansing like a run. It's suffocating. I'm being crushed by stones, added one by one, and it's hard to concentrate on the road through the thickening fog in my head. For an instant, I want to laugh at the way my mind mirrors the weather. Instead, I grip the steering wheel tighter and jut my head forward a bit, like a turtle, but it doesn't help me see through the fog any better.

"I'm not wearing fleece pajamas. You only think I am."

"What?"

Slowing the car a bit, I risk a glance at Astrid. But then I don't look back at the road—because she's right. She's not wearing fleece pajamas. She's in... what? Her green, sixth-birthday dress? Her childhood play clothes and frog rain boots? Her preschool Lily Frog costume? What the hell is wrong with me?

"Focus, Kyurp. Do you want to die?"

Yes.

I shake my head to clear the image of Astrid's shifting, morphing outfits and turn my attention back to the empty road, swerving to stay on my side. I speed up more than I should, and the headlights fade from my rearview mirror. Ahead, the road dips and rises, curves and twists. Despite the fog, I let my foot rest heavily on the gas until we're shooting forward like we're on one of those in-the-dark roller coasters, where you can't see what's happening until you're practically in the turn, or right at the top of the first, most intense drop. There's a steep slope to our right, and I think I see water at the bottom through a break in the fog. We might even be on a dirt road, the way the wheels slip a little as I steer. But I'm all turned around. Am I driving north or south? Is that the Merrimack? Or a pond?

Beside me, Astrid's got one hand on the Oh Shit bar and another on the armrest console.

"So?" I ask again. Maybe I am losing it, but I'm still her big sister. I can't let her self-destruct without trying to stop her.

I'll catch you every time.

"Can I at least convince you to live with me and go to college?"

"I'm not going to college."

"What, then?"

Shakes her head again. "Nothing. I'm not going anywhere. I'm not doing anything." Her words are gritty and hard, like she's telling me something she's told me twenty times before.

"What do you mean 'nothing'? You never learned to drive. You've never even held a job scooping ice cream at Callahan's. You've got to do something."

"I'm not going to do anything."

"I don't understand…"

She looks out the window. "Mom and Dad understand."

"Seriously? They're okay with you just deciding to lie around all day watching childish videos? Because if you stay with me, you can't do that."

Which is the biggest reason for her to run off back home.

"They're not okay. But they understand."

The car rises and falls, swerves left and right, and I can barely see what's coming. It sounds like Astrid's fiddling with the seatbelt buckle, but it's not safe for me to check.

"Kyurp, stop," she says.

She hasn't called me that in forever.

Since Monday morning.

"We're in the middle of nowhere."

She unlatches her belt. "You need to let me go."

Holding the steering wheel with my left hand, I slow down and fumble around with my right, trying to re-buckle Astrid's seatbelt. No way am I letting her out, alone, in the dark, when I don't even know where we are.

But in one swift movement, Astrid pops the lock, opens the door, and jumps out.

I can't catch her.

On the slick road, my dinky old compact becomes a top when I hit the brakes. Spinningspinningspinning, the fog a blur around me and inside me until I think *I'm gonna die* and a wild, high scream that can't be mine bounces through the car —my head lolls on my spring of a neck—and there's a *bang!* as the airbag deploys and the car stops—*thunk*—facing the wrong way and buckled against a row of trees.

The airbag collapses, its powder settling onto my clothes and everything else and making me cough. Something inside me crumples, too.

The radio hisses, Emily Snow singing

> *gone*
> *gone like the clouds*
> *torn apart by the wind…*

When did I turn the radio on? I reach over and switch it off, then stare at the passenger door. It's closed. It must have swung shut during the spin. My heart pounds, and whoever is adding the stones to my chest piles on two more. I feel disconnected from my body—like I'm engrossed in a movie, only the slightest bit aware it's not actually happening to me. But it hurts so much, it has to be real.

My hands are shaking so much I need both of them to undo my seatbelt. The door is jammed, the window shattered by a branch that missed my head by a few inches. I scramble through the car and climb out the passenger door, grabbing my purse on the way.

As I move, my vision blurs and everything swims around me. Bracing myself against the car, I lean over and throw up.

I must have hit my head when we crashed. I wipe my mouth and stand up, slowly.

One of the car's headlights is still on, but it cuts only a few feet into the foggy night. Where's Astrid? Did she roll free before I lost control?

"Astrid?"

The mist swallows my voice. She'll never hear me. Leaving my purse on the hood of my car, I take a few unsteady steps into the swirling grayness.

"Astrid!" I slip in the wet grass, sliding downhill and landing on my hip with a muffled splash. I'm at the shoreline—of a pond or the Merrimack, I still can't tell. It's hard to think. I try to stand, but I'm stuck, my feet sunk into the silty mud. Sitting down, I pull one foot, then the other, from the mud with a squelching, sucking sound. Leaving my shoes buried there, I turn back toward the car. Stumbling uphill in my slimy, muddy socks, my feet go cold fast, making the rest of me shiver more. Every movement makes my head throb harder and my tilt-a-whirl vision change direction more errat-ically. Once I'm closer to the car, keeping my hands out before me as if I'm negotiating an unfamiliar dark room, I call out again and again.

"Astrid! Astrid, where are you?"

What if she's unconscious? What if she can't answer? I won't cry; I don't want her to know I'm scared. I want her to know she can count on me. That I'll get us out of this.

"Astrid, I'm sorry. We'll sort it out. Just tell me you're okay!" *I'll catch you every time.*

"Kyurp?"

Her voice is tiny.

"Frog Breath, where are you?"

She whimpers. "It hurts."

"Keep talking. I'll find you."

"I—can't—"

Following the sound of her breathy cries—tripping over rocks, brambles, and downed branches I don't see until it's too late—I finally reach her. I almost can't take those last steps.

She's dashed against a log, one leg bent at an angle legs aren't made to bend at, the bone poking out of her shin. There's a branch sticking out of her chest and her breath comes in shallow gasps. I kneel beside her in the mud, stones and whip-thin twigs pressing into my shins and knees.

"Kyu... Kyu..."

She flicks her gaze toward the branch. It's big enough around to serve as a clothing rod.

"Shhh. No, no. Look at me."

She looks at me, but her eyes are glassy. Unfocused. Fighting against my own roiling vision, I stroke the back of her head the way I did when she was little. Her hair is wet and my hand comes away slick. I swallow my panic.

It's mud. It has to be mud.

I fumble for my phone and press the HOME button, grateful I've never bothered to use a lock code. The screen is shattered. I try to pull up the dial keypad, but only cut my fingers on shards of glass.

"Fuck…" I look around, but we're too far from the road for anyone to see us in the fog. "Astrid, I need you to hang on. I need to flag down help…"

"Stay—"

I shouldn't stay. If I stay…

I sit beside her in the mud, and wrap one arm around her as best as I can. "I won't leave, Astrid. I promise. I'm right here."

"Kyu—urp. Lis—en." Her voice is weak and burbly.

I know what she's going to say, and I don't want to listen. I take her hand in mind.

"I'm listening." My tears make it hard to see. This isn't happening. It's not. It's not. It's not.

"I need you to listen." Her voice is stronger. That's good, right? It means it's not as bad as it looks.

"I am."

"Promise me something."

"Anything, Frog Breath. Anything you want."

She laughs a little and shakes her head. "You say that now. I need you to mean it." She's talking now as if she's not injured at all. She's going to be okay.

I brush my tears away with the back of my hand. "I mean it. I'll do anything."

She takes a deep breath and meets my gaze. "You have to forgive yourself, and you have to let me go."

"What? Don't talk like that, Frog Breath. It's okay. You're going to be okay. I'll climb up to the road and flag someone down."

"You know I'm not okay. I know you know it."

"You're just in shock. Shock does strange things to the body, and to the mind."

"I know," she says, with an odd smile.

I smooth her hair, brushing a few wet strands off her face.

She grabs my hand and clenches it. "Promise. Promise you'll let me go. It wasn't your fault. We had an agreement."

I shake my head. "I can't. I... don't want to do that... it's too impossible."

"You have to. You can't stay here, stuck like this, forever. You have to keep going."

"No. I don't want to. You're going to be okay. I just need to get up to the road. I'll find someone and come right back and sit with you until the ambulance gets here."

"I'm already gone, Kyurp. You know that."

"No, I don't. I refuse to accept that."

"You have to."

Her breath hitches, and her face seizes up in pain. When she speaks again, her voice is young and high-pitched, like when she was just turning six. Like she's talking to me across the years. Her words come in gasps, each breathier than the last.

"I hid... your charm... real... good."

"What? What charm? I don't want a charm. I want you."

Her eyes look glassy and unfocused again.

"Keep… looking."

"I don't need a charm. I need you. Hold on, Astrid. It's going to be okay. *You're* going to be okay."

"Kyurp…"

She relaxes into my arms, and doesn't move again.

I hold her for what feels like hours, something in the back of my head screaming as I try to figure out what to do. Leave her and climb to the road? Or just wait for someone to find us? It's probably only been a few minutes, but…

Nobody knows where we are. I don't even know where we are.

My head is throbbing. Maybe I'm dying too. All I know is, everything hurts.

I'll stay with her for a few more minutes, then figure out what to do.

I rest my head against Astrid's shoulder and close my eyes, just for a minute.

Everything hurts.

I'm shivering despite the humidity.

"I'm here, Kirsten. You're gonna be okay."

"Astrid?"

"It's Josie. I'm here. Oakley's up the hill, watching for the ambulance. We lost you in the fog, and almost didn't see your car in the ditch." Her hand holds mine. Warm. Soft.

"Help Astrid…" I mumble, then close my eyes again.

Soon the crackle of radios and unfamiliar voices stab my aching head, replacing the early morning stillness. My head feels like there's a tourniquet around it, being pulled tighter and tighter. I turn to face Astrid, and she's gone. In her place are a man's boots, attached to a man's legs and, I guess, the rest of the man.

I turn away and close my eyes again. He sets something—a medical bag?—down with a *pwump* and unzips it; the zipper rips open my head, leaving everything exposed.

"Hi there," he says, his voice clipped but kind and lightly accented. "I'm Raul. I'm going to check everything out, make sure you're okay. Can you tell me your name?"

"Astrid," I say. "I'm cold."

Raul puts a hand on my shoulder; it's warm and heavy and I'm so glad he's here I start crying.

"Okay, Astrid, can you open your eyes for me?"

I try to shake my head but it hurts tootootoo much, so I just keep my eyes closed and answer. "No. Astrid's my sister."

"Astrid is your sister's name? Can you tell me *your* name?"

There's rustling in the brush nearby and the murmur of three voices—Josie, Oakley, and one I don't know—as Raul pulls open one eyelid, then the other, shining a bright light into them. I whimper and try to turn away.

"Ow…"

"Pupils dilated but reactive," he says. The unfamiliar voice—a woman—responds too quietly for me to hear the actual words.

Raul addresses me again. "Can you tell me your name?"

"Kirsten."

"Your name's Kirsten?"

Like he doesn't believe me. Like I don't know my own name.

"Yeah. My name's Kirsten."

"Okay, Kirsten. Can you open your eyes and look at me?"

"Don't shine the light."

"I won't shine the light."

I open my eyes and try to focus on him; there's still a light coming from somewhere, but it's not skewering my eyes anymore, so I squint against it and try to look at the man attached to the voice. I can make out dark skin and dark, close-cropped hair and I think he's smiling, but the world is Dorothy's house, spinning in the tornado. "Everything's moving," I say. "Everything's blurry."

"You hit your head pretty hard," says Raul. "You probably have a concussion, but we're going to get you taken care of. Do you understand?"

"Yeah. What about my sister?"

"Your sister. Astrid?"

"She was in the car with me. I think she got thrown when we spun around. I thought… I thought she was right here. I'm cold."

He turns and exchanges a few words with the people I can't see.

"…Winslow Elementary…" Oakley's voice.

"Are you certain?" the woman asks. "We need you to be certain, or we're going to have to do a search."

"Yeah," says Oakley. "I'm certain."

"Can I stay and hold her hand?" Josie's voice.

"Yeah, but you gotta let me work." Raul.

There's more rustling and the sound of twigs snapping. Josie's beside me, her hand back in mine. Warm. Safe.

Raul faces me.

"Okay, we're looking for Astrid, and we'll take care of her, too. I need you to focus on me, though. Think you can do that?"

"Yeah. But I need to find my sister. She got thrown. She's supposed to be right here."

I try to sit up, but he holds me in place. "Kirsten. You're staying here. I've got someone looking for your sister and they're going to find her. But I can't let you up. You've been hurt bad and I need you to cooperate. Are you going to do that for me?"

"Oh. Yeah. Sorry." I lean back against the log and he checks my blood pressure and my reflexes does a bunch of other stuff I can't see because my eyes are closed.

As Raul works, he talks to me. Asks me where I live and where was I going and does anything else hurt besides my head.

"I'm cold," I say. "Why am I so cold?" I stutter the words out with chattering teeth.

"You're in shock," he says. "We're going to warm you up real soon, now."

The woman's boots crunch through the twigs as she comes back down the hill. She sets something on the ground and Raul says, "Oh, good. Is the striker ready?"

"All set," says the woman. "And her friend up there filled me in. We're good to go as soon as we get her up the hill."

"Who's up there?" I ask, opening my eyes again. "Is it Astrid? Is Astrid safe?" Did she get thrown free and land in the grass instead of against the trees and rocks? I remember sitting beside her, right here. I know what happened.

"We've got everything under control," says Raul. "Remember, you promised to cooperate."

"Okay…"

Together, they put a stiff collar around my neck and shoulders so I can't turn my head anymore and they roll me onto the woman's legs, then backward onto the backboard. The world becomes a carnival Scrambler, everything risingfallingspinningswerving in directions that are all wrong. Raul covers me in a warm blanket, then puts those big wedges around my head like on TV and I can't see anything except what's right above me. I'm strapped down everywhere, even across my forehead, and I start crying again.

"I don't wanna die, I don't wanna die. Please, I need to get to Astrid… I need to make sure she's okay… she's my responsibility…"

But the world spins around me as they carry me up the hill. Stars pinwheel in the clearing, blueing sky, looking just like that painting by van Gogh. Everything comes alive around me, dancingspinningswirlingtwirling wild starscolorsshapes and then it all goes black.

FINALLY

18

SATURDAY MORNING, LATER

I WAKE up in a curtained alley in the Emergency Room.

Everything hurts.

My head is pounding, and I'm vaguely aware of the IV in one hand and the blood pressure cuff inflating around my upper arm. Squinting against the sick, flickering fluorescent lights, I get my bearings. Mom is in the chair, crying silently. Her eyes are closed. She's wearing shorts and an old t-shirt, her hair pulled messily back into a ponytail. Dad's standing beside her. He's still unshaven and his eyes are red-rimmed and bloodshot, but they're not sinkholes anymore. He's wearing a ragged pair of shorts that sag from too many days of wear in a row, but his t-shirt is clean and tucked in, in that dorky way he does. He's holding my bracelet on two fingers and staring at it.

Do they already know what I did? If not, how am I going to tell them?

I guess I make some kind of noise, or I move or something, because Dad looks up from the bracelet.

He sees I'm awake and stretches his mouth into a tight, broken smile. "Kirsten. Kirsten, hon… we're right here…" He puts his free hand on my arm.

I don't want to escape.

I don't need to.

Whoever that was last night is gone, now. My Dad—my real Dad who I've known all my life, who always caught me when I jumped off the big-kid swings at the park—is here, shifting his weight from foot to foot the way he does when he's nervous but trying to stay calm. "You're in the hospital. You're going to be okay."

I wish he were right.

I'll never be okay again.

Mom opens her eyes and her sobbing gets louder. She reaches a hand through the gap in the bed rail and clutches my shoulder. When I wince and moan, she loosens her grip.

"Oh. Oh, I'm sorry, sweetie. I didn't think…" she brushes the hair out of my eyes, even though my hair isn't in my eyes.

It makes me think of Josie and Oakley, who found me slumped against the log beside Astrid and called 911 and stayed with me until the ambulance arrived. Who held my hand the way I held Astrid's.

How did they know where to find me? Where are they now?

Even the feel of Josie's hand in mine is foggy.

I want to confess. Want to say, *Mom—Daddy—please, let me explain. I didn't mean to—I tried to re-buckle her seatbelt—I only wanted to save her—*

But I can't make my voice work.

Because I'd have to tell them I was speeding on wet roads. That I could barely see the road in front of me. That I was careless—reckless—irresponsible—and it's all my fault.

They're both leaning over me, holding my hands, smoothing my hair, and making reassuring noises.

"Shhhhhh. It's going to be okay. It was an accident."

But it was all my fault.

"You're safe. You're still with us. That's all that matters."

But Astrid's gone. How can it not matter that Astrid died because of me?

I open my mouth to try to explain, but my breath hitches and I start crying.

Because they wouldn't be so kind if they knew what really happened. But they must know, because Dad says, "after everything that's happened this week, I couldn't handle it if we lost you, too."

I think I can finally get it out. They let me order some food and there was a shrink who talked about—

What did he talk about? I don't remember. My head hurt too much to listen, so I closed my eyes and tried to figure out how I was going to explain the accident to Mom and Dad. But I kept thinking of Josie. I kept seeing her hand brush against mine, then hold fast, kept seeing her blow her bangs out of her eyes with a quick puff. I kept feeling the tingle of her hand in mine. How could I feel the tingle of her hand in mine when she wasn't there?

And how do I stop thinking about Josie long enough to figure out what to say to Mom and Dad?

The shrink said, "What do you say, Kirsten?"

I opened my eyes. "About what?"

He made a note in his notebook. "About talking to Ms. Knox again later today."

"Yeah. Sure. I guess that's cool." They're probably going to make me go for a while, to help me sort out the accident.

The shrink says something else to Mom and Dad that I didn't listen to. Then he left. The nurse came in with my discharge order and Dad drove us all home.

Now they're sitting across from me in the kitchen booth. It's just the three of us. Like it will be, forever. There will always be an empty seat where Astrid should be.

There's a small pile of packages pushed up against the back of the booth. I run a finger along the edge of one of the colorful boxes.

I take a deep breath. "I need to tell you what happened," I say. But I don't look at Mom or Dad. I just stare at the packages as I explain.

We were driving, I say. *It was back roads, somewhere. I don't know where. I wasn't paying attention. I should've been paying attention... it's just that I was trying to talk some sense into Astrid, trying to convince her to... I don't know... do stuff. Like college. Or a job. Normal stuff.*

No, honey, says Mom. *You weren't.*

You don't understand, I say, shaking my head. *You weren't there. You can't know.*

They nod.

Mom holds my hands in hers.

Tell us, says Dad.

I'm trying, I say.

But it's so hard. I run through it in my mind again, but can't make sense of it. Everything is jumbled and my head hurts and I wish we'd left the lights off. Thinking is like walking through molasses. Maybe it will come out okay if I just say it.

We were driving along the back roads, arguing about her future and how she was setting herself up to not have one. Then she jumped out of the car and I slammed on the brakes and the car spun out of control. Astrid landed… she landed against a downed tree branch.

There was nothing I could do.

Wait—

I made a mistake—

I start over.

Astrid and I were fighting again about how I need to let her live her own life. About how I can't write her life like a book. And told her how she can't spend her whole life lying on the couch watching old videos. How she can't live in the past, or let the past paralyze her. And I'll admit I was mad and driving too fast on the back roads. It was dark and I lost control at the exact moment that Astrid unbuckled her seatbelt. It just happened. The car spun and she crashed through the front window—

Wait. That's not what happened—

What happened was, her door swung open and she fell out and landed against a fallen tree. I tried to find her but I couldn't find her until it was too late. She died before the ambulance arrived. Before I could even call one.

That's not right, either.

I couldn't call 911. My phone was busted. So I climbed up to the road and—

No—wait—I think I stayed with her—

Or did I get the all-circuits-busy message?

I don't remember, exactly.

Why is it so hard to remember?

I shake my head, wince, and try one more time.

I took my eyes off the road to re-buckle her seatbelt and I must have hit a slick spot or debris or something in the road because the car was spinning and spinning and the door flew open and Astrid was gone before I even knew what was happening and I couldn't find her by the side of the road in the fog and the brush and the dark until it was too late. I tried to get to her. It took too long to reach her. By the time I got there, I couldn't save her. I was too late. Astrid is gone-gonegonegone—

Mom and Dad are crying and I must be, too, because my face stings and I taste salt.

I'm sorry, I say. Please don't hate me. I didn't get to her in time—

Kirsten, Dad says. *Kirsten, honey—it's not your fault.*

But it is, I insist. *It was an accident, but it's still my fault.*

Sweetie, says Mom. *Astrid wasn't with you last night.*

No, I say. *That's not right.*

I look at the packages. They're not just boxes. They're presents, wrapped in paper of varied shades of green. One package has frog stickers all over it.

I used to do that to the presents I gave Astrid.

Kirsten, Mom says.

I shake my head. *No. I don't want to hear it…*

I think you need to, says Dad. Mom nods.

I don't want to. My head hurts. I should lie down.

I know, hon. Soon. But first we really need to talk, says Mom.

I reach out and touch the stickered package. *Who is this for?*

It was for Astrid, says Mom.

What's in it?

You wouldn't tell us, says Dad. *It was some big surprise.*

I dislodge the rectangular package from the pile and pull it toward me. Fingering the thin green ribbons I can never get curled all the way, I blink slowly, trying to clear the fog in my head.

I untie the ribbon, then slide my index finger along the edges, unsticking the tape. Though I'm not sure why, I fold the paper carefully, tucking the ribbon inside where it won't get lost, and slide the paper toward the center of the table. Mom touches it lightly, then pulls her hand away. Dad reaches his hand across the table and rests it on my elbow.

My chest is tight and my heart is in my throat and I'm holding my breath and I don't know why. Beneath the table, my legs twitch like they're itching for a run.

My hands shake as I tug the lid of the box up. Inside, a few sheets of green tissue paper cover the actual gift. I remove the paper. Side by side are a small, 1980s style metal lunchbox and a handmade green canvas backpack. Lily, rolling with laughter, is embroidered onto the outer pocket of the back-pack. The lunchbox is painted green and decorated with Lily and Shelley, their friends Echo Bat, Zippy Dragonfly, Flash Goldfinch, and Button Mouse, and even Mama Frog and Lily's little brother Tad. The characters dance all around the container, in front of a background of cat-tails and lily pads and fallen, half-submerged logs.

The fog lifts. "Omigod…"

Mom nods and reaches across the table. She takes both of my hands in hers again.

"No—" I pull away, scramble from the booth, and head for the door.

I need to run—but I turn back toward the booth, walk a few steps, then shake my screaming head and turn toward the back door again. "I can't… she's… she was… only six. Just barely."

Dad takes hold of my hand.

"No." I pull away again. It's not fair. It didn't happen—I can't stop trying to reach the door. And I can't let myself run away again. "It was her birthday."

"What do you remember?" asks Dad.

"What day is it?" I ask, still pacing. I need to know how long I've been out of it.

"That doesn't matter," says Mom.

"It matters to me. What day is it?"

"Saturday," she admits.

I stop pacing. Put one hand to my mouth, as if I could take all the stupid things I must have said and cram them back in. Brent steps into the doorway and leans against the frame. He takes one look at me and nods.

My tears are a flash flood, sweeping me up, carrying me away, and dumping me in some unfamiliar, lonely gully. I sink to the floor. The past five days explode like a hundred fireworks all set off at once.

"What do you remember?" Dad asks, again.

I remember running with Oakley—Josie—Brent.

Kissing Josie at the concert.

Brent crashing in the den, and tearing into me on the footbridge.

Turkeys and nestlings and cats and runningrunningrunning.

I don't know what order everything goes in, and there are huge black holes swirling through everything, threatening to suck away the pieces that I do remember before the images solidify. "Flashes," I say. "I think… I think Oakley and Brent and Josie were always around. Is that right?"

"That's right," says Dad. "Brent is staying with us. Permanently."

Brent nods again.

"And… Grandma is here, but… staying in a hotel?"

"That's right," says Mom.

"It's all jumbled up," I say. "I don't know what's what, or what day anything happened on, or… even what was real."

"Jamaica said, as long as you weren't a danger to yourself, it was best to let your mind sort it out on its own," says Dad. "She said it's understandable, and not uncommon, after a traumatic incident."

I don't want to listen, but know I need to. I shut my eyes tight. Tears keep streaming out anyway as Mom and Dad sit on the floor, on either side of me, to explain that Uncle Nick grabbed Kevin Adams and dragged him out of the cafeteria so the teachers and parents could lock the doors. I imagine Uncle Nick lying there and not breathing on the floor outside the cafeteria.

Oakley's brother Luther lost his left eye. Hunter Adams died at the hospital, along with Ellen Walsh and Harmony Luc. But eleven other kids never left school that day. Including Astrid.

Astrid died in the cafeteria, right where she was sitting beside Lexie.

Waiting for me.

I just wanted to be able to hold hands with my girlfriend in public. I just wanted to stop sneaking around. But I should have been there on time, like Mom expected me to be. Instead, I suggested to Astrid that I should always be late. *You can hang out with Lexie and play* Lily's Pad *until her dad gets there,* I said. *Everybody's happy.*

Astrid is dead and it's all my fault.

Jamaica Knox is wearing the same sandals she wore on Wednesday.

It's only been a few days since I was here, on this sofa. Not twelve years.

Even so, the lavender polish on two of her toes is chipped almost completely off. There are puffy bags beneath her eyes.

She smiles anyway.

"How are you today, Kirsten?" Her voice is soft and kind. It feels like a parent peeking in on a sleeping child. I think she'd sit beside me and hug me if it would be appropriate.

I'm clutching the little packet of tissues Mom had in the glove box. I'm afraid to open it and use one, mostly because I'm certain if I use one, I'll use them all and still need more. Like a whole big box more.

"Um… not good."

I'm stiff and bruised; I'm achy all over. Once I'd remembered on my own, Mom made sure I took a short nap. She pulled the blinds down and the curtain closed, and tugged my quilt up as far as my shoulders, and I slept for a few hours. But my head still hurts a lot and lights are all too stabby.

Dad called Jamaica's emergency number while I was in the ER and she agreed to meet us at her office, even though today is Saturday.

"Why are you not good?"

"I…"

I don't want to say it.

I know I have to say it.

Why, though? Isn't it enough to know? Isn't it enough that I realize now, all those fights Mom and Dad had with Grandma were over me? Over the way they followed Jamaica's advice and let me believe Astrid was okay?

Let my mind work it out?

Isn't it enough to think of all the things I did and said—in front of Dad, Brent, and Oakley—that made it seem like I didn't care? Like I was mocking them? And they stuck with me, anyway.

I take a deep breath and glance at Jamaica. She's waiting. And she's watching me, but not like she's annoyed I'm taking too long. More like she knows what I'm going to say but wants to let me say it in my own time.

I lower my eyes. Study the neon orange packet of tissues. It's a little squashed from being in the glove box, but otherwise, it's new and full. I could pull back the sticky tab and break the perforated slit and take one out.

I shake my head *No.*

"What are you thinking, now?" asks Jamaica.

"That I don't want to say it."

I glance at her.

She nods. "What would change if you say it?"

"I... I don't know. Nothing, I guess. Not really."

And everything.

I lean back against the sofa. Pull back the sticky tab on the tissue packet. Remove a tissue. Unfold it. Smooth it out on my thigh. Fold it once, in half.

It rests there on my thigh.

Waiting for me.

Astrid waited for me.

I look up at Jamaica. Her dark brown eyes meet mine and it's like she does hug me.

I swallow, hard, around an enormous lump that came out of nowhere, and take another deep breath.

"Astrid died." My breath comes fast. "At school." Tears rush out, hot and furious. "On Monday. In the shooting."

I have to stop. And out of nowhere, I'm shivering. Freezing cold, but all I can do now is shiver and cry and cry and cry. So hard I can't catch my breath. So long my face feels swollen. My eyes sting, my nose runs, and there aren't enough tissues in the packet Mom gave me. My hands trembling violently, I reach for the box of generic tissues on Jamaica's desk. It takes both hands to get the tissues out and they're rough and thin and I don't care as I burn through three of them blowing my nose.

Jamaica doesn't say anything. She just gives me space to lose it.

"I keep thinking, though..." I say, when I can finally talk again. "I keep thinking, if I'd gotten there on time, she'd be okay." I'm still shivering a little.

Jamaica finishes up the note she's making and looks at me.

"That's possible. Do you know what time the shooting occurred?"

"Not exactly. Just that it was after school. Dismissal time."

"And you blame yourself for Astrid being there."

"Yeah," I say. "At the beginning of the school year, when I agreed to pick her up every day so Mom could take the promotion at work, I promised I'd be responsible. That I'd pick her up on time."

"And Monday was an exception?"

I shake my head *No*. "We worked out a deal. Astrid and I agreed I would get there toward the end of pick-up time. Her best friend, Lexie—Lexie's dad was always late. He always left work late and got stuck on the bridge. So, I said I would be late, too, so Astrid and Lexie could hang out and play this make-believe game they had. Plus, it gave me more time to be with my friends."

Jamaica nods and jots.

"The thing is, we also agreed to keep it a sisters-only secret. I mean, we weren't hurting anyone, so Mom and Dad didn't need to know. Right?" I look at Jamaica for reassurance, but her face is neutral.

How do therapists do that?

"You and Astrid worked out this arrangement, and you were both happy with it?"

"Yeah. Anytime I accidentally got there too early, Astrid gave me an earful. 'You promised to be late. We were right in the middle of our game. Can't I go back in and stay till Mr. Oh gets here?' So I tried really hard to not get there until almost the end of pick-up time. But I should have known something like this would happen."

She makes a note, then says, "Kirsten, we have to make decisions trusting that things will be all right. Otherwise, we would be paralyzed in the face of all the possibilities, the vast number of things that could go wrong but usually don't."

"I know" I say. "But…" I stop myself, thinking of all the times I let Astrid climb around on the slick rocks in the creek. All the times I get behind the wheel of my car, go to a concert, use my headphones while jogging…. What was the Astrid I invented like? Was she as fearless as the Astrid I knew? I wish I could remember. I hope she was.

Jamaica glances at the clock that faces only her, and shifts in her seat. "I know it's Saturday, but we need to stop for now."

I fiddle with the soggy tissue I've been using to dab at my eyes.

"When we last met, your parents scheduled another appointment for you for this coming Wednesday. So between now and then, I'd like you to do something for yourself."

"What?"

"I'd like you to find out what time the shooting occurred, and give yourself permission to feel whatever emotions come to you. But I'd also like you to remember what I said about the way we make decisions. We'll talk about it more when we meet again. Does that sound like something you can do?"

"Okay. Yeah. I think so."

She stands up and so do I. She opens the door and leads me back to the waiting room that's empty except for my parents.

I melt into Mom's warm arms as Jamaica disappears into the back again, closing the waiting room door.

Dad leads the way out to the car.

"I'm so sorry…" I mumble. Mom strokes my hair the way I used to stroke Astrid's. "All this week… everything crazy I did… I'm so sorry…"

"It's okay, Kirsten. It's going to be okay."

I glance at her. "Is it? Really?"

She nods.

"How? How is it going to be okay? Nothing's the same anymore. Astrid's dead. How are we supposed to move on from that?"

"I don't know, sweetie. You're right—nothing is the same. But we *will* be okay, somehow. Someday."

19

SUNDAY MORNING

It's eight o'clock.

This time last Sunday, I was sneaking Astrid a sip of my coffee and getting ready to plant her willow.

Come on, Kyurp! You said I get to help today. Trees are big. We should start early.

Today—showered, my cuts and scrapes rebandaged, my still-throbbing head dosed with ibuprofen—I'm dressing for Astrid's funeral in the dark blue dress from Mom's closet. The one she was ironing the other day. Something I know for certain was real.

Mom's wearing the black dress with white cuffs, the gashes on her left arm unbandaged. Revealed to the world.

Brent slept here last night, then cut through the back yards to get dressed at home. Grandma promised to swing by there and drive him to the funeral parlor—but only after she saw with her own eyes, yesterday, that I'm okay and that I know what's going on.

Uncle Nick's funeral was one of the first, on Thursday. I remember sitting in the church, but I don't remember anything else. Not the prayers or the songs, not even the eulogies. What did my mind do during that hour? I hate that it stole those last moments with Uncle Nick from me.

I braid my hair, use a few clips to hold back some loose strands, and fasten my bracelet before grabbing my purse from the closet knob and stepping into my heels.

Wobbling a little, I head to the living room. Dad is in Astrid's spot on the couch, waiting. He's dressed in a suit, his tie still a little loose. On his phone, he has the theme from *Lily's Pad* on repeat.

> *...in the weeping willow's shade...*
> *that's Lily's Pad...*

He's holding Mr. Ribbit in one hand and his baseball glove in the other. After Astrid's funeral, Mom and Dad are taking me to visit my still-unnamed cat at the emergency vet. Then we're all helping Brent go through some of Uncle Nick's things. My breath catches in my throat and the tears start again, coming from nowhere and everywhere.

From deep inside me, so much worse than in Jamaica's office yesterday.

Every cell in my body is crying for Astrid. My whole body is one enormous wound, gaping like a fish's mouth—and I think, for a flash, about running into the kitchen and slicing myself open with a knife to make it stop.

I want it to stop.

I need it to stop.

I'm a heap on the floor, sobbing and choking and practically vomiting and I can't breathe.

How do I make it stop?

How do I do this?

I can't do this.

Dad is beside me, now, on the floor. He's holding me tight and crying so hard his tears dampen my dress.

Mom is on my other side, crying too, shushing me, and stroking my hair like I used to do Astrid's.

I got that from Mom. She used to do it for me when I was a kid. It only makes me cry harder because Astrid won't ever get to stroke some little kid's hair while she comforts them.

"You couldn't have done anything," says Mom.

"It's not your fault," says Dad.

But it is. They still don't get that Astrid is dead because of me. Because I hung around too long with my friends and Josie. It doesn't matter that Astrid wanted to hang with Lexie, too. I was supposed to be the big sister… the responsible one.

They hold me, and I cry, and they cry, until we all wear ourselves out. They stand, pulling me gently up. Mom makes me blow my nose, then they each wrap an arm around me and we step outside. The Channel Seven van is at the curb.

"They've been there all week. Don't look at them," mutters Dad.

The day is bright, the flowers along the front walk fully in bloom.

I was out here, weeding the irises, the day Mom's promotion to Library Manager had come through. It was just last summer. Astrid had jumped down the front steps one at a time—*ribbit, ribbit, ribbit*—and crouched beside me.

"Guess what?" she said. There was a lime popsicle stain around her mouth.

"What?"

"Mom said I could tell you about the lieberry manger—"

"Library Manager," corrected Mom, sitting on the porch steps.

Astrid stood and faced Mom, putting her hands on her hips like Mom always does when we try her patience. "That's what I said. Lieberry manger. You said I could tell it."

"Go ahead, honey." Mom smiled.

Astrid faced me again. "Mom gets to be lieberry manger and you and me get to come home, just us, after school. When I'm in kindergarten next year."

I glanced over and she had that explodey smile on. "Really?" I said. "So we get sister time every day?"

She nodded. "We can watch *Lily's Pad,* and look for frogs and turtles in the creek, and—"

"Whoa, Frog Breath. We can do that sometimes, but I'm still going to have homework. And we'll have to get dinner started a few nights each week."

"But I still get a snack," she said, in her demandy-voice.

"Duh." I stuck my tongue out like a frog snatching a fly and she giggled.

Mom shifted on the stairs. "You sure you're okay with this? I know you were planning on doing track and cross-country again with Oakley."

"It's cool. I'm not as into it as Oakley is. Plus, we can still run together in the off-season."

Seeing the peonies, irises, and columbine now, rising above the fading creeping phlox, I want to drop back to my knees and rip up every last plant. Shred their delicate petals. Grind the bulbs and roots to mush beneath my heel. Why should the world get to go on without Astrid?

It should be pouring rain today. It should rainrainrainrainrain until I say it's okay for the sun to come out again.

But it's a perfectly bright, breezy, early summer day, and I don't rip up the flowers.

Instead, I dart back inside, returning with the backpack and lunchbox I bought for Astrid.

Taking a deep breath, I lock my gaze on our SUV and walk past the flowers mocking me like party decorations. I climb into my seat in the back of the SUV.

Astrid's booster seat is still in its place. I tuck the lunchbox inside the backpack and set them on the booster seat.

Dad takes the passenger seat, and Mom slides behind the wheel. We back out of the driveway and head west toward 3A. Toward Randall & Torres Funeral Home.

Up front, Mom and Dad talk quietly to each other.

I stare at Astrid's booster seat, trying to force myself to recall the imaginary argument I had with imaginary Astrid in the car. But like so much of the past week, it's lost to the fog of what Jamaica explained was a dissociative state. My mind locked itself away from the truth, and took me with it.

The real Astrid sat in the cafeteria on Monday, in her green birthday dress, waiting—

Wait.

What really happened?

The sunlight hurts my heart almost as much as it hurts my head, so I put my sunglasses on and open my phone, even though I probably shouldn't use technology just yet. I stare at the screen, calling up the courage to do what Jamaica asked me to do.

My hands shaking, I open my messenger app and find the convo with Mom. Her first text came in at 3:12.

I usually leave to pick up Astrid around quarter past, and get there around 3:25.

I wasn't late, after all. Not according to my agreement with Astrid.

My vision gets a little swimmy, and it's not just from trying to focus on the screen with a wounded brain.

What time did she die? What time did he enter the school?

Do I want to know?

Maybe not—but Jamaica thinks I need to know. As much as I hate what my mind did to me this week, I trust Jamaica.

I open my browser app and do a search: WINSLOW SHOOTING.

The first hit is a conspiracy site, and I let my breath out in a rush. Why would someone make believe this hell? How could anyone think we would? I laugh—hard and sharp—because my mind went through acrobatics to make believe it *wasn't* true.

Dad glances at me over his shoulder. "Kirsten?"

"It's okay," I say. "I'm just doing what Jamaica said, and—"

"Are you sure you should be using your phone already?"

"I know. I promise I'll keep it short, but I need to do this."

He nods and faces forward again. "Don't overdo it."

I turn back to my phone.

The second link is an article from *The Globe,* so I click through.

I don't want to read it don't want to read it don't want to read it but...

Gunman Kills 19, Injures 11 in Elementary School Shooting

Tuesday

Globe staff writer Sondee Silverman

Winslow, Massachusetts — A 32-year-old New Hampshire man, armed with two semiautomatic pistols, several handguns, and a semiautomatic rifle, killed 15 children and four adults in a shooting Monday afternoon in eastern Massachusetts.

The shooter, identified by authorities as Kevin Adams, is in police custody.

Those killed were in the cafeteria and the foyer. The Boston medical examiner's office sent a portable morgue unit to Winslow to assist in the shooting's aftermath.

According to information released by authorities, Adams entered the school shortly after dismissal time, when the security system is turned off. He forced his way past school secretary Patricia Phan and parent volunteer Jeff Stocek, who were monitoring the front door, at 3:08 pm.

Once inside, Adams ran across the large foyer and entered the cafeteria, where approximately 200 students between the ages of six and eleven awaited pickup by their parents.

Upon reaching the cafeteria, witnesses say Adams argued briefly with his estranged wife, Winslow Elementary art teacher Marissa Adams. He then pulled out his weapons and began firing wildly. Teachers and parents present rushed to hide children anywhere they could.

"It was terrifying," said parent volunteer Samantha Wallace. "There was hardly anyplace safe to hide the kids. All we could do was have them crouch behind overturned tables."

Fifth-grade student Luther Washington helped five students reach the cafeteria boys' restroom before he was injured attempting to enter, himself. Washington is listed in fair condition at Boston Children's Hospital.

Outside, the school busses carrying the remaining students had already departed on-schedule. Drivers in the pickup line had moved forward into the bus lane, and several students were in the foyer, on their way to waiting rides. Upon hearing the gunfire, several drivers left their cars and ran into the school. Two parents, Claudia LeClerc and Stephen Klein, were injured.

High school junior Todd Roman, whose brother attends the elementary school as a third-grade student, was wounded as he aided Winslow Elementary principal Nick Broderick in disarming Adams. Broderick entered the cafeteria and wrestled the gunman out into the foyer, enabling teachers and parents to lock the cafeteria doors. Broderick and Roman succeeded in overpowering and disarming Adams, though Broderick was killed in the scuffle. Third-grade teacher Xiomara Cruz was also injured as she shepherded over two dozen students behind the service line equipment.

Fourth-grade teacher Malik Walker and custodian Betty Thompson restrained Adams until police arrived a few minutes later.

Though Adams's motivation remains unclear, colleagues and older students have their suspicions. "As soon as I saw [Adams] enter the caf, I knew we'd have trouble," stated Walker. "We all knew Marissa had filed for divorce, and it was messy. She had a restraining order—not that it ever stopped him."

"Mrs. Adams gets hurt a lot," recalls a fifth-grade student. "She always has bruises or sprained wrists. She tells us she's just clumsy, but I think it's something else. I think somebody hurts her."

Marissa Adams, injured in the attack, is in serious condition at Boston General Hospital. Her son Hunter, a kindergartener at Winslow Elementary, was among those killed Monday afternoon.

When asked about the gun models used by the shooter, or whether any of the guns had been bump-stocked (which is illegal in Massachusetts), Winslow police chief Caren Carter declined to comment. "We're still gathering information," she stated. "At this time, our priority is to ensure all students are reunited with their families, and reach out to the families of those killed."

Police evacuated uninjured students to nearby Winslow Indoor Gym.

Everyone was right—even if I'd been in the pickup line first thing, I probably couldn't have saved Astrid. He was already inside, maybe already shooting. And if I'd been there—if I'd gotten out of my car and run inside—I might have been injured or killed, too. Or Astrid might've been killed in the foyer instead of the caf.

It doesn't matter that I waited for Josie. Maybe it saved my life. I turn my phone off and shut my eyes tight. A few tears sneak out, but I don't brush them away. They trickle down my cheek and settle in the corner of my mouth; I lick away their saltiness.

It's not my fault.

I tortured myself and everyone around me for days, for nothing.

But it's not my fault. I made a decision, months ago, with Astrid. Like Jamaica said, we had to make that decision trusting that nobody would shoot up Winslow Elementary. Otherwise, how could Astrid get on the bus every morning?

I lean back against the seat, my eyes still shut, and just breathe until Mom turns off the car and opens her door.

Astrid's death was out of my control. Astrid's death was Kevin Adams's fault.

Before everyone else arrives, the mortuary director lets us sit in here for a while, with Astrid. Her rented casket is smaller than a casket should be allowed to be, and it's closed. I run my fingers along the edge of the smooth, shining pine.

Astrid's body is in here. After we leave, they'll take her body to the crematorium and put it into the whatever-they-call it and it will come out again as a little pile of bone and ash. They'll give us that little pile in an engraved metal container and we'll take it home.

It won't really be Astrid.

It'll just be a pile of dust that used to be my little sister.

I have to say goodbye. I never got to say goodbye.

"Can I see her?" I ask, resting my hand near the latch. "I need to see her one more time."

"That's not a good idea," says the director, his voice low.

"I need to. Just one more time." I tear up again, but the director steps closer to the casket, almost between it and me.

"You don't want to remember her this way." He touches my elbow lightly, nudging me toward my parents.

"But I never got to say goodbye."

He nods. "I understand."

"No. You don't. I need to tell her I love her. She has to know I'd trade places with her if I could. I didn't mean for this to happen. I…"

Mom and Dad are suddenly beside me, Mom's arm around my waist and Dad's hand on my arm. Brent and Grandma join us, each putting a hand on one of my shoulders.

"It's not fair," I tell them, as if they don't agree. "She was just barely six. She didn't deserve to die."

And why should the shooter get to live when he stole so many lives? Astrid died right beside her best friend, and Lexie will live the rest of her life with that trauma.

I think, for a fraction of an instant, maybe if I raise the casket lid, it will be empty. Maybe this whole thing is a nightmare and all I need to do is wake up.

And it *is* a nightmare—though I know, now, I'm fully awake.

Astrid is gone and her absence is a bullet.

What happens next? How do I get past this?

I'm still standing in front of the casket when people begin arriving. Oakley comes to my side and wraps her arms around me. "I'm sorry, K."

I lean into her.

"Thanks for watching out for me." My voice is low enough for just the two of us. "Did I say anything stupid or cruel? I'm sorry if I did…"

I feel her shrug. "I'll admit it was unnerving, but your parents explained what was going on. That made it a little easier. Josie and Brent helped, too. Still… I'm glad you're back."

I can't say I'm glad, too—that would be the same as saying I'm glad Astrid died. I slide one arm around Oakley's waist. "How's Luther? I know he got hurt…"

She nods. "Yeah, he only lost his right eye."

"Only?"

Oakley snorts. "I know, right? He's more pissed than anything else right now. I'm sure it'll hit him hard at some point, but Luther's gonna be okay. He's here."

I nod, not sure if she means *he's alive* or *he came today*—probably both. We hang onto each other a little longer. Later, I see him sitting between his parents. The patch over his eye keeps his glasses from sliding down his nose the way they usually do.

Eventually, I join my parents. We talk to everyone coming in —Mr. & Mrs. Martin, with Jeremiah in tow, his cowlicky blond hair spit-combed down; several others from the neighborhood; Mom's coworkers and Dad's, too; even my boss and a bunch of people I know from school—kids and teachers. They all say the same things over and over. *Unimaginable. A tragedy. She was so young, so bubbly.* When Lexie and her dad arrive, Lexie clinging to him like a vine to a tree, he gives me a tense smile.

I'm nervous, too. I don't remember exactly what I said to them, but I know I need to try and fix it. Astrid's backpack is behind me on a little table. Taking a deep breath to quiet the fluttering in my chest, I pick the gift up and turn to Lexie and her dad.

"I'm sorry about the other day…" I say. "I don't remember it all, but I'm pretty sure I scared Lexie."

"She still hasn't cried," Mr. Oh admits.

Nodding, I squat down to meet Lexie's eyes. "Lexie?"

She gives me a wary look, arms still wrapped around her dad's leg.

"Lexie, I'm sorry for scaring you when we met outside the park. I was… I was a little mixed-up. But I'm better, now."

She loosens her grip on her dad.

"I miss Astrid a lot," I say. "How about you?"

Her mouth turns down and tears rise in her eyes. "Uh-huh," she whispers, then buries her face in her dad's pant leg. He squats, too, and wraps his arms around her.

I hold out the gift. "This was supposed to be for Astrid, but I think she would want you to have it."

She turns back toward me and regards the backpack out of the corner of her eye. "Why?" she asks, her voice mouselike.

I swallow around the sudden lump in my throat. "You were her best friend, Lexie. Astrid loved you. And *Lily's Pad* was something special you shared."

Mr. Oh scoops her up.

"There you go," he says, patting her back as she gives in, her shoulders heaving. *Thank you*, he mouths, then turns toward the seats. "I know…"

I follow them and place the backpack on the seat beside Mr. Oh.

Eventually the mortuary director comes over and escorts us—me, Mom and Dad, Grandma, and Brent—to the front row. He steps up to a small, light oak podium and waits as everyone takes the hint and finds a seat.

I want to turn and scan the seats behind us for Josie; I didn't see her come in. Maybe my mental break scared her off.

I can't say it might not have scared me off, if it had been her break.

The director welcomes everyone, and Grandma gets up to deliver the eulogy.

That's another thing my mind stole from me—the chance to memorialize Astrid the way only a sister can.

I tried to pull something together last night, but my head hurt too much and my vision got blurry the longer I stared at the blank page.

But Grandma says enough of the right things.

As soon as the memorial is over I seek out the bathroom, where I lean against the cold, marble tile on the wall for a few minutes, until the crowd of well-wishers has moved into the reception room where the mortuary staff has laid out all the food.

When I arrive at the reception, Josie is hugging Mom. As I approach, they part and Mom steps away.

We stand there awkwardly, a little further apart than conversation-normal.

She runs a hand through her hair. "So… you're better?" she asks.

"I guess that depends on what you call 'better' but… yeah. Thanks for finding me and calling 911. And following me and everything."

She blushes and nods. "Brent texted me and Oakley. We caught up with you just as you passed the park."

She takes a step forward, pauses, then moves closer and takes my hands in hers.

"Are you sure? What about your parents?" I ask, quietly. "Are they here?" I don't want to turn and look.

She shakes her head. "Do you remember… anything?" she responds.

"It's all mixed up, and the concussion doesn't help but… I remember bits and pieces."

She flashes me a tight smile. "Short version? Mom read my journal while I was out with you and Oakley, after Mr. Broderick's funeral. She figured out I'm gay and kicked me out."

I nod. I recall walking in on their fight the night of the concert. Count that as one more piece of the puzzle I can fit into place.

"I've been staying at my Uncle Stu's while he and Dad try to talk some sense into Mom."

"Wow.… That's not what you expected."

"Yeah. It's kind-of weird. She's started asking stupid questions, but I think it's going to be… tolerable, eventually. But Uncle Stu said I can consider his place home, permanently, if I want to. I mean, I'm eighteen, so in a way it doesn't matter where I call home, but… I'm pretty sure I'll move in with him and Keith."

I'm about to ask what this means for us, but she answers before I can get the words out. "I know this isn't the place to get into everything, but… I'm so sorry I put you through all that closeted angst and panic. Thanks for sticking with me."

"Omigod, Josie, you're worth it." Even though we're in a funeral home, I bounce a little on my feet and tear up.

"Damn," I say, blinking uselessly against my emotions.

Josie smiles and lets go of my hands. Somehow, the magic of the tingle remains. She unties her bandana from her purse-strap and hands it to me.

"Now I have *two* reasons to stop by your house tomorrow," she says, and I laugh through my tears as I dab them away.

By the time she leaves, everyone else is gone; even Grandma and Brent have departed for Brent's house.

Mom and Dad thank the director and we step outside into the still-bright morning. Again, I'm struck by the cruelty of the world's continued existence in the face of Astrid's death—but this time, it's survivable. Why? Because we had a brief service and people ate meatballs and tiny sandwiches? Because I saw and touched her casket?

Because it's what is, now. Having to face the truth, and talking to Jamaica, has helped me understand that we don't move on from grief. It's always there. I'll never stop missing Astrid—but even with my grief, I can move forward, and the only way forward is through.

In the car, as Dad navigates the back roads toward Westford and the emergency vet's office, I look down at my charm bracelet. I finger the charms in order, beginning with the simple disc with a braided border and the words *big sister* engraved on one side, and ending with last year's tiny silver-and-black ghillie. Six charms.

I can't find the charm Astrid picked out to give me last Monday. I remember, now: I've been going through her room all week. Rummaging through boxes in the basement. Checking behind the couch, the TV, her bed, *my* bed… searching everywhere. All those times I stepped out of a fog to find myself in a room I didn't remember entering, I must have been searching for the charm.

Astrid was right—she hid it real good.

20

ONE YEAR LATER

Today is Astrid's seventh birthday.

There's a candlelight memorial service this evening, and we're attending with Brent. This morning after breakfast, Mom, Dad, and I opened the rest of last year's gifts. Then we donated them to Gate City Cares, along with a bunch of her old books and toys. Yesterday, we took most of her clothing and bedding to Lowell Wish.

Not her frog books or favorite *Lily's Pad* play set, though. Those are on the lower shelves in the living room, beside Dad's photo albums. The cat, Foggy, kept knocking them off the top shelf. Next weekend, Brent and I are painting Astrid's empty room, and he'll move his stuff out of the den and into his new room.

It'll be weird, at first… but it's way past time.

My social media feeds are full of {{{hug}}} and <3 <3 <3 u and Hey K thinkin of u 2day

I'll respond tomorrow.

Today, Astrid and I are having a picnic lunch at her willow.

I spread the blanket and pin down the corners with a few softball-sized rocks from the rock pile. I set out a box of cold fried Wicked Chicken, a small tub of deli counter macaroni salad, a bowl of edamame, and a few cans of lemonade.

It's chilly for June, but I've pulled on a sweater and it's warm enough for the irises, so it's warm enough for us.

For me.

I stretch out on the blanket and gaze up at the long, whippy branches. Astrid's willow grew over six feet last summer, the canopy widening more than any of us expected. Some of the height is because I overfed it massively during my dissociative state, but Maura says it'll be okay in the long run. After the funeral, she even came over and helped me fix the mess I'd made during my midnight breakdown—which wasn't too hard, actually, since the tree had only been in the ground for a week.

Sunlight dances through the swaying branches and shines in my eyes. I close them and take several deep breaths, inhaling the earthiness of the moss at the edge of the creek and the damp, earthy scent of the bobbing irises.

When I open my eyes again, Astrid is here, in her green birthday dress, sitting on her knees beside the willow and staring at me.

"Hey, Kyurp."

"Hey, Frog Breath. Happy birthday."

She glances up at the willow.

"You've been doing the fairy dance for me."

I nod, unable to see her through the tears suddenly filling my eyes. "Yeah," I manage. "Every chance I get."

She smiles like she knows something I don't. "You know there's no such thing as fairies, right?"

"I know." Laughing, I wipe my eyes on my sleeve, take a few deep breaths, and watch her count the rocks in the ring around the tree. "I miss you, Frog Breath."

She keeps counting the rocks.

"You don't have to tell me," I say. "The trunk is already bigger. I'm going to have to move these."

I lie there and imagine her beside me for a few more minutes before getting up and shifting the rocks along the downhill side of the ring. Making the circle larger means I need more, so I steal the ones I've used to anchor my blanket. When I go to move the rocks on the uphill side, I add a few from the rock pile, but I'm short one rock, and there are no more in the pile that will fit. What else is there that the elements won't ruin? The nodding irises catch my eye, and there it is—the bird-watching frog Astrid moved last year. It's perfect.

Ignoring the footbridge and stepping carefully across the narrowest spot in the creek, I retrieve the large, hollow metal frog. It's almost as heavy as a fieldstone. How on earth did Astrid get this down the hill without smashing a toe? Holding it sideways so I can grip the hollow edge like a handle, I turn toward the creek.

My fingers brush against something inside—something that's not dirt or leaves.

What I pull out is a rectangular blob of plastic about the diameter of a tennis ball. Setting the frog back down among the irises, I examine the package.

In triple layers of slide-lock baggies is a small cardboard box, the size you'd use for earrings. The box, wrapped inexpertly in rainbow paper and practically covered in tape, is a little smushed, but otherwise okay.

My hands shaking, I fumble with the package, trying to peel away the tape or tear it, but nothing's working until I think to slice it open with the jagged end of a small, pointy rock.

Inside is a small silver charm—a heart, with the words *my favorite* engraved on one side. I'm crying again. Big, messy tears that all rush out at once and make my knees buckle out from under me.

"Oh, I miss you, Astrid. I miss you so much, sometimes I can't breathe..."

I kneel there, beside the irises, in the chill of the early afternoon shade, sobbing until my face is raw and chapped and my head throbs and my eyes sting and my nose runs and I'm sweating despite the cool air.

When there's nothing left but sniffles, I dab my eyes dry with the cuff of my sweater.

Taking off my bracelet, I pry open the link to Astrid's heart with my fingernails, slip it into place, and bite it shut again.

Stuffing the paper in my jeans pocket, I carry the frog across the creek and fit him into place near the willow, then clean up the picnic.

As I fold the blanket, Astrid's heart shifts—there's something engraved on the back, too.

Love, Astrid.

RESOURCES

GRIEF

Eluna
https://elunanetwork.org/
Supporting children and families impacted by grief or addiction. Resources include:

- Camp Erin for youth grieving the loss of someone significant
- Camp Mariposa for youth affected by substance abuse of a family member
- Team Jesse, providing support for families of fallen soldiers

Experience Camps
https://experiencecamps.org/
No-cost camps for kids and teens coping with the loss of a family member

HealGrief
https://healgrief.org/actively-moving-forward/
Resources include virtual support, and national and local support organizations

SLAP'D
https://slapd.com/
Surviving Life After A Parent Dies
Social media platform for teens who have lost a parent

BOOKS FOR TEENS AND YOUNG ADULTS

The Empty Room: Understanding Sibling Loss
by Elizabeth DeVita-Raeburn

Finding Meaning: The Sixth Stage of Grief
by David Kessler

It's OK That You're Not OK: Meeting Grief and Loss in a Culture That Doesn't Understand
by Megan Devine, forward by Mark Nepo

I Wasn't Ready to Say Goodbye: Surviving, Coping and Healing After the Sudden Death of a Loved One (A Compassionate Grief Recovery Book)
by Brook Noel and Pamela Blair

On Grief and Grieving: Finding the Meaning of Grief Through the Five Stages of Loss
by Elisabeth Kübler-Ross and David Kessler

Weird Is Normal When Teenagers Grieve
by Jenny Lee Wheeler, forward by Heidi Horsley Psy.D.

When a Friend Dies: A Book for Teens About Grieving & Healing
by Marilyn E. Gootman Ed.D.

BOOKS FOR YOUNGER CHILDREN

Ida, Always
by Caron Levis, illustrated by Charles Santoso

Is Daddy Coming Back in a Minute?: Explaining (sudden) death in words very young children can understand
by Elke Barber and Alex Barber

The Dead Bird
by Margaret Wise Brown, illustrated by Christian Robinson

The Rough Patch
by Brian Lies

Something Very Sad Happened: A Toddler's Guide to Understanding Death
by Bonnie Zucker, illustrated by Kim Fleming

NATIONAL AND ONLINE LGBTQ+ ORGANIZATIONS

Believe Out Loud
for all identities, sexualities, faiths, and denominations
https://www.believeoutloud.com/

Bisexual Resource Center
https://biresource.org/

CenterLink
The Community of LGBT Centers
https://www.lgbtcenters.org/

Gender Spectrum
https://www.genderspectrum.org/

GLSEN
https://www.glsen.org/

Human Rights Campaign
https://www.hrc.org/

It Gets Better Project
https://itgetsbetter.org/

Keshet
For LGBTQ equality in Jewish life
https://www.keshetonline.org/

Mental Health Warmlines
directories of support lines for non-life threatening situations
https://screening.mhanational.org/content/need-talk-someone-warmlines/
https://warmline.org/warmdir.html

Muslim Alliance for Sexual and Gender Diversity
https://www.themasgd.org/

NQAPIA - National Queer Asian and Pacific Islander Alliance
https://www.nqapia.org/

PFLAG
https://pflag.org/

Planned Parenthood
https://www.plannedparenthood.org/

Soulforce — confronting religion-based violence against LGBTQI people
https://soulforce.org/

The Marsha P. Johnson Institute
https://marshap.org/

Suicide & Crisis Lifeline
988

The Trevor Project
https://www.thetrevorproject.org/

TLDEF – Transgender Legal Defense & Education Fund
https://transhealthproject.org/

Trans Lifeline
US (877) 565-8860
Canada (877) 330-6366
https://translifeline.org/

TSER – Trans Student Educational Resources
https://transstudent.org/

Youth Pride Association
https://www.ypapride.org/home

FOR HOMELESS LGBTQ+ YOUTH

Covenant House
https://www.covenanthouse.org

National Coalition for the Homeless
https://nationalhomeless.org/references/need-help/

National Network for Youth
direct link to their guide for obtaining photo ID:
https://nn4youth.org/a-state-by-state-guide-to-obtaining-id-cards/

National Runaway Safeline
1-800-RUNAWAY
https://www.1800runaway.org

FOR LGBTQ+ YOUNG ADULTS IN FLORIDA, OHIO, & TEXAS

PRISM Florida
Serving LGBTQ+ youth in South Florida and beyond
https://www.prismfl.org/

Visuality
Fort Myers, FL
https://www.visualityswfl.org/

Full Spectrum Community Outreach
Youngstown, OH
https://www.fullspectrumcommunityoutreach.org/

Greater Dayton LGBT Center
Dayton, OH
https://www.daytonlgbtcenter.org/

Borderland Rainbow Center
El Paso, TX
https://www.borderlandrainbow.org/

LGBTQ Saves
Fort Worth, TX
https://www.lgbtqsaves.org/

For more local resources serving LGBTQ+ youth in the United States, visit my
website at wendymmcdonald.com/resources

GUN VIOLENCE

Brady
https://www.bradyunited.org/

Everytown for Gun Safety
https://www.everytown.org/

Giffords
https://giffords.org/

Moms Demand Action
https://momsdemandaction.org/

Students Demand Action
https://studentsdemandaction.org/

Sandy Hook Promise
https://www.sandyhookpromise.org/

SAVE Promise Club – Students Against Violence Everywhere
https://www.sandyhookpromise.org/our-programs/save-promise-club/

FOR SURVIVORS OF GUN VIOLENCE

Everytown Survivor Network
https://everytownsupportfund.org/everytown-survivor-network/

Gun Violence Survivors Foundation
http://gvsfoundation.org/

National Child Traumatic Stress Network
https://www.nctsn.org/

The Rebels Project
https://www.therebelsproject.org/

Survivors Empowered
https://www.survivorsempowered.org/

Trauma Survivors Network
https://www.traumasurvivorsnetwork.org/pages/home

You can find out more about my thoughts on some of these issues in the Author's Note.

AUTHOR'S NOTE

Kirsten's story is about survival—about finding the will to embrace and celebrate life again—even when you'd rather die of grief.

I wrote *The Willow* because, on the day of the Sandy Hook Massacre, my kids heard me sobbing in front of the television. All I could do was hold them both tightly, and cry harder, thinking of all the families who would never again be able to hold their children. As I draft this note—almost ten years after Sandy Hook—already forgotten by the news are the recent grocery-store massacre in Buffalo, New York and the mass shooting at the Taiwanese church in Laguna Woods, California. Just hours ago, children and teachers were slaughtered at Robb Elementary School in Uvalde, Texas. All within ten days. By the time this book is for sale, there will likely be over a hundred more on the list, whether they've made the news or not.

It makes me sick to my stomach, every single time.

Every single time, our government provides the same non-response—thoughts and prayers—while stalling legislation and cutting funding for services that would make a difference. What we're left with are families and communities eviscerated. Lives that cannot be lived in safety and security—but still we must go to school, to work, to the store, to the movies, all with the threat of mass murder hanging over us. Yet, to change our behavior out of fear of that threat is to let terror win. And so we numb ourselves, and go about our days. We're told that the threat of mass-murder is the price of freedom. But terror is the opposite of freedom.

And I didn't want to put another story about the shooter out into this world. I wanted to write about survival, about one family—one small circle—that would never be whole again.

That's how and why this book began, but *The Willow* is only partially about gun violence—it's also about grief and about navigating loss, especially when it's unexpected or unjust.

I began revising *The Willow* while my brother Daniel was dying of cancer, and I continued revising after his death. Several of my critique partners asked me, *Are you sure this is the book you should be working on right now?*

My answer was always a steadfast, immediate *Yes.*

From my first close experience with death, when my dad's father died, I've worked through my grief by writing. At 13, it was the only option I had. Now, after so many years, dumping my grief onto the page and exploring the pieces until they become something beautiful is the only thing that makes sense to me. That's not *all* I do—I think about my brother's leather riding pants that I still have in a drawer, waiting for me to discover what they'll be next. I remind myself I want to clean up his old Millennium Falcon and hang it from the ceiling in my office. Sometimes I still cry a little—at a song, a memory, the sight of one of his favorite movies that's now in my collection. Every day, I see my brother's smiles on my kid's face—the wry one, the mischievous one, the ecstatic one—and I see, in my other kid as she reads or works on her laptop, the way my brother slouched in his chair and held his head when reading. I wonder which parts of my brother live on in my nephews.

Here's the thing—grief is intensely personal, and there's no right way to go through it. It doesn't look the same for any two people, even two people who've lost the same person or gone through the same horror. And though many have heard of Elisabeth Kübler-Ross's work with David Kessler on the five stages of grief, one thing that's not evident unless you've experienced them is: they're not really stages. People often think they're a checklist: denial, anger, bargaining, depression, acceptance. They sound like a roadmap, dependable and linear—but also inflexible. Grief will do whatever it wants to.

The five stages are more like a buffet. You don't have to go through them in order—you probably won't. You'll probably skip around or jump back and forth, get stuck on one for a while, or even miss one altogether. And grief clings to you, like onion or jalapeño on your fingers, for the rest of your life. The idea of making a loss matter in some way must have been instinct for me—and I'm glad, because that instinct led me to writing. It helped me become who I am. Kessler's 2020 book, *Finding Meaning: The Sixth Stage of Grief,* covers in-depth the concept of making loss matter. Writing *The Willow* is one way I'm trying to make matter the loss of so many lives to the rage of white men… and to make matter the loss of my own sense of security.

Because beyond death, there are countless opportunities for loss in our lives. We can lose our sense of self. We can lose our physical or mental abilities. Our expectations, comfort, hopes. Our safety. Financial security. Health. Our homes. Irreplaceable possessions. Emotional security. Our faith in another person, or our belief in a god. And we grieve each loss—how can we not? Something was ripped from us, something we knew and possibly loved—though even things that are despised can be grieved for when lost.

When our kids were very young, my husband and I fell into the habit of telling them we loved them several times each day—often before naps or at moments of transition. Sometimes just because. To this day, we continue to cloak them in random but frequent *I-love-yous*. I now take comfort in what I once worried might be excessive—because as citizens of the United States, the threat of mass-murder hangs over our lives, especially their lives. At least they'll have heard *I love you* recently.

ACKNOWLEDGMENTS

Thanks, foremost, to Dr. L. A. Mirabelli, for her assistance in my understanding of PTSD, dissociative state, and psychological function, disfunction, and recovery. When I spoke with her during the early stages of drafting, her interest in the premise was encouraging as I moved forward with telling Kirsten's story. Dr. Mirabelli's feedback on a middling draft helped shape several crucial scenes. All mistakes and creative risks are mine.

Jeremy Rhodes shared his experiences as an EMT—his comments and input on those scenes was invaluable.

Karen Dent, Roxanne Dent, and Pam Marin-Kingsley—your support as I dusted off my keyboard has led not just to this novel, but to the one about the ghosts (which actually came first), as well.

Heather Kelly, the founder of The Writers' Loft, created a welcoming and nurturing writing community at the exact time I was looking for one. The fellowship I've found at the Loft has been inspiring. Thanks to Kate Messner, Linda Urban, Annie Cardi, Jen Malone, Karen Boss, and everyone else I've ever taken a workshop from—be it through the Loft, at the New England Society of Children's Book Writers and Illustrators conference in Springfield, or elsewhere—for so generously opening your writer's toolbox and sharing your tools. All my friends at Swinger of Birches: I missed the camaraderie and productivity during our pandemic-induced hiatus, and our return to Plattsburgh this past July was its own magic rock.

I started making a list of all the writers I've met through the Loft, the SCBWI, and Swinger of Birches who have helped feed my writerly soul, but there are just too many of you. You all know who you are, though, because every time I see you, I give you a hug and sometimes there's even a squeal of delight.

Sarah Darer Littman, Tara Sullivan, and Nancy Werlin: your commitment to telling tough stories gave me the courage to not just begin this novel, but to keep going even when it seemed I'd written myself into an impossible situation.

Thanks to Pam Vaughan, who coached me on the basics of lacrosse, Brook Gideon, who shared her expertise as a veterinary assistant, and Mary Cronin, for helping me get Kirsten and Josie's relationship right. Deborah Sosin provided feedback on a few late-stage scenes. Julie Morgenlender and River McMican helped with providing entries for the LGBTQ+ portion of the resources list.

The staff at Mahoney's Garden Center in Chelmsford explained the effects of over-fertilization on a weeping willow sapling, as well as how to help the tree recover. Speaking of plants: it's because of Kristin Russo, Sheryl Schmidt, and Dianne Simonini, who all helped me out with gardening content, that I didn't have daffodils blooming in June! Nancy Poydar wins a prize for naming the plant nursery where Kyurp works—Dirty Knees forever!

I rely on my critique partners to tell me not only what I'm getting wrong, but also what I'm getting write. (Yes, I did that on purpose.) They never turned away from a brainstorming session, and read multiple iterations of this novel yet somehow remembered which version was reality—no mean feat, given that I, myself, regularly referred to the five-foot-long timeline tacked along one wall of my office.

Nandini Bajpai and Marissa Doyle, my critique partners during early drafts, helped me find and shape the overall direction of Kirsten's story, and encouraged me to trust my inner sense that this story was important to tell.

My Monday night crit partners are the Tups—Sandy Budiansky, Shannon Falkson, Jane Kohouth, Julie Reich, Jean Stehle, and Laura Woollett. In particular, the Tups helped me shape Grandma Villi's character, and assured me the tiny moments of humor speckled throughout the story not only worked, but came at just the right time.

My Thursday night crit partners are Table for 7: Gary Crespo, Erin Dionne, Megan Mullin, Phoebe Sinclair, and Annette Trosello. It's thanks to Tf7 that Kirsten's parents are as supportive as they are broken, and that Brent, Oakley, and Josie got more time on the page. Extra thanks to Erin, who asked questions that made me stop and re-think everything—then re-think it again—and who assured me that the weird, risky elements of this book are part of what makes it so amazing.

It's hard to find beta-readers who will tell you, from a reader's perspective, what they're seeing or missing in your novel. My good friend Julie Holmansky rose to the challenge. Thank you for the time and attention you gave to my project. You didn't just read my novel—you spent an evening geeking out with me about *The Willow*'s structure, timelines, pacing, and character arcs in a way that only another former English teacher could appreciate. That discussion helped me firm up the timeline and pacing of this story.

I'm sure my parents caught me reading under the covers with a flashlight—then pretended not to have noticed—more times than any of us can count. I know they don't understand how I can read as a passenger in a moving car, or while walking, or eating... but thanks, Mom and Dad, for letting me read just one more chapter.

My early-bird sister Debbie—who shared a room with me for over 10 years—deserves a medal for all the times I kept her up far too late, inventing stories. Thanks for indulging this night-owl. I hope you don't mind, but I gave Mr. Ribbit to Astrid—though your Mr. Ribbit was three feet long, and didn't have a sucking foot.

Daniel: when you were born, I was too young to understand that having you as my brother would eventually mean splitting a block of cheese as we watched our regular late-night episode of *Quantum Leap*. Those moments of bonding over our shared love of story are my favorite memories of you. I wish you were here to share this story with me, but you're part of it nonetheless.

Most especially, thanks beyond measure to my husband Dan and our kids Penelope and Zephyr, for believing in me and my vision for this novel. Your interminable patience as I read aloud scenes—then revised them and read them aloud again —did not go unappreciated. All three of you helped me come up with some of the funny bits—they were small, but essential.

Pen and Zeph: I started writing again, after too many years away, because I knew I couldn't expect you to follow your dreams if you didn't witness me following my own. You have kept me young in ways I never expected, but for which I am profoundly grateful. Thanks, too—though you didn't really have a choice—for letting me mine the atmosphere of your first rock concert for the Emily Snow show. I told you I'd get you back later!

Dan, you gave me Wicked Chicken, *Tornado Alley*, *War of Ages*, and Emily Snow. You didn't blink when I came home with an antique writing desk, even though I needed your help to lug it up two flights of stairs. You never complain when I spend time with my imaginary friends instead of you. And you've already answered too many texts that read "can you be my rubber duck?" with "on my way!" but I can promise there will be many more... you're the one!

ABOUT THE AUTHOR

 Wendy M. McDonald lives outside Boston, where she pens darkish stories in the garret of her home. A former high school English teacher, Wendy now works for educational publishers, reads banned books, donates to Everytown for Gun Safety, and calls her Senators and Representatives even though they already support laws for gun safety.

Wendy's short stories appear in two anthologies: Chaosium's *Once Upon an Apocalypse* ("Mary Had a Little Limb") and *Firsts: The Writers' Loft Anthology* ("First Comes Love"). She also has two poems in *Friends and Anemones: Ocean Poems for Children.*

Find out more about Wendy at wendymmcdonald.com and at tablefor7press.com. You can follow her on Instagram and Twitter.

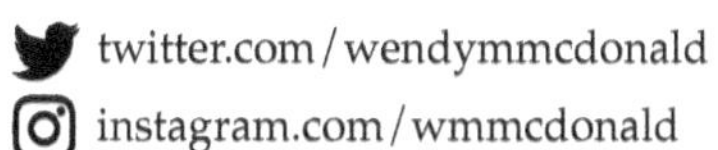